Cut The Blue

Ao

For Ethna Margaret Mary Cassidy

December 1915 – December 2012

Oh the laughs you gave us during your extraordinary 'dash'.

ABOUT THE AUTHOR

Aoife Sheridan has been writing for nearly thirty years, sadly mostly in her head. But the reading public need wait no more! Cut the Blue is the first story that has gone the distance, from light bulb moment to ink on paper. Born in Dublin, she enjoys writing quirky, character-based fiction, interwoven into the fabric of Ireland's capital city.

Her mission as a writer is twofold: First and foremost to entertain. She guarantees her books will give the reader at least one giggle and will definitely not hurt their heads. Secondly, she is determined to help the people of the world pronounce the name 'Aoife' correctly. It's 'Eefa' if you're interested.

She lives on Dublin's north side with her partner and two giant, alas imaginary dogs.

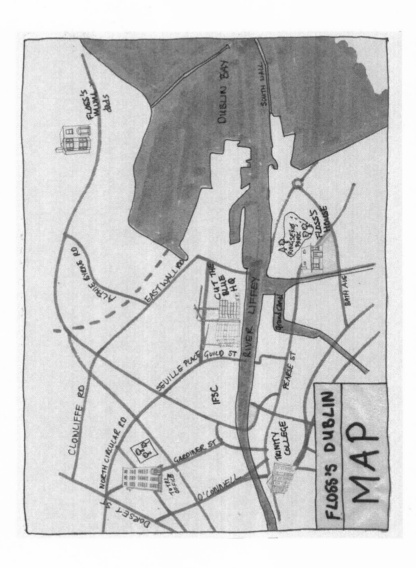

Aoife Sheridan

PROLOGUE

My name is Florence McFarland, a.k.a. Floss, and I'm ninety-nine per cent sure I'm going to die in the next few minutes.

I never really imagined it quite like this. I always thought of slipping gently into the night at the tender age of eighty-seven, off my head on morphine, with Grandad Dermo singing a slightly ropey version of 'I Did It My Way' in the background. I'd have said my 'Up yours' and 'I love yous' and be smiling serenely on my way to the Pearly Gates.

But there is nothing serene about this version. This is more Tarantino-style, and I'm putting up a serious fight. Not so much a physical fight, more of a verbal attack. There are words coming out of my mouth that would make a trucker cringe. This verbal onslaught is directed at Neander Man in the crane below me. I'd have a proper go at him, unleash the full arsenal of my half-learned Aikido moves, but no can do. I can't move.

I'm strapped to my Bond-bad-guy office chair, my face mashed up against the main window of my prefabricated office that's currently dangling precariously over the River Liffey. The guy beast below is laughing menacingly and threatening to hit the release lever on the crane, which is the only thing that stands between me and a murky end.

I'm not really in the mood for a full life flashback and fond reflections. I'm livid. My rage is partly directed at this vicious goon, but mostly at myself. I would kick myself if my legs weren't tied to the chair. In between curses, I hear myself shouting 'You utter, utter eejit!!' at the top of my lungs.

And, in all this mayhem, I can hear Mum's voice in my head,

smugly saying that phrase that nobody ever wants to hear, "I don't want to say I told you so, love, but ..."

1

It's Monday morning and, judging by the sounds of the racket outside my bedroom window, there's an absolute shitstorm blowing outside. I'm worried that the tree branch which has been lurking just a little too close to the back of my house for the past two years risks becoming a permanent fixture in my bedroom suite. A sneak peek through the broken bit in the blinds confirms my suspicions. Holy crapola! Horizontal rain and gale-force winds. Nora's garden next door is a disaster area. Meteorological hell or, as we say in Ireland, a 'grand soft day'..

I make a mental note: *get the bloody blinds fixed.*

'Morning Ireland' is blasting out its usual doom and gloom on the radio alarm clock. I swore off national radio about six months ago due to the relentlessly depressing reports and the black mist that used to descend after every programme. I hold that radio station partly responsible for talking us into a recession. Sometimes a bit of state-sponsored, positive propaganda can be just the ticket. But as a way of getting me out of the scratcher, 'Morning Ireland' has no rival. I'm up and at it before the seven o'clock beeps have finished. Not a snooze button in sight.

Today's a big day for me. It's the start of a new era in Floss-world. No more moaning about pretty much everything: Dublin weather, the price of a pint, the evil bank moguls, my creaking business, my terminally single status, my lack of boobs (are these last two related?). It's all on the up-and-up from here on in. Got to change the old tune.

Leon, my dog (and soulmate), did not get the memo. He's whimpering on the other side of my bedroom door.

"Yeah dude, I'm on my way. Keep your fur on."

I open the door and brace for impact. Leon is a Leonberger, which translates into a giant, brownie-black, four-legged fluffball with a heart of gold and the patience of Saint Monica. I know, I didn't exactly push the boat out when naming him, but if you met him you'd just know he was a Leon. Honest.

His whimpering stops and we have our morning rumble. I always come out a lot worse for wear after these episodes. Leonbergers are classed in doggy terms as extra-large. I think the doggy-chart people are underselling their size here. They need a new category for my Leon, something along the lines of horse-dog.

"How about some brekkie, big man?"

When he hears the magic word, he releases me from the Stepover Armlock Camel Clutch he has me in and makes straight for the fridge.

"Lumpy, brown jelly crap for you, coffee and Coco Pops for me. The breakfast of champions, eh fella?"

I'm pretty sure he nods at this, but it could just be a nervous twitch due to Bitsy, Nora's dog next door, being in heat at the minute.

I slurp down the last of the milk straight from the bowl, ignoring Mum's voice in my head: "What way were you reared?" One of the joys of having my own place is doing the opposite of what I was taught. Rebel with a capital R.

"Okeydokey, Leon. Out you go and destroy the garden."

He makes straight for Nora's garden fence and does an

almighty crap. Well, what goes in and all that. He comes back in with a proud did-you-see-that-Mum? expression on his face.

"Yes I did and seriously dude, you're not going to win over the ladies with that sort of display."

I jump in the shower and let out a yelp at the freezing water. The tiny mounds of my boobs (they've been referred to as M&Ms) invert themselves and disappear back into my chest. I spend two awful minutes sticking bits of me in and out of the stream of ice-cold water, trying to spread the pain – followed by three lovely minutes hugging the radiator.

What to wear for a power day at the office?

Ted Baker, it's got to be. I whip on the sharp, black, wool dress and jacket. My new hoosh-up, ultra-tech bra almost gives me boobs. Quick mirror check. Good job, too. My ridiculous black mop has gone into epic frizz proportions. I grapple with a bobbin for some minutes until the wildness is contained in a ponytail. Flash balm, mascara, eye and lip liner, and the image before me is transformed from a mess into a slightly better-disguised mess.

"Let's go, Leon."

Out the door ... and disaster looms. I spot my elderly neighbour Eddie exiting his apartment. Eddie drives a snazzy, red-for-faster, two-seater Mercedes at a top speed of thirty-five kilometres per hour, and he's likely to get ahead of me on the road. It's a single lane all the way to work. Getting stuck behind Eddie is a pretty frustrating way to start the day.

Not today, no way José.

I dash through the lashing wind and rain to my car, with Leon in pursuit. Leon loves the 'beat Eddie out the gate' game. My 2001 Nissan, 'The Jalopy', starts first time. The gods are on our side. I floor that puppy and screech through the gates, narrowly avoiding Eddie's passenger wing mirror. I toot and wave and briefly catch a glimpse of his stunned expression in the rear view before we hit the bend.

"We own today, Leon."

He nods. I'm sure of it.

We head over the East Link, up Sheriff Street, then left into the IFSC centre. I drive past the glistening glass and chrome buildings of Dublin's financial hub and pull into what was intended to be the car park of the new Anglo Irish Bank building. After the economic crash and all the grand plans that went astray, what's left is a concrete shell, overlooking the Liffey and a two-acre gravel car park. The building stands as an ugly reminder of all that went wrong in the overly-ambitious years of the Celtic Tiger.

In the corner sits a dark, grey prefabricated building, the humble headquarters of my personal business. CTB Investigations might be based in a trailer in an abandoned car park, but it is *my* trailer, *my* empire and *my* master plan.

I'm actually a qualified actuary, but about two years ago I had a complete meltdown. Not a complete Krakatoa job, where furniture gets broken and medication is required. Just a 'what the fuck am I doing with my life and where's the vodka tonic?' kind of meltdown. I'd been working for a large consulting firm and had just completed a complex benefits calculation for a global insurance company. I know, I know – the glamour. The job went really well and the project team went out for a few celebratory scoops after the final wrap-up. It ended up being a late one: tapas and cocktails, finishing at one of Dublin's ostentatious and overpriced wine bars.

I was having a great night, with lots of mutual backslapping and ego-boosting. Late on, I was getting my round in at the bar, when this absolute dish started chatting away in my direction. I had to check behind me to make sure he was talking to me. Auburn hair, a sprinkle of freckles and sparkling green eyes, all smiles and cheeky chappie. Definite marriage material! We were getting on swimmingly and I'm pretty sure some sparks were zinging back and forth – until he asked me what I did for a living. I took a deep breath and started my mind-numbingly boring spiel.

"Well, I'm an actuary specialising in insurance benefit calculations and …". Not long after there was a loud thump. My husband-to-be had actually fallen asleep mid-way through one of my sentences, face planted onto the bar. He sprang back up, rubbing his forehead, and tried to rally with a "Sorry what was that you were saying, gorgeous?" but the moment was lost.

I jumped in a taxi and retreated home. Mortified.

The next morning, with the mother of all hangovers, I wrote my resignation letter and dropped it in to my boss. The feeling of lightness and exhilaration, mixed with a tiny bit of hysteria, was out of this world. I was high on life and its possibilities. Then Mum called.

Being on a roll, I told her my news.

"Holy Mother of the divine sweet Jesus. You're after doing what?" she almost screeched down the phone.

"Resigned, Mum. I can't help feeling I'm supposed to be doing something else, something more useful and noble, maybe …"

She was so not going to buy this.

"Oh really? And what would that be? And, more importantly,

does it have a pension?"

Her voice became muffled. I could picture her covering the mouthpiece.

"Bert, Florence has resigned from her job … permanent and pensionable. Will you talk some sense into her?"

"Christ, Mum, I can hear you, you know! Look, it's not about the money. It's about being able to enjoy what I do. I want to be able to tell people about my job without their eyes glazing over, you know?"

"Enjoy? Enjoy? I'll give you 'enjoy'. I see the future and it involves me getting your single room ready here when you're evicted."

"Thanks for the vote of confidence, Mum. Look, just give me a chance to figure it out, ok?"

"It's not too late to take it back, love. Write an unresignation letter or something." Then again in muffled tones: "Albert James, get your fat arse off that lazyboy and tell Florence to take it back."

"Goodbye, Mum."

"This conversation is NOT over."

"It is now," I said, and quickly hung up.

Well, that went well.

I got pretty much the same reaction from everyone else I told.

Generally, it was along the lines of "Hold on a second. You're practically printing your own money and I'm busting a gut, day in day out, to sell vibrating hairbrushes. How dare you resign?"

Or similar.

Of course, that was nothing like the reaction I got when I dropped the pearler that I was starting up my own private investigation firm. Mostly I got stunned silence. Followed closely by:

"Are you alright? In the head, I mean? Do you need to talk to someone? Not me ... someone in a professional capacity, like?"

Mum, needless to say, was having a complete conniption. She ran the full gamut from hysterical shouting to guilt-inducing whispers, plus everything in between. She even sent her parish priest around to talk some sense into me. That backfired badly. Father Brendan thought it was an outstanding idea.

"Sure isn't catching the bad guys God's work. I can't fault ya for it. Good on ya, girl. But Jaysus tell your ma I gave you a stern talking to ... tell her I said things like, 'that Cagney & Lacey is not all it's cracked up to be' and the like."

We left it at that and watched the Antiques Roadshow together with a nice cup of tea and some slightly stale custard creams. My type of religious experience.

The only other person who supported my radical life-change was my best friend Penny. After she'd picked herself up off the floor, she simply said:

"Why the flip not? Although I'm worried that I'll be alone in my status of 'person with the most boring life on the planet'."

Bless her little heart.

Penny is probably my oldest friend (in longevity rather than age). We met at St Anne's National School when we were eight years old. I was new in school and a bit lost. She was a bit of an outsider, all credit to her ridiculous but free milk bottle specs. She looked like a forty-year-old biddy, dressed up as a

*

school kid.

Our friendship started when I was being picked on at little break by the class bully, Fran Fitzpatrick, a stocky wee fella with an eye for where to land a good dead leg. All I remember is being pinned against the gym wall and hearing the chants of "A-G ... A-G-R ... A-G-R-O ... AGRO" by the audience that had gathered, sensing a good schoolyard scrap. I was pretty close to losing control of my sphincter when in swooped a flash of mousy-brown hair, dodgy headband and two-inch lenses.

Before I knew it, Fran the Man was doubled over in pain and I was being rushed away from the scene of the crime by Penny. He never gave us another moment's trouble after that.

Penny and I have been inseparable ever since. I've even become the third wheel in her marriage to Conor, her doting husband. I think they view me as some form of charity initiative. "Wayward and in their thirties. Please give generously ..." They feed me, listen to my rants, console me when my heart has been mashed by the latest 'bad choice' and generally treat me like one of their kids. I've even gone on romantic weekends for three with them, but not, it must be said, in the 'throw your keys in the bowl' way.

Conor's a clueless genius. Last time I checked he knew everything about absolutely everything but has zero cop in the street smarts department. I refer to him as The Oracle.

What The Oracle doesn't know is that his wife is a complete adrenalin freak. She will try anything and is scared of nothing. She lives a kind of double-life. At home she's the clucky mother of two and mothering wife of one; on the street, she's a totally different beast. The Oracle thinks Penny works at the information centre in the National Gallery. In fact, she works for me: Assistant Private Investigator Penny.

Clearly, Penny's concern about being the world's most boring person was no passing complaint. On day two of CTB Investigations, her over-magnified eyes were peering imploringly and insistently though my prefab window. She talked for thirty solid minutes on why she would make an invaluable addition to the CTB team. I was powerless to resist.

Of course, for the last two years, she has been pretty much going cold turkey from adrenalin fixes. CTB has not exactly been inundated with spine-tingling adventures.

CTB stands for Cut the Blue, reduced from Cut the Blue Wire. Yes, that moment in the movies when the hero or heroine has to pick which wire to cut to diffuse a bomb that is seconds from detonating. As the time ticks towards 00:00:000 on the giant red digital clock (which the bomb nut has kindly provided for added suspense and clarity), the loyal sidekick finally screams "Just cut the blue wire!"

What has that got to do with being a private investigator? I'm glad you asked … the answer is absolutely sweet 'f' all.

Actually, it had more to do with the kind of decisiveness that leads to people throwing in the towel on a well-paid job and setting up outfits like CTB. Like, just grow a pair, make the bloody decision, go on! Chuck in your job, ditch that loser, have a baby, have two, tell your folks you like to dress up in ladies' clothes, hire someone, fire someone, dye your hair purple, shave it all off. But whatever you do, you absolutely cannot do nothing.

Deciding to quit Important Bods & Snobs Actuarial & Sons was my Cut the Blue moment. I like to think there's also a hint of 'cut the crap' to the name. Having worked in a consulting firm for many years, I waded up to my neck in buzzword claptrap and industrial jargon, to the point of near drowning. In rebellion, CTB is a strictly straight-shooting, straight-talking outfit.

The name just seemed to work.

Of course, when Penny and I are in full sales pitch mode, we tell our clients that the name CTB is inherently linked to investigations. Our theory is that by making the decision to even talk to a private investigator, our clients are at risk of inviting a major upheaval into their lives. Deciding to survey their husband's potential extramarital shenanigans or taking a closer look at a business partner's hand hovering in the area of the till will more than likely lead to a wire-cutting episode. In our initial meetings, we insist on giving clients the full eye-opening speech on what may lie ahead. We ask them directly if they're ready to wield the pliers, so to speak.

CTB specialises in insurance fraud and corporate espionage. I love that! It sounds very Jason Bourne. Our business cards say 'CTB Investigations – Between the lines'. Not so Jason Bourne … but catchy.

Well, although we'd like to specialise in white-collar crime, we really do whatever our clients ask us to do. In the last two years, we've searched for missing wives, husbands, kids, cats, dogs and documents, snooped on dole bludgers, cheating spouses, rogue employees, crèche workers and pets (yes pets!). No job is too small for CTB.

If asked to pick my all-time favourite, it would have to be the case of the demented cockatoo.

Mrs Grymes, a dear and gentle lady with the most beautiful bouffant blue rinse I've ever laid eyes on, came to us in a perplexed state, worried that her cockatoo had completely lost the plot at the tender age of two. Penny and I had already done our pre-pitch research and were up to speed on the typical timing for the onset of dementia in cockatoos. Which, if you're interested, is NEVER. They don't go mental, they just kark it. One second they're saying "Who loves Polly?" and the next they're lying on their back with their feet in the air.

The protagonist in this case was Elvis, a Black Palm Cockatoo. An aptly named fella, with a taste for Tayto Cheese and Onion crisps and an uncanny ability to mimic human speech. Yes, I know that all cockatoos and parrots have this ability, but this bird did accents! He actually spoke with a Belfast twang, inherited from his owner. He could recite the 'Our Father' and chunks of the 'Hail Mary', and burst out with catchphrases such as "Give us a kiss", "Say your prayers" and "Ain't nothin' but a hound dog" (I made up that last one). He actually looks like Elvis, if Elvis had been a bird.

Our feathered Elvis, being of the Catholic persuasion, had been trained to head-butt his little bell when the gong for the Angeles came on the telly every evening at six. It was kind of scary to witness.

Anyway, Elvis's problem was that he had started to speak gibberish, punctuated with little moans. Mrs Grymes thought he had succumbed to some form of parrot stroke. We told her to leave it with us and we'd have it wrapped up in a week.

After Mrs Grymes had left, Penny looked at me with her 'where's-the-craic-in-that' face. I retaliated with my 'don't-start-we-need-the-money' look.

Penny kicked into surveillance mode and had the case wrapped up by end of day one.

It turned out that Elvis's room in Mrs Grymes' flat was separated from her neighbour James Redhand's living room by paper-thin walls. Mr Redhand's guilty pleasure was the filthiest of filthy French porn. He liked to watch it at top volume in the afternoon when Mrs Grymes was at bridge. So, although Elvis sounded like he had gone gaga with all his gibberish, in fact he was speaking X-rated French and doing a remarkably good impersonation of a French porn star's moment de joie.

As is often the case with private investigations, this left us in a delicate situation. If we revealed the truth behind Elvis's new party trick, Mrs Grymes herself might have a stroke. After much debate, we agreed that French opera would be a more palatable, if less plausible, explanation.

Mrs Grymes bought it, hook line and sinker. The cheque was in the post that day. Job done.

2

Having locked the car, I start unlocking the six bolts and padlocks on the door of my office. There is nothing of value in my office, but the local rascals and ruffians are bored easily and love the challenge of a mindless break-in. Three in two years.

Leon lets out a low warning growl behind me. I know without a backward glance that one of the aforementioned local kids must be in the vicinity. Sure enough, Whacker, the leader of the pack, is leaning on one of the parked cars on the far side of the car park. He's leering at us with a fag dangling from his lips. He thinks he's James Dean.

"Starry missus? How's about a ride?" he asks in his strong inner-city accent.

"Mmmm ... now let me reflect on that for a second, Whacker ... mmm ... no, not now, not ever."

"Seriously disappoint'n. We're goin' t' take that trailer of an office o' yers for a spin someday. Dollier Strand 'd be a grand spot, wha'?"

"Go to school and get an education!"

"Good wan, ma ... an education, good wan," he says, giggling away to himself.

I finally get inside and shut the door. That little fecker always manages to get the last word. Leon makes his way to his makeshift doggie bed in his favourite corner of the office.

I flick on my laptop and make some coffee. The boot-up normally takes around ten minutes, a nagging reminder that I need to get an upgrade. The laptop's on its last legs. It makes grunting and grinding noises as if there's a little band of tiny laptop elves inside, scurrying around trying to get the thing to work.

Once the elves have done the bizzo, it's straight into email to see if there have been any bites over the weekend. Nada. One bill query from a fraud case we closed last month and a discount offer on radical new penis-enhancing pills called GrowMyPeen. Eeeuwh! Delete.

What to do on Mega Monday – my day of fresh starts? What to do … A To Do List! That will kickstart the day.

I grab my notepad and pencil and start jotting down my tasks for the day ahead:

1. Deal with local vagabond. Tick
2. Check email. Tick.
3. …

At point three I begin to struggle.

I flick back through my notebook to find last week's to-do list to see if there's anything I can carry forward. Nice one. A couple of odd jobs there for me to tackle. I need to check with Penny as to what's happening with our Google campaign. We had a bit of success early on but it seems to have dried up now.

As usual I've managed to avoid doing any of my dreaded money-chasing calls. We always have a few clients who are either chancing their arm or genuinely struggling to come up with the cash. In Ireland right now, forty per cent of all daily mental energy must be spent on chasing unpaid bills and writing off bad debts. If we could all just have a group hug and agree to pay on time, we'd save a serious amount of wasted effort in the economy. Then we could all focus on other things such as more group hugs and selling more stuff.

Debt-collection calls … an outstanding task from last week, and from the week before that … transferred in a kind of limbo status from one week's list to the next. I move it to this week's list, and put an asterisk beside it and a giant exclamation mark. Not exactly textbook 'Time Management Skills 101', but this day of days is Mega Monday after all.

I decide to ease myself into the day with Penny's Google campaign. I hit speed dial 2 and Penny answers on the first ring.

"Have we got a new job?" she asks.

"Sadly, no. But that is half the reason I called."

"Oh-oh. I'm just an easy task on your list. So how is the to-do-list avoidance going?" Penny has an annoying habit of zeroing in on my weaker points.

"I think you've forgotten that it's Mega Monday. Strictly no gnarly job evasion," I say smugly.

"Well, excuse me! So, exactly how many cold calls have you made this morning so far, then?" she asks, her tone dripping in sarcasm.

"Well, hold on, let me just look through my target list … eh, none," I reply sheepishly.

Silence.

"Ah Penny, don't do the Strategic Silent Pause on me. You know I can't handle it. I'll just babble right into the thick of it. Look, I'm already doing it …"

More deafening silence. Excruciating. I'm just about to start waffling into the void again when she breaks it with:

"I gather you're calling about the Google stuff. It's all in hand. I'll fill you in when I get in. Now please, hang up and start making some flippin' calls!"

I do exactly what she says. Her and her pregnant silent pauses have that effect on me.

First up is Archer Insurance. These guys are a good example of positive energy being channelled into negative pursuits. They must have a whole department dedicating to not paying bills on time. They will be a bunch of bean counters in a dark basement office with 'Credit Terms Management Department' on the door.

Before I make the call I have to do my pre-call prep. This involves awakening angry Floss from deep within my core. I do this by thinking about middle-aged male Jaguar drivers who speed up when you try to overtake them. I am instantly livid and ready for a fight.

"Good morning. This is Florence McFarland of CTB Investigations. I'm calling about an outstanding invoice."

"Floss! It's Niall. How the hell are you? I've been meaning to call you for weeks now, but ..."

"Oh really? And was that intended call going to be about a cheque that's in the post? Or was it just for a general chit-chat? A bit of breeze-shooting?"

"Ah you know how it is, Floss."

"No, actually I don't! What I DO know is that you owe me eleven grand for over two months now, despite the invoice having a seven-day payment policy. It's nothing short of daylight robbery. I'm honestly of a mind to ..."

"Whoa! Slow down there, Floss. "

"Slow down? Slow down? If I went any slower I'd be statuesque." I'm getting into the swing of things now and my face is roaring red with the power of my fury.

Niall butts in: "Give me a second to ..."

"I'll give YOU a second."

"What? That doesn't make sense."

"I'll give YOU some sense."

"Ah for God's sake Floss, you've gone off the deep end. Look, the cheque IS in the post. We got paid by Pfizer yesterday and a batch of invoices got paid, including CTB."

"I'll give YOU ... what? It's really in the post? Not just 'pretend in the post'?"

"I saw it with my own two eyes."

"Well ... right ... in that case. Um ... well thanks Niall. Nice talking to you again."

"Apology accepted, Floss."

I hang up the phone gently, my earlier fury being rapidly replaced by mortification. What a complete numpty! I slap my forehead twice to try and clear away the embarrassment.

This is why I hate these calls. I'm either too softly-softly or I'm a complete crazed loon on the rampage. I've never perfected the art of in-between.

But hey, eleven grand. Happy days!

I skip over to Leon singing 'We're in the money' and give him a giant hug. He's not impressed.

Well, if I'm on a roll, I might as well keep on trucking. Next on the list is Jennifer Gillen. We did a snoop job on her long-suffering husband back in June. She was one hundred per cent convinced he was having an affair with some young floozy in his workplace. After two week's full-time surveillance, it became abundantly clear the poor bloke was just escaping to the library for some quiet time before heading home to face his wife. She refused to believe us and questioned our investigative process and due diligence. She also refused to pay on the grounds of services not rendered. To Penny and me, this was like a red rag to a bull.

However, after the previous embarrassing incident with Niall I decide to go easy on Mrs Gillen.

"Good morning, Mrs Gillen. This is Florence McFarland of CTB Investigations. I'm calling about an outstanding invoice for the case closed for you back in June."

"CTB? Does that stand for Can't Trap Bastards? Or Complete & Total Bullshit?"

"No, Mrs Gillen. As you know it stands for Cut the Blue. It should be printed quite clearly on the top of that invoice we sent you three months ago. Any luck with paying that?" This is said through gritted teeth.

"Why should I pay for your pathetic efforts? I think you're in on it with him," she says, warming to her theme.

"Mrs Gillen, I think you're being a little harsh there. We spent two weeks tracking your husband's every movement ..."

"Fuck off and check my bowel movements."

Lovely.

"Ok, Mrs Gillen. I've tried to be nice. But here's the deal. You've seen my dog, right? He likes nothing better than to hear the 'Attack' command."

In the background, Leon starts to growl. It's a party trick I taught him years ago when I moved into my new place. Of course, if anyone actually went near him, he'd probably crawl under the desk and pretend to be dead. He has been known to run scared from chihuahuas.

Mrs, Gillen, who is terrified of all things canine, has no idea what a softy he is.

"Don't make me come over there with the dog. It won't be pretty."

This has the desired effect.

"I'll pay you half this week and the rest in two weeks' time, when Arthur's support cheque comes through."

"Nice talking to you, Mrs Gillen!"

In case you hadn't gathered, Jennifer Gillen is a nasty piece of work. She is a good example of when PI cases go bad. Her husband, having somehow heard about our investigation, decided he might as well get some enjoyment out of the crime he had supposedly been committing, so promptly started shagging a young intern at the library. I've learned in this profession that sometimes it's better to let sleeping dogs lie.

"Well done, Leon. You played a bloody blinder." I chuck him over a Rich Tea biscuit. He looks at me as if to say, "Cool, but I do prefer them with butter." It's gone in one bite.

I've never had two successful bad-debt calls in one week, never mind one morning, so I take this as encouragement that this whole turning-a-new-leaf gig just might work!

I check the office clock. Ten forty-five. Coffee time.

"Leon, stay there and hold the fort, I'm just nipping out for a coffee." He whimpers. He doesn't like being left alone.

"Oh, come on then ya big wuss!" He shoots across the floor and does a huge skid on the lino as he tries to take the corner for the door.

The rain has eased off. We head across to the little coffee cart that sits right on the quayside near the new pedestrian bridge over the Liffey. It's my favourite coffee place in all of Dublin, even Ireland. It's partly the coffee and partly the kick I get out the daily catch-up with Massimo, the main barista and owner. Massimo is a full-blooded Italian male who is as serious about coffee as he is about his womanising. Coffee is not a transaction, it's a ritual.

"Buon giorno, Massimo."

"Buon giorno, Flossimo. Latte extra dry?"

"Please."

Massimo gives me a full look over. "The lady she wear black today, no? Did someone dead?"

I laugh. "Ha! No, just trying to look sharp. It's the new me – big push for new clients this week."

"Is sharp … is ok. But too much. Scary job. Scary suit. Ze men, they run very fast away."

"Well thank God you've cracked it, Massimo, the mystery of my celibate status. Find me a strong silent type then, who won't run away."

"Ok, I keep my eye to ground," he says pointing at his ear.

"You do that, Massimo," I say resisting the temptation to correct him.

"No problem. Latte for you, extra dry. Biscotti for Leon."

"Thanks Massimo. Catch you tomorrow!"

"Si, si … domani, bella Floss. Domani."

I wish Massimo was my type. I'd say he's the absolute business in the sack. He's certainly had enough practice. Four out of five days, there's some blonde hottie dropping by the coffee cart on a blatant walk of shame back from his place down the quays.

Leon pads across the road ahead of me. As we come into the car park, Penny's emerging out of her car.

"Morning Penny!"

"Morning, boss."

"Don't call me that, you lemon. How are we this morning? How does the world look through your crazy glasses?"

"Grand. Conor slipped a disk in the shower this morning so it was pandemonium at our place."

"Ouch! Is The Oracle pulling his usual 'woe is me' caper?"

"With bells on top. He's propped up in bed at home making appeals for the Purple Star."

"Should I send flowers and one of those old-style bottles of Lucozade with the orange, crinkly plastic bit?" I ask.

"God no! He'd love that. He'd be telling me how much more sympathetic Florence Nightingale is and I'd never hear the end of it."

"Alrighty, I'll hold off so. So what's the story on our advertising push, Pen?"

"Yep, let me just fire up the PC and I'll give you a full debrief." Penny's PC operates at similar speeds to my own.

"Full debrief no less? Very fancy."

I was named Florence after the Italian city. Thanks Mum. One of my Dad's throwaway comments about my black hair being the texture of dental floss led to the nickname. The name stuck. Thanks Dad.

"So, it seems we've reached our budget. I know you hate the technical stuff, but we have to specify an upper limit of clicks through to our site and we reached that at about week two."

"What was the budget?"

"One thousand euros for five hundred clicks."

"What the …? If that gave us a hundred clients … fuck it, even five clients, I'd be delighted, but all we have is a trickle of queries and a shed-load coupons for penis enlargements."

She giggles. "I know, but it's a numbers game, hon. You have to think of them as qualified leads."

"Qualified my arse," I retort with arms crossed. "I've a feeling there's a recommendation coming …"

"Yep, pay evil giant Google the money. It's worth it. We don't get much corporate stuff from it, but it seems to be great for the individuals out there looking for small-scale stuff. Thirty-three per cent of last month's customers in fact. If you look at the value of each …"

"Stop right there! You're hurting my ears and wasting time that I'll never get back. Buy the extra thingies that you need, because today we're officially minted!"

"You made a few calls?" she asks, incredulous. I nod smugly in reply.

"Well done you! I know it's not easy for you."

"Want to know who coughed up?"

Penny nods eagerly.

"Archer and you'll never believe this … Gilly the Witch."

"No way! How did you manage that?"

"I threatened to set the mighty beast on her. Leon is a highly under-valued member of staff. If there are ever any cutbacks around here, it'd be touch and go between the two of you."

"Go easy on the motivational pep talks there, Floss."

"Just keeping you on your toes … but seriously, do fire ahead on the Google stuff, maybe up to 2K."

"On it," she says as she parks herself down with her coffee.

I go back to my list, thinking that two successful money-chasing calls surely must constitute an honest day's work. Yes? I'm starting to think about what I can do for the rest of the day when the silence is broken by the shrill tone of CTB's telephone. Leon, Penny and I all stare incredulously at the contraption that has rung a total of twenty times in two years. There's a prolonged pause before Penny and I both lunge for the phone. I make it just ahead of her but she hits the speakerphone button.

The voice is polished and female. "Page five of The Times. It's happened again."

Aoife Sheridan

,

3

Almost a year ago, we were engaged by Trilby Wealth Management Ltd to investigate repeated leaks of information that were supposed to be available at board level only. These leaks were killing the company on the stock market as the recipients of the juicy insider info were able to jump ahead of the market every time. They were laughing all the way to their Cayman Islands accounts, while Trilby's share values were decimated.

We went down the route of trying to find the outfits that would be benefiting most from the leaked information, but got lost in the rabbit warren of holding companies and offshore parent entities. 'Wicked web' does not even begin to describe it.

We were making slow progress when I decided to go slightly gung-ho. We put in a proposal to place an undercover director or consultant in the company. I spent ages on the pitch and then proudly presented it to the company's chairwoman and majority shareholder, Janet Barry.

Janet is old everything. Old school. Old money. Old value system. A gentle lady in life, but all steel and cold calm in the workplace. Her staff and colleagues both revere and fear her. She and her key partner sat through our entire presentation with a look of bemused horror on their faces. At the end, knowing I had lost the room, I bravely asked, "So, what did you think?"

Janet's offsider began to reply, but she stilled him with an authoritative hand.

"I'll take this one, Clive." Then, looking at me. "Florence ..."
She always insists on calling me by my full name, due to an
apparently longstanding abhorrence of pet names and
abbreviations. She has never once referred to us as CTB.

"While I appreciate the effort and ... ingenuity that has gone
into your presentation today, I cannot help but feel that it is
somewhat convoluted for our needs. I think we need some
old-fashioned blood, sweat and tears rather than high drama.
More Sherlock Holmes, less Miami Vice, if you will."

And with those imperious words, we had lost our first ever
client.

Devastated, I went into a mindless tailspin of recriminations
and self-accusations. How had this come about? Where had we
gone wrong? How could we avoid it happening again? Was I
cut out for this investigations malarkey at all?

But the "Page five of The Times" phone call is from none
other than Janet herself, returning to us with cap in hand,
seeking our help after nearly a year.

I feel completely vindicated, and Penny even more so (she'd
come up with our original proposal). I don't need to look over
at her; my Spider sense tells me she's beaming from ear to ear.

I hang up the phone having agreed to a nine o'clock
appointment in the morning. We tend to prefer to have our
meetings on client sites. One glimpse of the prefab would be
enough to send anyone running ... nevermind the sight of
Leon and our local pal Whacker.

"Well, well. A rather contrite Ms Barry don't you think?"
Penny chirps with arms folded.

"Her type don't do contrite, but sheepish ... that she did pretty
well. And more importantly, she does cheques. Big fat cheques!

I'm pretty close to doing a cartwheel here."

"Do NOT do a cartwheel," Penny cautions. "Last time you ended up in A&E."

"Fair point, but in my defence, I did not see the manhole. Right, down to bizo. Dust off that proposal from last year and let's see what tall tales we spun in their direction."

"Course, you do know if we win this job, it will involve a certain you know who?" says Penny.

"Don't remind me. I am painfully aware of that," I reply. "But I can't afford to think about that right now. Let's just focus on nailing this tomorrow and we can worry about 'he who cannot be named' after we're rolling in the first down-payment."

"Like it," Penny announces.

We spend the rest of the day reviewing the proposal and updating our slide deck to make it relevant for CTB as it is today. We have a couple of practice runs to make sure it's nicely polished, and call it a day at five o'clock on the buzzer. Penny has to get home to prepare the dinner for the gang. We do our usual ritual of inventing some gallery adventures (she really works in the gallery, remember) and mishaps for her to share with Conor. Today's 'incidents' include a heroin addict who mistook the gallery for a methadone clinic and an American lady who asked if she could buy the Monet.

I'm also keen to head home early and bask in the glory of a pretty promising start to CTB's new trajectory. The only way is up, it seems.

On my way home I stop in at the local one-stop-shop to pick up a celebratory bottle of Chardonnay and the makings of my favourite dinner ... spaghetti hoops on toast. Culinary bliss. I make a silent promise to try not to polish off the bottle by myself.

I pull up at the front of the house and sigh with the contentment of a relatively new house-owner. The novelty has not yet worn off.

My home is a Tardis-like cottage in Irishtown, a characterful suburb on the south side of the city near the mouth of the River Liffey. Having grown up on Dublin's northside, my mother was heartbroken when I moved across the river. It was as if I had run off and joined the Moonies.

Of course, that age-old rivalry between the north and south sides of the city, with skangers on the northside and snobs on the southside, is utter rubbish – particularly since the Celtic Tiger. The suburbs on both sides are peppered colourfully with all manner of social demographics, forming our own mini Irish melting pot. Gone are the days of having to make up an address to avoid being ignored in job applications. Now it's all equal opportunities Ireland. And we're much the better for it, despite still having a ways to go.

The house is my pride and joy. Back when I was earning the big bucks at my actuarial job, I spent a good chunk of cash on renovating the place. God knows it needed some serious TLC. It had a sordid history, starting with a prostitute and ending with repossession and a gang of squatters. By the time I rolled up to view it for the first time, the place was a shambles. The stink of stale cigarettes, beer, cats and worse almost forced me to turn around and run home to Mum. But my buddy Stace, artist and art teacher, was with me, and she sees the beauty and potential in everything. While she had the vision for my home as it is today, I had a nightmare of Dickensian proportions.

It took a lot of convincing on Stace's part. Her powerful vision combined with the name of the street, Ropewalk Place, almost had me. But it took Nora, my future neighbour, who came out onto the street and begged me to save her from the reprobates (her words), to finally nudge me across the dotted line.

Stace spelled out her little idea – demolish everything except the cute old-world cottage façade and build a large extension out and up. Eleven months later, after a serious makeover job and the sinking of all my savings, I was the proud owner of a killer gaff in an up-and-coming area within walking distance of the city.

The back of the house is south-facing and composed mainly of glass, supported by red-brick and steel. The front of the house faces onto Ringsend Park, which Leon looks at longingly from the front room. There are three bedrooms, an office, kitchen/living-room, utility room – and a modest garden relative to the size of Leon. My favourite room is the utility room. Having lived on and off in apartments and flats where my washing was constantly hanging off the cooker and the bath rails, the idea of having a room dedicated to laundry and, well, just storing stuff was a dream come true. I can often be found in there twirling and swinging my arms about like Julie Andrews in the Sound of the Music.

No. 17 Ropewalk Place is a little gem. More than enough for Leon and little old me.

We dash through the downpour and I wave to Nora who's stationed at her front window in the role of Ground Command Leader, Neighbourhood Watch. Those bloody Neighbourhood Watch stickers give nosy neighbours carte blanche to pry into all the goings on in the area. But it's good to have these vigilante neighbours close at hand. They never miss a trick.

I deactivate the alarm and start straight into the vino.

"A toast to CTB, Leon!" He licks his lips messily and looks at me with eyes that ask: "Dinner is when exactly?"

"You're worse than any man, you know that?" He gives me the blank dog face.

Once dinner is dealt with I sit down to watch 'Strictly Come Dancing', one of my many guilty pleasures. I'm ten minutes in, but find the pairing of the former rugby player and the pixie-like glitterbug not enough to distract me from my thoughts.

I'm not worried about losing the pitch tomorrow. We lost them once so I can handle losing the Trilby account again. I'm more worried about what it means if we win the damned job.

In our pitch to Trilby last year, we needed a guy, partly for gender balance and partly to go undercover as a director of the company, somebody arrogant and charming enough to be able to pull it off. The only option we could come up with was McCarthy & Co; the competition and potential co-opetition in the investigative space. They specialise in undercover work.

We'd had some initial contract negotiations and dealings with their head sales guy, Neville, and both sides were keen to hammer out a deal. Everything was going swimmingly until the head man, Milo McCarthy, walked into our office. 'Hurricane Milo' is how Penny now refers to him, due to the trail of destroyed females he leaves in his wake.

He was everything my mother warned me about. Tallish, body of a boxer, face of a Marlborough Man, the faint trace of a real tan and enough wrinkles to hint at character. His dark-brown hair was slightly receding, highlighting the delicious scar below his left eyebrow, and he had these strange, hazel eyes with an 'I'm gonna mess with you' mocking twinkle. If Helen of Troy's face launched a thousand ships, this fella's eyes must have popped a thousand cherries.

It took every ounce of my willpower and a stern 'get-a-grip-on-yourself' look from Penny to stop me from throwing myself across the desk at him. I'm not sure what my face was doing but my loins had gone into hyper-drive. Never in my life had my body reacted so instantly to the sheer presence of another human being. But then never in my life had I met a specimen quite as delectable as Milo McCarthy. Trouble with a capital T.

During our meeting, I managed to make an utter muppet of myself. I couldn't remember our proposal (not even the name of our client) and I eventually had to hand over the reins to an eagerly awaiting Penny. Thank Christ for Penny. She pitched our idea in her clear and concise manner, and Milo immediately indicated he'd be keen for McCarthy & Co to be involved, on one condition – he himself would be the undercover man.

"I'm just the guy for the job," he said, oozing confidence. "I'm the right age profile, I've a background in financial services, I'm a sharp dresser and am oozing with charm. They'll be putty in my hands." As he said this, he did this strange form of double-wink in my direction that nearly undid me. Surely a double-wink should just be a blink? But no, with Milo's eyes, it took on a life of its own. It sent out an electric pulse that shot straight to my fanny, kicking off the loin lambada again. Was I drooling? Milo's double-wink should be illegal.

"Yes, well …" I stammered, and looked at Penny, wondering if I was still visibly drooling. She nodded and jumped in to save me, "What Floss is trying to say, is that Trilby are a very conservative firm, who have been around for generations. They do not trust blow-ins, so a sharp suit will only take you so far."

"Care to take a wager on that, princess?" he said with an

infuriating smirk.

I finally found my voice again. "Princess? Really? Let's not worry about the who and how until we have them in the bag."

"You're the boss!" Milo piped up.

Arrrrgh! The phrase 'you're the boss' is near the top of my 'Ten Most Annoying Phrases' list. While it implies agreement and subservience, what that person is actually saying is, "This is a ridiculous decision which can only end in disaster but I'm going to agree to it now and I look forward to wallowing in smugness when I'm proved right".

When mere mortals use this phrase around me, I slam-dunk them with one of my razor-sharp put-downs, but when Milo uttered it with another wink, it sent another sonic boom through my nether regions.

For the love of God, get a hold of yourself, Floss. Say something sensible.

"Yep, that's right I'm the head honcho around here." What? Was this the best I could do? Penny was staring at me open-mouthed with an expression that said "Did you call yourself a honcho?" I couldn't help it! This man, with his tapered suit and open-necked crisp blue shirt, had turned me into a raving lunatic.

He was regarding me with a quizzical look, not quite sure what to do with my last comment, but eventually he came to my rescue with "Well I better get going, I'm sure you ladies have a busy day ahead. Keep me posted on how the gig goes down at Trilby."

He tipped an imaginary hat to us both and strutted out the door, leaving us with the delightful image of his fit little butt, which seemed to have taken on an independent swagger of its own.

As soon as the door shut, my forehead hit the desk.

"Hello, what just happened there? Is Zelda awake?" Penny was laughing away to herself.

"Zelda is not only awake, she's on fire. I cannot possibly work with that man."

Zelda is my name for my hoohoo, front bum, down there or whatever you want to call it. I was inspired to give it a name after watching a play called the Vagina Monologues. If you haven't seen it, it's a fantastic show, which does - quite literally - involve a lot of monologues about vaginas. One section is dedicated to listing all of the various names for a lady's unmentionables, including contributions from the audience. What became clear is that guys have all the fun with naming their man bits, giving them colourful personalities like lad, mickey or willy, while women are stuck with words that sound either medical or violent ... vagina, gee, gash (eeuwh!), snatch and, the pièce de resistance, the C word, the most violent of words.

I wanted my genitalia to have a presence, a voice and an attitude, even. And so Zelda was born. Penny, who came to the show with me, is the only person on the planet who knows about Zelda. I reckon most men would run a mile from a chick with a named vagina, so it's better to keep it on the down low.

"Down girl," scolded Penny. "You cannot seriously fall for that? I mean, 'the gig goes down'. What does he think he is ... a rapper?"

"Mmmmm ... Mc Milo ... badaboom!" I reply laughing.

Oh, I had fallen alright. Zelda had just discovered her kryptonite.

Aoife Sheridan

4

So, when we lost the Trilby account, I was devastated. But a tiny piece of me, the libido part, was swimming with relief. Milo represented everything I didn't want in a man: over-confident, threateningly handsome and an out-and-out womaniser.

In the intervening year, I'd spoken to Milo twice when he flipped some overflow work our way. He had the same impact on me every time. All roads led to X-rated thoughts. But I was always too grateful for the work to turn it down.

And here I am again, back in Milo McCarthy's orbit.

I agree with Penny that we'd only call him if we got the go-ahead for the proposal from Janet at Trilby. This gives me a little more breathing space and also ensures I won't be distracted by thoughts of him swaggering into the boardroom, in a Clint Eastwood-style poncho, to whisk me away for a good seeing to. I'm not kidding. These are the notions that are flying around my head.

I go through my presentation notes again and do another run-through for Leon. He falls asleep half way through.

"Thanks for the vote of confidence, ya big hairy rascal."

I hit the hay early and sleep the sleep of someone who drank just a snifter too much white wine.

I wake up at six-thirty on the buzzer and take Leon for a run. I say 'take' as if I'd some form of control. In reality, Leon drags me around Ringsend Park four times. Someday, I'm going to buy him a sled.

I had arranged to meet Penny at the Insomnia café near the Trilby offices in Fitzwilliam Square for a mutual psych-up and coffee-fuelling session. I get there first and order two full fat lattes.

Penny arrives wearing what she describes as her 'finery'. This entails a brown and mustard tweed two-piece number that my mother's mother's mother might have worn if she'd been raised on a country farm in West Sussex. Style is not Penny's strong suit. But I can't fault her for lack of effort.

"So, how did you explain the rig-out to Conor this morning?" I ask.

"I told him the mayor was coming to the gallery to rehang the Monet," she says, smiling proudly.

This story is actually quite credible as the Monet was slashed by some nut-job last year and has been in restoration for months. It caused quite the stir at the time.

"Brilliant. Your creativity never ceases to amaze me," I say. "How are you feeling?"

"Charged. You?" she asks, knowing I'm in bits.

"Sick as a dog and this coffee is not helping," I moan.

I get very, very nervous before pitches. I'm fine once I get in front of a crowd and get going, but beforehand, my insides take an absolute pummelling. As does any toilet within range. Sorry, but it's true.

We spend the next twenty minutes talking about anything but the presentation. Penny knows after two years working with me that she just needs to distract me.

At five to nine, we head across the road to the imposing Georgian offices of Trilby Wealth Management Ltd and are ushered upstairs and straight into the boardroom. We decline the offer of more coffee from Margaret, the matronly receptionist, opting instead for water.

We're sitting at a large oak table, fidgeting nervously, when in marches Janet, all business and professionalism.

"Morning ladies," she booms.

"Morning, Janet. How are you?" I reply.

She arches one eyebrow at me. "In light of yesterday's article in The Times and a further drop in our share price of 3%, I'm not doing that well today. In fact, I'm starting to get angry."

Janet saying this is, frankly, terrifying. Her delivery is both ladylike and menacing. I'm glad we're the good guys. I nod in what I think is a wise and sympathetic fashion.

"Completely understandable," I say. "Are we waiting on any others or do you want us to get started? We may just need to organise a projector. Maybe I should go back to reception to …"

Janet shakes her head impatiently: "There's no need for a projector. I remember your proposal clearly. And nobody else will be joining us."

Interesting. I glance over at Penny and raise my eyebrows. She shrugs.

"I need this arrangement to go through me and me alone. Understood?" she demands rather than asks.

We nod like chastened school kids.

Janet continues: "Yesterday's leaked information was only released during the board meeting the previous day. Therefore, I'm assuming only a director can be responsible. The only director who definitely didn't release the data is me. Ergo I am the only person I can trust. I have floated the idea of a new non-executive director among my colleagues in preparation for our little charade. How quickly can you get your undercover detective in place?"

"Let's see," I say, "pending confirmation of our undercover agent being available, it will take us at least one week to get a credible profile out into the ether. Once we have that set up, we can arrange interviews with your directors. Presuming you can get them to agree to the new guy, we could be up and running in one to two weeks. Which should fit nicely with your next board meeting."

"Excellent. Make it happen," she barks. "Margaret has a cheque for you at reception on your way out."

We have been dismissed.

Penny and I gather our things and file out the door, stopping to pick up the 'golden ticket' on the way out. We just about make it as far as the street before ripping open the envelope with the cheque. And oh what a cheque! I let out a "whoop whoop" before Penny clamps my mouth shut. Written in beautiful, almost calligraphy-style writing is a cheque to the tune of twenty-five thousand Euros. This is the single biggest retainer CTB has ever received.

I show Penny the cheque. Her eyes nearly explode with wonder behind her glasses. She drags me round the corner onto Baggot Street where we do this awkward part-hug part-victory dance.

"Let's celebrate! Where's open?" I shout, bursting with excitement.

"May I remind you, Floss, that it's nine-thirty in the morning. Nowhere's open. Unless you want to hit an early house." Early houses are pubs that open at 7.30am in the guise of providing after-work drinks to shift workers, but are, in reality, the first port of call for the city's winos and alchos. They are generally less than salubrious establishments.

I contemplate it for just a second but then say "No, of course you're right. Besides, the early houses generally don't stock bubbles."

Penny just shakes her head. "Speaking of bubbles, I don't mean to burst yours, but you're going to have to make that call …"

And then it dawns on me. I'm going to have to face Milo.

Milo McCarthy, in the investigative world, is the real deal. He worked for ten years in the Garda Special Branch before taking a bullet in the ass during a botched bank robbery and, not long after that, he took early retirement. He was only thirty-two. Rather than sitting round on his punctured butt cheeks, he quickly set up McCarthy & Co and has spent the last eight years building it into a very successful private-eye firm. If CTB is fighting for relegation in the Vauxhall League, McCarthy & Co is near the top of the Premiership.

His firm manages to be extremely successful, while keeping a low profile – which is key to being able to credibly go undercover. Milo himself would rarely go undercover; he has a team of crazy cats who risk life and limb in precarious situations for moderate pay. So I wondered why he was insistent on being the undercover director in the Trilby caper.

We head back to the office but I stop at Massimo's for two lattes and some caramel slices for Penny and myself. As celebrations go it's pretty muted, but we share the idea that all significant achievements should be marked with an upsurge in calorie intake.

When I get to the coffee cart, Massimo is laying on the charm with some blonde, but all credit to him, he can still take an order without missing a beat in the conversation. I briefly think he's bucking the trend with his male multi-tasking until I realise that flirting for Italians is synonymous with breathing. Effortless. A poor Irish guy would have scalded his hand with the milk steamer by now.

As I'm paying for the coffees and treats, Massimo briefly interrupts his pursuit of blondie and turns to me. "There is girl in car park. She looking ... no, she watch your office."

"Oh yeah?" I reply distractedly as I load the two sugars into my coffee.

"She is blonde with ..."

"Ah surely you've got your hands full in the blonde department, Massi?" I wink at him.

He shakes his head "No, no, not for me this lady. Not my type."

Not a looker is what he's trying to say.

"Grand, thanks for the heads up. I'll keep an eye out for her. Thanks for the coffees and I'll see ya tomorrow."

He waves, but he's already back in full eye contact with his prey.

I cross the quays and head back through the car park, expecting to see Massimo's lady, but the place is deserted, apart from Whacker. He's over by my car door, dragging on a cigarette as if it was his last breath. He can't be more than fourteen, but you'd be forgiven for thinking he was forty plus.

"Are you scaring away my clients with your local charm, Whacker?" I ask him as I approach.

"Me? Jaysus no. It's your partner's scary woollen number that's scarin' the shite out of everyone around here. Bleedin' extreme makeover is what yiz need."

"I'll give you an extreme makeover, you little pup." (God, I really need some new retorts.)

"I can hear you, you little shit!" from Penny through the door.

I go through into the office, but just before I close the door, I hear Whacker saying, "Hey bud, if it's the tiny little blonde ting you're after, she left ten minutes ago."

I pop my head back out the door. "Thanks Whacker. Let me know if you see her again? If you find out who she is, there's a tenner in it for you."

"Fuck off with yer tenner. I don't get outta bed for less than fifteen." He's trying to sneer like whoever is his role model.

"Your loss, darling," I pipe back at him as I head back inside.

Penny is fuming inside her tweed number, which must be hot work.

"The cheek of that little so-and-so. He's shifting around out there in his Adidas tracksuit and stolen runners and he's giving me a hard time" she exclaims, incredulous.

Although for the first time ever I'm in complete agreement with Whacker on this, I manage to tut-tut: "Yep, the little twerp. What does he know?"

The truth is that, with all that patterned wool and Penny's slight frame, it's hard to see the woman inside. But I would never change anything about Penny, particularly the way she dresses. Her crazily conservative dress sense and the first impression she gives of meekness always lead our clients and their bad guys to underestimate her. They see the 'little lady' or the secretary and are clueless to her hidden talents. She is often completely ignored in client meetings. And that suits me and CTB just fine.

"Penny, can you nip over to Reads and pick up some of that extra thick paper? We need our undercover director to have his CV printed on some decent stock. Grab a twenty out of petty cash there."

"No problem, hon." She gathers her things, takes the cash and is heading out the door when she pauses and turns to me with a knowing look.

"Don't you for a second think I don't know what's going on here. You're sending me off on a noddy job so you can call Hurricane Milo."

I blush and wave her away. "Do what you're told," I snap back. After twenty-five years of friendship, there's not a lot I can get by her.

I *was* trying to get rid of her. I have to call Milo and I can't possibly do it with Penny in the office. It's going to be tough enough without having her watching over me. I rummage through my rolodex until I come across his business card. I pull it out and stare at it for a few minutes before picking up my phone. I take three deep breaths, and dial.

It rings for long enough to make me think I'm going to get his voicemail, so when he actually answers, I'm a little flustered.

"McCarthy & Co. Milo here."

"Eh, hello. Can I speak to Milo, please?" I stutter.

"As I mentioned earlier, this is he," he says, a touch of mirth in his tone.

"Right, yes. Well, this is Florence McFarland of CTB Investigations."

"Well if it isn't my favourite private dick." He's toying with me. "How may I be of assistance on this fine winter's morning?"

"It's investigator. Private Investigator."

"Well, I sit corrected, but my question is still valid."

God, he knows how to push my buttons. I'm infuriated, but also wishing desperately that he would push a few of my buttons. Nobody's been near them for ... I've actually stopped keeping track it's been so long.

Gather yourself, Floss.

"Right. It's the Trilby case we pitched together on last year? We had a meeting with Janet Barry this morning and they have given us the go ahead."

"And now you need my help," he asks.

"I see it more as mutual back-scratching than you helping us." I can hear myself getting defensive now.

"Mmmm, mutual back-scratching. Tell me more about that, McFarland," he says, lowering his voice to a throaty murmur.

"Look, do you want the job or not?" I'm straining to avoid the squeaky pitch my voice tends to get when I'm annoyed.

"Alright, keep your clothes on. Let me just look at the diary ... let's see now ... from memory this gig is just part-time, dipping in and out of meetings, and you're on top of all the surveillance and fun stuff. Is that about right?"

"That's right," I squeak.

"I should be able to fit that in, but I think we should meet first to talk through the arrangements."

"No way! Out of the question," I say a little too quickly, and then backtrack. "I mean … em … yes that's a very good idea, but my associate Penny will brief you on the plan of attack."

"I'd rather deal with you than your associate, if I'm going to be on point on this one."

"Firstly, I am on point on this one. You are a sub-contractee. Secondly, well I don't actually have a secondly." *Nice one, Floss.*

"OK, whatever, but how about I meet you at the Pearl Brasserie tomorrow at two o'clock for a full briefing. My treat. Think of it as McCarthy & Co's thank you for sending this job our way."

"Well …" I flounder. Resist the temptation to babble and fill the silence! Resist!

"I won't take no for an answer, so see you then," he replies, followed by the dial tone.

The cheeky monkey! Presumptuous and arrogant and … who am I kidding? … delicious. My heart's still racing.

About five minutes later, I am still staring at the phone as Penny comes back with a couple of reams of the good paper. She takes one knowing look at me and says, "I'm going to use my superior powers of deduction now. Judging by your rather flushed facial complexion and the tiny bit of drool on your bottom lip, you managed to call the infamous Milo. Yes?"

I nod.

"So, how did it go?"

"He's available for the Trilby job and I have a debriefing with him at two tomorrow afternoon."

"Great, where are you meeting?" she asks matter-of-factly.

"Em … the Pearl Brasserie," I say sheepishly.

"Floss, you and I both know that the Pearl Brasserie is not a typical business luncheon location. A start time of two in the afternoon lends itself more to a late boozy lunch, followed closely by a hotel check-in rather than a business get-together. I'd be careful that he's not trying to de-brief you, if you get my gist."

"Whoa there, Penny. I think you might be getting ahead of yourself. This is all fully above board and tomorrow will be strictly professional." I'm getting tetchy, I can hear it in my own whiny tone.

"If you say so, hon. But I just don't want you getting your heart broken and messing up a great job for CTB, all in the one afternoon. So what are you going to wear?" Penny has this great way of dishing out warnings and advice and then briskly moving on to the next topic.

"Oh God. I don't know. Help!"

"I'll lend you one of my suits. That would keep everybody grounded."

We both laugh out loud, then my laughter turns into on-the-edge-hysteric, and Penny stares at me with a concerned expression. It's the same face she turns to her son Oscar when he has run head first at something.

I've started chewing my nails. My brow is furrowed.

"No seriously, I need help."

Aoife Sheridan

5

The following day I decide, with Penny's much-needed help, that the best approach for the big Milo showdown is to dress down for the occasion, so it's clear that I'm not trying to impress. After a morning of pulling my wardrobe apart, I finally land on a pair of skinny jeans with a cream chiffon blouse and cowboy boots. To me, it says, 'Femme, but don't fuck with me'. This is precisely the message I want to convey. My hair refuses to be tamed this morning so I just have to let the 'fro' breathe and take on a life of its own. It's not pretty.

I head to the office first, leaving Leon behind to mind the house. He hates being left alone and on the way to the car I can hear him whimpering and scratching my beautiful oak front door. I'm in the car park at work before I know it, thinking, how did I get here? Did I drive on autopilot the entire way? *Worrying.*

Once in the office, I check my phone for messages. Penny has rung to say she can't make it in today as Conor's slipped disk has reached crisis levels. She has to stay at home and pander to his every need. Marital bliss.

I head out to grab a coffee from Massimo. No further sign of the mystery blonde. I wander back to the prefab and, as I open the door to the office, a small piece of white paper flutters to the ground. My 'post no bills' sign has obviously been totally ignored by the poor sod who is delivering the flyers. I am sympathetic but still annoyed.

Flopping into my chair, I cast a casual glance at the piece of paper. This is no junk mail with the latest Lidl or Aldi offers.

Somebody has left me a note. Very exciting. It is written in small, elegant handwriting – definitely a woman. Or a very camp man.

You must to help me. They steal my friend.'

Elegant writing, but not so hot on the English grammar, so definitely a foreign national. Now, I am intrigued. If I were a betting woman, I'd have a flutter on the mysterious blonde girl being the author.

"Well sweetheart," I say out loud. "You have definitely got my attention, but without a contact number or some way to find you, there's not a whole lot I can do for you." I create a new case file for her so she doesn't get lost in the chaos. I file it under 'Jane Doe', mainly because it sounds cool.

I while away the rest of the morning putting together the brief for Milo's fake director profile. I have to be careful that his schooling and places of employment do not overlap with any of the directors at Trilby.

CTB – Cover profile

Name: Magnus Flynn

Age: 43 (I add on a few years to his age just to annoy him; a form of Irish flirtation)

Education: Bachelor of Business Studies, Trinity College Dublin, 1992
MBA Harvard, Boston, 2005

Employment: 1992-2005 Deloitte Financial Services, from graduate programme to Partner in 2000
2005 – Study at Harvard

2006-2012 – Phoenix Investments, Partner & Shareholder

Directorships:	Dublin Airport Authority, Non-Executive Director NAMA, Non-Executive Director PaymentsOnline.ie, Executive Director
Marital Status:	Divorced, no children
Interests:	Formula 1, golf, kite-surfing.

When I'm happy with the profile, I email it to Penny for actioning. She will get a bogus profile set up on LinkedIn and Facebook, along with some fictitious web articles and white papers that will give the profile some added credibility. The first place the other directors will look will be on Google. Janet will mention that the Trilby recruitment team had done a thorough background check on Magnus. Fingers crossed, the combination should do the trick.

Just before heading off to meet Milo for lunch I make a quick call to Neil O'Connor, aka Zippy, my electronics whizz-kid (he is a kid – no more than nineteen years old). He was working for Peats Electronics while developing a sideline in selling and installing high-tech surveillance equipment. When Peats got into financial difficulties, he decided to make the surveillance gear a full-time endeavour.

The phone rings for ages before he picks up. "Yep," says a distinctly disinterested, high-pitched male voice. I note that setting up on his own has not improved Zippy's phone skills.

"Hey Neil, it's Floss here over at CTB."

"Yeah?"

"I need some top-end surveillance gear for a corporate outfit."

"Details?" *Charming.*

"Three cameras, two bugs and a bug sweeper. It's a fixed date as it's a board meeting."

"When?" Seriously, kid, where are your manners?

"Monday, November 12th."

"Self-install or my guys?"

"It's a DIY job. So, how are you placed?" I ask, resisting the temptation to scold him for being so monosyllabic.

"I'll make it work." This constitutes chatty.

"Can you flick me a quote? Come to think of it, make it three listening devices instead of two – and top of the range."

"Cool."

"Pleasure doing business with you, as always, Zippy."

"Yep." He hangs up.

Zippy's nickname comes from his unnerving resemblance to one of the characters from the Seventies and Eighties kids TV show, 'Rainbow'. All of the characters were just plain creepy, from the giant bear with his mushed-up tiny face to the uber-camp hippo, and a presenter with the tightest pants I've ever seen on daytime television. How he kept his blood circulating I'll never know. Zippy was this camel-coloured thing with a big round face and a mouth that spanned his entire head, and in place of lips he had a giant zip. See what I mean? Creepy. And our Neil was the spitting image. Bless him.

What Zippy lacked in telephone skills and physical appearance, he more than made up for in the geeky underworld of surveillance gear. He always had access to the best stuff and his team were slick performers in terms of efficiency and discretion. His appalling phone manner was a minor extra cost.

I touch up my mascara and lip liner before heading out for lunch with Milo, glad that Penny is not there to give me her I-am-thoroughly-disgusted-with-you look. I walk over, hoping the wind will put a bit of colour in my cheeks. It does, but also whips my mass of black curls into a mess of black candyfloss. The 'fro' I left home with has taken on gigantic proportions. I should have a 'Wide Load' sign on my back.

So it's with this boost of self-confidence that I breeze downstairs into the Pearl Brasserie, a socially acceptable 10 minutes late. Milo is already seated at a cosy table for two in the back corner. He gets up quickly to greet me and I notice that he too has dressed down for the occasion: casual white shirt open at the neck, a well-worn pear of Diesel jeans and some industrial-strength Timberlands. I'm momentarily transfixed, as is, apparently, our waiter. He gives me a knowing look as he pulls out my seat. My right hand immediately goes to try and control my hair, feels the frizz and retreats quickly underneath the table. *A lost cause.*

"Ms McFarland," he almost purrs, raising a bemused eyebrow at my coiff.

"Milo," I nod (a distant satellite records an unusual movement on the earth's surface as my hair sways back and forth).

"How about an icebreaker?" he asks, drinks menu in hand.

"Just a sparkling water for me, thanks." I'm determined to remain sober and in control.

"Really? I have a nice red Burgundy on the way. You wouldn't let me drink alone now, would you?" he asks with that infuriating little smirk.

"Maybe a small glass with my meal," I say quickly, to keep the peace.

"That's the girl. We need to celebrate our upcoming venture in style."

I have to redirect where this is going, urgently. "I see this more as a project brief rather than a celebration. I'll be keen to celebrate when we've found the leak at Trilby."

"Why do I always feel like I'm the bold boy at school when I'm around you, McFarland?"

"Can I suggest that you save that question for your therapist?" I say. "He will love that, I'm sure."

"*She* will love that. Excellent suggestion."

The waiter arrives with the water and vino and Milo orders: "Sirloin, medium rare please, and the lady will have the Caesar salad,." His cheeky grin provokes an urge to smack him across the chops.

"Actually, I'll have the ribeye, rare. All the trimmings."

The waiter rolls his eyes and swishes back towards the kitchen.

"Ah, Floss's fighting spirit. Fantastic. So you were saying about the project brief ..."

"Em, yes. That's right. I've prepared your profile. If you could take a look at it, we'll get it out into cyber space over the next week." I hand the one-pager across the table. His index finger manages to briefly touch the back of my hand. Electric shock. I jerk back my hand, spilling my sparkling water. I leap up and start fussing over the spillage, my face roaring red. *Mortified.*

Milo leans across and grabs my hand. "Just leave it. It's not going to do any harm." The strength in his arm is urging me firmly back to my seat.

"I'm going to need that Burgundy after all," I say quietly. He nods, laughs and begins to pour.

"So let's have a look at this," he says starting to flick through his profile. "Divorced, so that makes me single. Interesting." Again he smirks at me. "Mmm, hmm, ok, looks good, except for the kite-surfing. This guy should be ultra-conservative. Formula 1 and golf are perfect, but the closest this guy gets to kite-surfing is through the window of his Mercedes as he's driving along the coast road."

"Actually, on the car front, I've already lined up a rental Jaguar for you – a 2011 XF."

"A Jaguar even? A woman after my own taste. This job is really becoming attractive … in more ways than one." I glance at him to check for hidden meaning but he's back looking over the profile.

Fighting to get the meeting back on track, I start on my spiel. "Just to give you a quick reminder of what we need to do. We'll need to make a few brief appearances in the office, starting pretty sharpish. There'll be an interview of sorts with the other directors. Then you'll need to be seen swanning in and out of Janet's offices for a couple of meetings."

His hazel eyes are zeroed in on mine. "Swanning, I can do," he jibes.

"Naturally, it's why we chose you."

"Ouch," he says, holding an imaginary knife to his heart.

"The big date we're working towards," I say, again trying to redirect the conversation, "is the next board meeting, which is on November 12th. I plan to sweep the room for bugs before and after. We'll have the room rigged for sound and vision so we can review the meeting and compare notes on whether any particular individuals are acting hinky in any way."

"Did you say kinky?" he asks, innocently enough apart from the raised eyebrow.

"No, hinky, as in out of sorts."

"Oh. Shame. Really, is there such a word as hinky?" *Down eyebrow, down.*

"Dictionary.com. For definite."

"Care to take a wager on that, McFarland? Say loser buys lunch."

"First, you are paying for lunch out of your kindness and gratitude for having business sent your way. Secondly, I bet you a tenner the word hinky exists."

"Ok, how about loser pays a tenner and shouts the next lunch?" he asks with a twinkle in his eyes.

"You're on," I say, laughing while trying to hide my growing excitement.

We spend the next few minutes chatting amiably. He is a surprisingly attentive listener when not making fun of me. When he forgets his role of schmoozy charmer, everything about him softens and becomes ... damn it, even more attractive.

He's regaling me with tales of his last investigative adventure involving a drugs ring when lunch arrives. The waiter tops up our wines and I'm feeling that nice alcohol buzz and glow. The beer goggles will be next.

Don't get me wrong. One does not need to look at Milo McCarthy through vino-tinted goggles. Without them he is an out-and-out 'ten'. But I trade strictly in the 'seven to seven point five' range, with personality appreciation sometimes bumping me up to an eight at a stretch. So, allowing for the fact that there are roughly three good-looking native men in the whole of Ireland (and no, Craig Doyle is not one of them), Milo McCarthy is well out of my league.

I've obviously gone into a bit of a trance while I have this inner conversation. When I look up, Milo is staring at me quizzically. "What is going on in that head of yours, McFarland?" he asks gently. "I'd pay good money to find out."

"Was just going over some numbers in my head," I say quickly, with a slight blush.

"Oh right. Always focused on the job at hand. You know, too much focus on work can make Floss a very dull girl."

With that, he's taken me from a place where I wanted to tear his clothes off to wanting to punch him in the face.

"Oh-oh. I seem to have woken the beast." He backs his chair away from the table with his hands raised in a defensive boxing pose.

"You wouldn't like me when I'm angry," I say, in an attempt to diffuse my own emotions, but feeling the blood still flowing through my face. The curse of a fair complexion. Every 'redner' I pull is front and centre for all to see.

"I might surprise you." He unleashes one of his trademark double-winks.

I'm about to melt into my chair when my mobile phone bursts over the quiet afternoon hum in the restaurant, breaking whatever was going on across the table between us. The spell, if you will.

"Howareya Floss. It's me, Whacker. Yer tiny blonde wan is knockin' around the car park again. You owe me a tenner."

I look at Milo with a disappointed feeling in my stomach, both for me and for the half-eaten steak on my plate.

"Gotta go."

6

I wobble my way out of the restaurant, feeling the anaesthetic effect of the wine on my legs. I flag down a taxi and direct the driver back to CTB headquarters.

"Not a bad day now, thank God," the cabbie says, hopeful of a good natter with his new fare.

"Sorry my friend, but I need to focus on sobering up and not puking in your taxi, so I won't be able to do the chat thing today." The cabbie looks as if I'd smacked him in the face – which is effectively what I have done. There's nothing more insulting to a Dublin taxi driver than rejecting 'the chat'.

He puts the boot down and we are back at CTB within seven minutes. I pay the guy and give him a hefty tip.

Whacker is standing by my car, chewing on a matchstick. He obviously thinks it makes him look tough. It doesn't.

"Where's the girl?" I ask, as I climb unsteadily out of the taxi.

"Steady on there, ma. She's after leavin' 'bout five minutes ago. Ya took yer time."

"Damn it. We practically broke the land speed record getting here. What type of snitch are you if you can't get me here in time?" I ask, frustrated - though mainly with having walked out on a delicious lunch and even tastier company.

"I'm no snitch, ma, but I did get yer wan's digits. The number's under your door. I'll take that tenner whenever yer ready. Cash on delivery, ma, if ya don't mind."

I root through my purse and scramble together ten euros, mainly in coins. Whacker is not impressed.

"It still works, you know, Whacker!"

"It's not good for me image to be janglin' around the place with all them coins. Are you on the bread line or wha'?"

"Not far off, Whacker, not far off. I could be getting a dig-out from you in the not too distant future. Thanks for your help. Keep on keeping an eye out if you don't mind."

"You're the boss!" he says with a military salute.

"Whatever," I reply absent-mindedly. Back in the office, I pick up another small, white piece of paper. It's the same handwriting:

Please call 085-7865438. Nika.

I grab my mobile and try the number. It rings out. No voicemail.

"Shit, girl. How can I help you if you won't pick up the bloody phone?" I say out loud.

I try to distract myself with paperwork and more lists but my mind keeps going back to the mystery of this elusive foreign girl and the spot on my hand where Milo McCarthy touched me 'accidentally' over lunch. I can't help but wonder where the afternoon would have taken us, had I not been called away by Whacker. I've butterflies doing the rumba in my stomach just thinking about the possibilities.

Eventually the lunchtime wine catches up with me and I curl up under a fleece blanket on the sofa at the back wall of the office. It's one of those corner couches, so I have to make myself into a proper foetus shape to get comfortable. It doesn't take long for me to pass out.

My sleep is consumed by a disturbing dream about a giant wheel of camembert chasing me and Mum over Howth Head.

The cheese starts ringing a loud bell and we've just run into a dark alleyway, since there appears to be nowhere else to go, when I'm abruptly woken up by the CTB landline ringing for the second time in one week. I am momentarily wondering if it is still the cheese ringing the bell before I fully come to.

I scramble across the office with the blanket entwined in my legs and fall clumsily onto the desk. "Hello, CTB Investigations," I say, slightly out of breath.

"Just checking up on you, McFarland," Milo drawls.

"Great, two dads. That's just what I need." The wine-induced nap has left me grumpy and ready for a fight.

"Well now I am offended. I might have five years on you, but surely you can't think I'm old enough to be your father?" he asks incredulously, but with a trace of humour. I sense the wine has not fully worn off him yet.

"Maybe you started young."

He giggles with his unexpected schoolboy charm, both infectious and disarming.

"An answer for everything, McFarland. Look, I just wanted to make sure everything's ok. You kind of left lunch in a hurry."

"It's all good, just a potential client I've been trying to track down."

"Wow, if you offer that prompt service to all your clients, where do I sign?" he chuckles.

"Sadly for you, you remain in the CTB sub-contractor role and, therefore, are expected to be at *my* beck and call."

"I am at your disposal," he says, all formal.

"Proper order."

"I'll be in touch on the Trilby gig, McFarland." He rings off.

I am still gathering myself and trying to still my beating heart, when my mobile makes the sonar sound for a text message. I flick it on and read:

> Hinky: .adjective (hinkier, hinkiest), US informal: (of a person) dishonest or suspect: he knew the guy was hinky; (of an object) unreliable. Source = Oxford English Dictionary. Guess I owe you another lunch? M

O to the M to the My God. That is a flirtatious text if I ever saw one. Milo McCarthy, Stud McMuffin is batting his SMS eyelids at moi!

After deliberating long and hard whether to smiley-face or not to smiley-face, I text back "And a tenner ...", opting for the non-committal dot, dot, dot.

I sit for a while with my feet on the desk, allowing myself to indulge in some x-rated thoughts before calling Penny.

"Hey missus. How's Red Cross Command Central?" I ask when Penny answers. I can hear a lot of noise in the background. "Not good by the sounds of it."

"Well, Sean just jumped on Conor in his usual life-is-but-a-climbing-frame way and the dying cow-like sounds you can hear in the background are the result. His back has gone into spasms now, allegedly. Honestly, I think I'd rather he had man-flu. At least you know what you're dealing with then. Meanwhile, Sean is out the back crying his eyes out. So all in all, just your average day here in the Firth household. How did your date go?"

"It was not a date. It was a business briefing."

"Honestly, Floss, I can hear down the phone how red your face is. You can't hide from Aunty Penny. Tell me all."

"In terms of the profile, he liked what he saw."

"I'm sure he did," she chuckles.

"Stop it! The only change is to remove the kite-surfing. He reckons it's too adventurous for our fictitious director friend. I tend to agree, so let's replace it with 'avid reader' or something along those lines."

"Fine, done. But how did it really go?" Penny asks, not letting me off the hook that easily.

"Well, if you must know, I was like a dribbling mess at the start, never mind by the end of it. The combination of red wine, his testosterone and that bloody double-wink had me ready to promise him my first-born child."

"Oh God. This is not good. Tell me you didn't end up in the sack?"

"How dare you! You know I never put out on a first date."

"A date! See? I knew it!" she shouts triumphantly.

"To be perfectly honest, had Whacker not called me when he did, I don't know where I would have ended up, but there was definitely a bit of mischief in the air."

"Mischief? Well Mary Magdalene and all her unholy sisters, is that what the young kids are calling it these days? Be careful, Floss. I've seen the double-wink and the arched eyebrow and believe me there are no honourable thoughts going on behind that annoyingly handsome exterior."

"I know, I know. It's infuriating. I'm a semi-successful business woman with an independent brain and a good degree of pride, but there's something about that Milo McCarthy that makes me feel like a hapless but horny virgin caught in his sights."

"Sweet Jesus, get a hold of yourself, Florence McFarland. You can never repeat that sentence to another living soul. Do you hear me?" She is using her 'mammy' voice and my full name, which means I am definitely in trouble.

"I'll try, I promise," I say meekly.

"Good girl."

Good girl? It's come to that?

I pause for a second and then decide to shake off this eau de Milo that lingers in the air.

"Listen, get the updated profile out there in the ether and we'll give this thing a whirl. If I'm going to make an idiot out of myself, I'd at least like to earn a few shekels while I'm doing it."

"On it," says Penny, picking up on my desire to drop it. "See you tomorrow, that is, assuming Conor's spasms have eased."

"Talk then." I ring off.

A chat with Penny always gives me the balance I need. She is part friend, part mum, part agony aunt, part teacher. She is, also, always right.

I try ringing Nika's mobile number again to distract myself from my wandering fantasies. No answer. I try a text instead. Some people feel more comfortable in text-world.

> Hi Nika. Floss from CTB here. Can we meet? I want to help.

Short, sweet, non-threatening. Sixty seconds later ... bingo. The sonar on my phone blips.

> Yes please. Café Kylemore O'Connell St. 9am tomorrow please. Thanks. Nika.

CTB specialises in corporate crime, so the possibility of something other than boring old fraud is triply scintillating. A clandestine meeting with a mysterious blonde foreigner has me practically drooling. I text back instantly to show my enthusiasm.

> Sounds good. I have a lot of black curly hair and will have a pink Filofax on the table. You can't miss me. See you tomorrow. Floss.

Given my slight hangover from the wine at lunch and a truly big day in CTB terms, I decide to call it a day and head home. On the way I am racked with the Irish guilts and decide to drop in to my folks for a long overdue visit. They live on St Lawrence Road in Clontarf, a beautiful, tree-lined street of red-bricked, terraced homes. The suspended street lamps dangle like hanging lanterns in the middle of the road, giving it a dash of uniqueness. Having lived there for twenty-five of my thirty-three years, it always feels like coming home.

When I get there, Mum is sweating over some pots and pans in full dinner-preparation mode. I give her a quick peck on the cheek and a squeeze and try to guess what she's cooking. "Chicken curry?"

"No darling. Delia's Moroccan Lamb. To die for. Although I'm free-wheeling a bit here with the ingredients, as I'm missing quite a few."

Dad is not in his usual spot by the fire.

"Where's Dad?"

"He's gone up to evening mass at the convent. He'll be back in half an hour or so. He'd better remember that couscous on the way home or I'll murder him. 'Serve it with spuds', he says to me. The cheek! It's not famine lamb, I said to him. How many

Moroccans do you see eating mashed potatoes?"

"I couldn't say, Mum. I don't see that many Moroccans on a daily basis, eating spuds or otherwise."

"Honestly. That man will be the death of me."

And you him, I think quietly to myself. Smiling on the outside.

"Will you stay for a bite?"

Picturing the contents of my fridge at home (a half-empty bottle of Chardonnay and some blossoming mould), I'm quick to take Mum up on her offer. I have to get some nutrients from somewhere.

"That would be lovely, Mum, if there's enough in the pot."

"That is couscous delivery pending, but you won't starve and it's better than take-away Chinese."

She has read my mind.

"So since when is Dad going to daily mass at the convent?"

"The last month or so. He goes with Des Connors. I'm delighted as it gets him out from under my feet for a little while each day."

"Sainthood still on the cards, so. Anything I can do to help on the dinner front?" I ask, knowing she will say no.

"Not at all. Make us both a cuppa though, would you darling? So how was work?"

I flick on the kettle and start the tea-making ritual. "A great week so far, Mum. We've won back a deal we thought we lost last year and I've a highly promising meeting tomorrow. Got a few bills paid so all in all things are on the up and up."

"That's great news, love. Who's the new client?"

"I'm not sure yet, but it's a bit more interesting than our usual run-of-the-mill stuff." I give her a brief synopsis of the contact from the mysterious foreign girl.

"Oh be careful, honey. Don't get in over your head. If it's not an area you're familiar with, would it not be better to outsource it to say … a more … experienced outfit?"

"And by 'experienced', you mean 'male'?" I say tetchily. This is an old bone of contention. Mum thinks my job is unladylike.

"Yes, darling, I do mean male. Really, secret meetings in town, it's all so unsavoury."

"Mum, just think of it as coffee and a cake at the Kylemore with my new foreign friend. Nothing unsavoury about that at all, other than perhaps the pastries at the Kylemore."

She looks at me seriously. "Give me a call when you're finished tomorrow to let me know you're alright."

"At nine in the morning, I'm unlikely to be clubbed over the head and dragged into a van in the middle of a busy caff by a small frail blonde thing," I say, rolling my eyes as far back into my head as they will go.

"Very funny. Just be careful, love."

"I will, Mum. Don't you worry. Penny will be backing me up, so there'll be witnesses if I'm kidnapped in broad daylight."

She laughs, but there's a slight furrow in her brow. She can't help herself. I know my new chosen career can't be easy on her and it's in a mother's DNA to worry.

Mum is sallow-skinned and dark-eyed, exotic to the point of almost unIrish. Lustrous, straight brown hair, like something from Charlie's Angels, particularly after a blow dry. She is sixty-one but doesn't look a day over fifty. These are the genes

I long for. Instead I got the whitest of white skin, blue eyes, a light smattering of freckles and unruly black curly hair. I am your average Irish colleen from the romance novels, but take it down a notch to a seven out of ten, like I already mentioned. My colouring comes from my Dad and in turn, his Dad. Mum always says I am cut out of my Grandad Dermo.

My memory of Grandad Dermo is bathed in the glow of childhood adoration. He died before I got the chance to find out any of his flaws through a grown up's eyes. The life and soul of the party. Always messing and laughing, with a mischievous twinkle in his eye. Fond of the drink but not to a damaging degree. A policeman by trade and a pretty good one by all accounts. Killed in his prime during a shootout with a cornered IRA escapee in Drogheda. The ordinary gardaí don't carry weapons, which makes shootouts a rather one-sided affair. But, as the story goes, Grandad Dermo was killed while trying to protect an innocent bystander, which makes me gush with pride.

I was twelve at the time and remember the devastating impact it had on Dad. It was the first time I'd seen a grown man cry outside of the telly and it nearly broke my heart. I'd been so busy thinking about having lost my Grandad that I'd forgotten that my Dad had just lost *his* dad. He retreated into himself for a long time, as if it knocked the fight out of him.

When I told him about CTB, I was expecting a tongue-lashing. He just shrugged his shoulders and said, "Sure, that figures. Not off the ground you licked it." And he turned back to the telly.

What Mum lacks in conforming to Irish types, she more than makes up for in fulfilling her role as the quintessential Irish mammy. She is all things to everyone in the family and the glue that holds us all together. She's the reason we gather around for dinner on Sundays. She's head tea-maker in times of crisis, chief worrier and generally the backbone of the family. Without her, we McFarlands would cease to function.

I hang around watching telly with Mum until Dad gets back.

"Here's Holy Joe," I say to him as he comes through the door. "I hope you prayed for the delivery of couscous," I whisper in his ear as I give him a hug.

"Shite! She'll have my guts for garters."

"Did you remember the couscous, Bert love?" Mum shouts from the kitchen, where she's resumed administrations.

I look at Dad with a grin and say, "You'd better go in and face the music."

"All's fair in love and war." He squares his shoulders and braves the kitchen.

It turns out that Moroccan, or rather Famine Lamb (as it's now called), is delicious - although that doesn't stop Mum from 'throwing daggers' at Dad all the way through dinner. I'm glad to leave the poisoned atmosphere shortly afterwards. I head home and take Leon for a long walk along the South Wall. He loves that walk. There are so many birds to chase and other dogs to fraternise with. He can hardly control himself with the excitement.

When we get home, I make a quick call to Penny to arrange for her to be at the Kylemore for nine the next morning. She's going to have to blend into the background. I point out that, given the demographic mix of the Kylemore clientele, she might need a velour tracksuit rather than a tweed number to truly go unnoticed, but she just scoffs at me.

I polish off the remaining charders and hit the scratcher. Big day tomorrow.

7

In Café Kylemore at eight-thirty, I get a bite and some coffee in advance of the big meet. I've been awake since six-thirty with nervous energy. Leon and I went walking until seven-thirty at which point he made it clear that exercise time was over. So at a quarter past eight, I headed into town.

Dress code for today is seriously low-key. Scruffy jeans, white shirt and pumps. I didn't want to intimidate my potential new client with a power suit. I often wonder if my clients have any inkling of the time I waste on picking outfits to suit them. If I could only bill them for it.

The crowd in the Kylemore at this time of day is quiet and mixed. Four lads, clearly on their way home from the night before, chowing down on the 'Full Irish', still slightly drunk but subdued. An old-age pensioner sits quietly over a pot of tea and a scone. And two yummy mummies sipping on lattes, chatting away while quietly comparing their two newborns, without being seen to be making comparisons.

I pick a seat at the back where I can see everyone coming and going and place my gaudy pink Filofax in front of me on the table, so Nika can spot it easily. I order a latte and a poppy-seed bagel with cream cheese and raspberry jam. Another one of my guilty pleasures. My eyes never lose sight of the door.

At five to nine, I clock Penny coming in the side door. She is hardly recognisable without her glasses and is sporting a Fred Perry hoody with jeans and trainers. I can't even imagine where she got this garb from. We make brief eye contact but don't acknowledge each other. If I did, I'd probably start giggling uncontrollably.

She grabs a window seat facing my way and stares out the window. I send her a quick text.

> Nice outfit, Pen. You could sell some weed or Halloween bangers in that ensemble. I hardly know you!

Her face doesn't show anything. She quickly texts back:

> I'm undercover. Living the dream, Floss. Living the dream.

Penny really does love this stuff. Undercover anything. It's what she signed up for.

At nine o'clock, my eyes are zeroed in on the main door like a laser beam. Five past. No sign of my mystery woman. I glance at Penny. She shrugs her shoulders and goes on staring out the window.

At precisely 9.07am, the door opens and gang of rowdy construction workers crowd in. They are in flying form, jostling for position to flirt with the pretty cashier, but they're blocking my view of the door. I'm straining my neck to try to see around the builders when I hear in my left ear "Hallo. Are you Floss?"

I almost jump three feet in the air, then fall out of my chair. I gather myself up off the floor and try to regain my dignity, while Nika looks at me with a wary eye. *Well done, Floss. Way to make a first impression. Positively slapstick.*

I finally manage to stand up straight and say "Great to meet you, Nika. I'm Florence McFarland from CTB Investigations. Will you take a seat?"

She nods and quietly sits down. I ask her if she'll take a coffee and again she nods her assent. I nip up to the counter and take this time to assess Nika on the sly. She can only be five foot four inches, a little whippet of a thing with dark-blonde straight hair, cut in a severe bob. Her complexion is so pale that it adds to her overall semblance of frailty. Distinctive cheekbones and colouring – no mistaking her Eastern bloc origins. Despite her small frame there is a steeliness to her that makes me suspect she'd be worth backing in a scrap.

I get Nika an Americano and a blueberry muffin (she looks like she could do with some extra calories). "Here you go!" I say cheerfully.

"Thanks."

"So, I'm guessing that you're the person who left a note for me regarding your friend being stolen," I say smiling. "Why don't we start at the beginning, maybe with where you and your friend are from and then we can get into more detail?" I am looking at Nika in an encouraging way, but what I am getting in return is a blank, confused expression. I'm starting to doubt if there are any lights on behind the eyes, when I realise there may be a language barrier at play here. I try again.

"English ok?" I say with a thumbs-up sign.

"Nyet, no. Not ok." She smiles sheepishly and gives me a thumbs-down.

"Ok, are you from Russia? Latvia? Lithuania?"

"Russia. St Petersburg. Russia."

"Ok, great. And your friend who is stolen? Is he/she also from St. Petersburg?"

"Da. Yes. She is … Anna from St. Petersburg … too."

"Ok now we're getting places. Is Anna missing?"

Her puzzled expression indicates that she doesn't understand. I try repeating my question, speaking slower and louder. She again looks puzzled and shrugs her shoulders in an apologetic way. I see a text flash up on my phone from Penny.

She's not deaf.

Fair point, I think, but I'd like to see her do better.

"My Engish eez very bad," says Nika. I want to give her a hug, she looks so helpless. She slides across a clipping. From a newspaper. Almost falling to pieces. Cyrillic script, so presumably Russian.

I smile back. "My Russia eez very bad", I say, giving the thumbs-down. She laughs and I see it is a huge release for her. She is wound up like a spring. Her worried face makes my stress wrinkles look like laughter lines.

"I think we're going to need some help with Russian and English, yes?"

She nods.

"Meet here tomorrow again at nine?" I am doing the slow loud speech thing again. Penny has turned around and is glaring at me as if to say, "Are you for real? They can hear you in Moscow now but they still don't bloody speak English!"

Nika nods. I squeeze her arm gently.

"Thank you," she says quietly as she slides out of her seat and heads for the door.

Penny comes over to join me. It's precisely 9.22am.

"Well, that went well," I say sarcastically.

"It was certainly the shortest sales meeting we ever had. I can't believe I got all dressed up for this."

"That my friend, is not dressing up, it's dressing down, with a capital D. Where *did* you get that outfit?"

"Well, you know how our house is a drop-off point for St Vincent de Paul clothing? Well, let's just say that this number is currently 'on loan' from one of the big black sacks in the garage."

"Good one! How did you get past Conor in that?" I ask.

"I changed in the car in the Ilac car park. If there is any sort of bank robbery in the area, I'll be the number one suspect from CCTV footage alone."

This cracks us both up.

"So," she adds, "I only heard bits of your conversation, that is, the bits you were broadcasting in news-for-the-deaf style. What's the story?"

"You know about as much as me. Between her lack of English and my lack of Russian, the conversation was not exactly flowing. I arranged to meet her here same time tomorrow, so I just need to find someone who can do some interpreting."

"We could try the Russian embassy, if there is one."

"There's someone I have in mind. Bit of a long shot but she might be able to point us in the right direction."

"Who's that?" asks Penny.

"A vague acquaintance, that's all."

"Mmmm, very mysterious. Now I am intrigued."

"If it works out, I'll fill you in tomorrow, ok?" I say, trying to cool Penny's curiosity.

"You're the boss."

"Yes I am. And you're skating pretty close to a dole queue at the minute."

"You wouldn't last jig time without me and you know it."

"Oh phnurrr." This is my response of last resort, when I know the other person is right and I can't think of anything else to say. It sometimes succeeds in confusing an opponent, at a minimum. But Penny is no ordinary opponent.

"Snappy comeback, Floss."

"Yes, I thought so."

But my mind is elsewhere. It's ten per cent occupied with Nika's worried little face and ninety per cent worried about having to touch base with my Russian contact. Her name is Natasha, or Tash for short. Nobody is aware that I know this lady and I'd like to keep it that way.

8

When I started CTB, Dad insisted that I do some form of self-defence in order to … well … not be so useless. He didn't kick up a fuss or try to dissuade me from my business idea like Mum did. He just quietly slipped me a bunch of flyers on various defence and martial arts courses, saying, "It would give your Mum and me a lot more peace of mind." Classic Catholic guilt-tripping power play. Who could argue with that? Having grown up in a Catholic household and been educated in a convent, I can see these manoeuvres coming at a hundred paces but am still powerless to resist. You can take the girl out of Catholicism but not the Catholic out of the girl.

So I browsed through the flyers and found a beginner's Aikido course in the Irishtown community centre near my house.

I liked the sound of it. An ancient martial art, using the attacker's aggression and motion as a force against him. Could come in handy (including against Milo McCarthy). I'd make a good Steven Seagal, after all … that lazily swift movement, where he appears to do very little but the bad guy goes flying. *Perfect.*

Of course the reality of it fell far short of my outrageous expectations. For me, Aikido was all about agonisingly long stretching sessions and throwing yourself repeatedly at a mat and shouting 'hai' at the top of your lungs. I trained once a week for six months and at the end was pretty confident I could tumble my way out of trouble at a moment's notice. If a bad guy approached me at just the right angle and tempo, I could probably break his thumb. On the other hand, if he didn't play by the rules, I'd be poked.

But if I'm really honest, what Aikido was really about for those six months was Tash. My Lithuanian Aikido instructor, single-handedly responsible for the most confusing six months of my adult life.

I arrived up at the Community Centre for my initial introductory session, thinking I'd give this two weeks max and then I could tell the folks I'd given it a shot, at least. The crowd was a mixed bunch, ranging from hard-core martial arts enthusiasts decked in white pyjamas to jokers like me, with my underused Pilates pants and yoga shoes. Plus a surprising number of older people who must have mistook Aikido for some form of meditation, like T'ai Chi. I was worried for their safety. As it turned out, I should have been worried for mine.

The class started with a demonstration by the more seasoned Aikido crew. It mainly involved pairing off and taking turns to throw each other around on the mat. They were all complete Aikido ninjas! One lady in particular, who was sixty-five if she was a day, hunched over and looking like she might keel over at any second, was called up for a demo against a likely-looking lad of about twenty-five.

Just as I was thinking *Jesus this is going to be a massacre ….* run for your life, nice old lady, the old dear transformed into Yoda, jumping around the mat like a Jedi, minus the lightsaber. It was one of the more magical and unexpected things I have seen in my life, and it ended with the young buck being pinned securely by Lady Yoda until he finally hit the mat in submission.

I found myself clapping and thinking *Where do I sign?,* when in walked Tash. She took the room's and, more disturbingly, my breath away.

Tash could be described as a Baltic goddess, but bombshell

wouldn't be too far off the mark either. She had long blonde hair, pulled back into a tight ponytail, a fringe that took the edge off it, cheekbones you could do your washing on and these ice-green eyes that had a way of seeing through people. No more than five foot nine, but with a frame that oozed strength and athleticism, she reminded me of a wild cat on the prowl, lazily languid but with a coiled-up energy, ready to be unleashed at any second.

Describing her physical appearance doesn't really do her justice though. It was more the impact she had on the class. The space became smaller in her presence; she simply commanded the room. I was mesmerised.

Tash introduced herself to the class by giving a brief background. She grew up in Lithuania, moved to Ireland when she was twenty-eight, having lived, it seemed, almost everywhere in between. Russia, Latvia, Iraq, Afghanistan to name but a few (she obviously liked all the tourist spots!). She was a six degree black belt in Karate and an Aikido Master. Everything was delivered in James Bond bad-gal accented English, grammatically not too shabby but with endearing Lithuanian quirks.

She then went around the class asking each of us individually what we wanted to get out of these Aikido classes. Most said a combination of self-defence and self-confidence. Some were quite specific about a particular level or Kyu they wanted to achieve. One of the younger guys piped up that he wanted to kick Steven Seagal's ass. This got a giggle out of everyone.

When it came around to me, I said, "My Dad wants me to protect myself from the bad guys."

Tash looked at me with those glacial green eyes and said, "I not ask what Dad want, I ask what *you* want." She was looking at me as if I was a kindergarten kid.

"Well, right now?" I asked. She nodded.

"Right now, I want the ground to swallow me up." Everyone sniggered. I tried to hold her gaze in a mild game of chicken. I broke eye contact first.

"Ah ha," she said, smiling. "I see we have found class wise-ass. It not take long."

"Sorry," I said, blushing puce pink. "Honestly, what do I want from this?"

She nodded once more, probably expecting another smartass comment.

"I'd give both my tiny boobs to be just like you." More chortles from my classmates. But I'd meant it as a compliment.

"Well, let's see what we can do, but perhaps without sacrifice of breasts."

It could have just been my imagination but she seemed to say this while raising one eyebrow and looking at my chest with a look that said "Honey, you cannot afford to lose anything off that non-existent chest of yours", but she was still smiling. I looked away again, sufficiently chastened.

Next, Tash asked us what the first rule of self-defence was.

I was determined to remain silent for the rest of my Aikido days, but everyone else chirped up enthusiastic suggestions like "Move like Bruce Lee" or "Defence is the best form of attack" or, my personal favourite, "Shoot first, ask questions later" (from the same youth who wanted to take down Mr Seagal).

Tash patiently listened, then shook her head gently, raising her right hand to quiet us. "First rule self-defence. Run!"

A brief pause. "What is second rule?"

Nobody was brave enough to guess.

"Second rule is run faster." She said this while staring straight at me. I felt as if she was telling me something or warning me in some way. I felt a shiver down my spine, followed by a tingle throughout my body, from head to tippy toes.

What the fuck, Floss? Pull yourself together.

Tash wrote the first and second rules up on the blackboard at the top of the gym. We spent the rest of the class doing stretches and watching more demos. At the end, she asked for a volunteer. Seagal Boy shot up his hand. I pinned mine under my arse to ensure they didn't shoot up involuntarily, keeping my eyes averted from Tash's gaze.

She shook her head and said, "I'm not sure I'm ready such testosterone, just yet." Everyone giggled. "How about my wise-ass friend?"

Oh-oh.

I could feel all eyes on me, but most of all I felt Tash's green laser beams burning a hole in the top of my scalp. I raised my head in dread.

"Yes, you," she said smiling. "What's your name?"

"Floss … McFarland," I stammered.

"OK, Floss McFarland, come to mat, please," she said encouragingly while smirking a smile that said 'I am going to hurt you'.

I walked hesitantly up to face my torturer.

Tash turned to the class and said, "I'm going to show you classic Aikido move. To be used only when option of escape, like first and second rules, is not possible."

Oh God, I thought, *I'm going to be maimed.*

She turned to me: "OK, Floss McFarland, I want you to come at me from behind as if you choke me."

"Do I have to? Really?"

Another raised eyebrow. "Yes. Just do it."

"Right," I said, "just like the Nike ad."

I paused for a second, circled around her slowly, trying to drum up courage, then made a half-arsed attempt at grabbing her neck from behind. She hadn't even glanced my way, but next thing I knew, she'd vice-gripped my arm and bent it in such a way that I was sure it would break unless I hit the deck. Which is exactly what I did. In a blur of motion, Tash jumped on top of me and pinned me firmly to the mat. Everyone started clapping and cheering.

Her lips were close to my ear. She whispered gently: "I won't hurt you, unless you want me to." She got up in one fluid movement and helped me up with an incredibly strong arm. I was looking at her in complete confusion when she gave me the tiniest of winks.

I wobbled back to my spot in the class. My classmates patted me on the back, murmuring things like "Good effort" and "Hard luck."

Tash bowed to us and said she hoped to see us all again next week.

I walked the short way home in a daze. Although my head was all over the shop, there was one thing I was sure of. While I'd been on the floor with Tash on top of me, something passed between us. Something physical. Something electric. And most of all something I did not want to acknowledge.

Pursuing that avenue of thought was a veritable Pandora's box, so I spent that evening repeating the mantra "I am straight" over and over to myself, resolving to put that crazy Tash episode down to a blip in my distinctly heterosexual landscape.

I filed that first class of Aikido under "interesting experience" in my deeply suppressed, internal filing cabinet. And then I went back the following week. And the week after that ... by about week six, I had to admit to myself that the excitement levels I was feeling on my way to Wednesday-night Aikido were not really in keeping with my appreciation of the martial arts. They were more in keeping with the intense infatuations kids have with their coaches and teachers.

After the sixth class, I came home to Leon and told him out straight. "My name is Floss. I am heterosexual and I'm obsessed with a lady." He looked at me as if to say, 'Bummer, but where's my dinner?' and then tried to lick my face.

I didn't tell another soul. Tash was my guilty secret, one I did not know how to handle. So, like any self-respecting ex-Catholic, I buried it.

Tash, for her part, did not effect a repeat performance of the intimate whispering on the mat over the coming months. She was the consummate professional; going about her business of flinging students onto mats and teaching them how to land properly. This *did* help to suppress the crazy infatuation, but did not reduce my obsession in any way. I continued to convince myself that the reason I bounced out the door, every Wednesday without fail, was because I loved Aikido.

Denial was suiting me just fine until I accidentally ran into Tash outside the classroom environment. I'd been attending classes for six months by that time. I had perfected the forward tumble and could just manage a backwards roll without dislocating any neck vertebrae. As progress, it wasn't exactly stellar. I wasn't convinced of how well I could maim the bad guys, but was happy enough with where I was at.

It was a stunning Sunday morning in early April and Leon and I were out walking in Ringsend Park. The vibrant spring colours were in full bloom and Leon and I were enjoying the swishing sound of the dew-drenched grass underfoot. I was in my own world, worrying about how we were going to drum up more business for CTB. Leon was rushing around, meeting and greeting fellow walkers in the park and scaring the crap out of the smaller dogs – i.e. all of them.

As I went around a bend, I could see Leon up ahead rolling around on his back having his tummy tickled. It's unusual for him to do this with complete strangers, so I was really curious. As the person straightened up to look out for Leon's owner, I saw with a start that it was Tash. We clocked each other immediately. My face went bright red. *Brilliant.* Thanks again Dad for the colouring.

She smiled in her super-calm way. "Well, what we have here? Floss McFarland, smart mouth and committed Aikido student."

"Actually, I believe 'wise-ass' is my official title," I said, trying to recover the ground lost due to my total redner.

"Is grissly bear yours?" Her pronunciation of 'grizzly' was delectable.

I laughed. "Yep, this is Leon. I'm pretty sure he's single-handedly responsible for all the reported sightings of the Yeti in the Ringsend area."

She giggled at this and those melodic chimes made my heart swell with pride at having earned them.

"Well, nice to meet you, Leon," she said bowing slightly towards him.

"Where are my manners?" I said. "Leon, this is Tash. Tash, meet Leon." Leon has been trained to give the paw when I introduce him to people, so up popped his paw with the timing of well-worn circus act. Tash, tough Aikido instructor, was putty in his paws. She looked up at me with delight. I realised she was a fellow dog nut.

Oh God. Not another thing to make her more perfect.

"Do you live near here?" Tash asked, after giving Leon a big bear-hug.

"Yep, if you look straight over there, the small cottage, backing onto the park with the red window frames. That's us."

She looked over and nodded in admiration. "I can see you spend lot of time looking all over Dublin for Aikido school." Her cool-green eyes softened slightly.

"Yep, after months of searching for the right Dojo, I just happened to find one on the same stretch of road as my house. Would you credit that?"

She laughed again. *Music to my ears.*

"Can I join you and Leon for walk? I live in apartment at top of building, so dogs not allowed. And I try steal every opportunity."

"No kidding. I thought he was in danger of being dognapped when I came around the bend there."

"So, it's a yes?"

"Yes, absolutely. You can use me for access to Leon anytime."
And with that I went puce again. What was I saying? I could
hear the attempted flirtation and the cheesiness of the line.
Horrendous!

Tash was looking at me out of the corner of her eye, mildly
entertained by my mortification, it seemed. "You have a deal,"
she said, with a blatant wink.

Queue another red face. I began walking again to hide my
embarrassment. Leon bounded off into the leaves and Tash
moved smoothly to catch up with me. "Which way are we go?"
she asked, probably to help me forget my hot flushes.

"Well, on Sundays, we normally walk along the South Wall. It's
quite the round trip but Leon loves watching the boats come
through the harbour entrance. Are you game?"

"Yes. For sure. I follow you."

What followed was one of the most wonderful interludes I had
ever spent with another human being. We walked slowly,
talking at length and then pausing for quiet spells. Never had
silence with another person been so comfortable. We laughed a
lot, mainly at Leon's antics and sometimes at other walkers'
expense: couples with his and hers matching tracksuits, a
jogger with an ungainly gait, a couple of lads with tins of cheap
lager, sitting on the pier shouting their heads off – it wasn't
clear if it was the end of the night before or they were just
getting started.

An hour and a half later we found ourselves back in Ringsend
Park. A slight tension had arisen between us we neared my
house. I wasn't sure what to do next, I just knew I didn't want
to say goodbye. Should I offer her a coffee? At my place or at a
café? Was it too early for lunch? Brunch?

She put me out of my misery. "Well thanks for the walk. I really have to get going as I have more class in afternoon."

"Oh, yes, of course … alright." I tried not to sound too disappointed. I was gutted.

She could see this: "Maybe we can do again another Sunday?"

"Ah yes, back to using me for Leon access again," I said laughing.

"No, Floss," she said and picked my hand up in hers, staring at me with warm eyes. "I mean us. Leon is of course, bonus."

I was rendered speechless, possibly for only the second time in my life.

"I think … I think I would … like that."

"Ha! I not believe you. You must say with little more definite," she said, laughing at me again.

Out of the blue, she hugged me to her. It was not a normal girlfriend to girlfriend hug. It was close and intimate. I could feel her hips pressing against mine. It lasted a delicious age.

My head was instantly reeling with an avalanche of emotions. I pulled away suddenly. Pointing at us both, I said, "This … I … I don't know how to do this." I could feel tears springing up in my eyes.

She went to take my hand again, but I shrank away from her. I was having a mild anxiety attack. I waved stupidly at her and ran away, back to the safety of No 17 Ropewalk Place. I could hear her shouting after me, "It's ok, Floss. It's not problem." As I went through the front door, I collapsed in a heap back against it. My knees had given way.

Leon was looking at me as if to say, "What happened there? She seemed nice."

"Don't go there, Leon." I was still gasping for air.

That night, I didn't sleep a wink. My mind was in hyper-drive thinking over the morning's events. How this could be happening to me? I had had boyfriends. I liked boys. Men. The male of the species. Their tackle. Not lady bits. I tossed and turned, remembering the heat of Tash against me. The slightly hurt look on her face as I moved away from her. There was sympathy there too, but definitely hurt.

The next morning, exhausted after a sleepless night, I decided to give up Aikido and Sunday morning walks in the park. I could not cope with what had happened the previous morning and the implications it could have for me. I effectively went cold turkey. And it was agony. Wednesdays and Sundays nearly broke my resolve each week. But I eventually weaned myself off my doses of Tash. After six months, the memory of Tash had begun to fade and I'd managed to categorise the whole episode as a figment of my wild imagination.

Until now.

9

Aikido is my only link to Tash. In the short time we spent together, she managed to extract my entire life story, while I was still very much in the dark about her background and what made her the formidable woman she was. The one thing I did manage to find out was that, apart from her native Lithuanian and fluent Russian, she spoke four other languages. Right now, I need her to help me figure out what's going on with Nika's missing friend Anna, even if it requires me facing up to the possibilities contained in Pandora's Box.

When Penny and I get back to the office after our brief meeting with Nika, I look up the Aikido club online to discover when the classes take place in the Irishtown community centre. There is an advanced class at three-thirty in the afternoon and a beginner's session at seven in the evening.

We spend the next hour and a half reviewing Milo's McCarthy's alias profile on LinkedIn before hitting the 'publish' button. Penny builds a series of links and endorsements to give his profile more authenticity. It's tedious work, but effective.

I nip out and buy two baked ham and coleslaw sandwiches from the tiny deli behind the Citibank building. As I horse through my lunch and Penny nibbles hers daintily, she looks at me and says, "Are you alright, Floss? You seem a little distracted. I hope it's not that 'strictly professional' relationship you're developing with Hurricane Milo?"

I snap out of my reverie. "Honestly, Pen, not at all. He does get under my skin, but the less I see of him, the easier it gets to forget he exists. I'm thinking about Nika and her mysterious friend. It feels like it's going to be big and you know I always get a bit nervy around the big gigs."

"You do, but you still deliver the goods!" she says encouragingly.

"Yep! Results and Irritable Bowels 'R' Us," I say giggling.

"Oh, God Almighty, Floss. That's disgusting." But she is laughing despite herself.

"I have to head out for an appointment at 3.30, so I might not see you till tomorrow morning at the Kylemore. You ok here by yourself?"

"Definitely. Off to meet the clandestine Russian contact, are we?"

Relentless.

"Something like that, but maybe without the glamour," I say in all honesty, thinking of the crusty old community centre.

"You're going to have to tell me some day. My curiosity has been piqued."

"No dice, Penny. Get back to work!"

"Yes, boss. See you tomorrow."

I jump in the car and head straight for Irishtown, resisting the temptation to nip into my local pub, The Oarsman, for vodkas and courage. It's only 3.20 when I park up at the centre, so I sit there chewing my nails – for ten minutes. Then I head inside. Des, the manager, who looks suspiciously like Rocky's first coach in the movies, is in the entrance hall.

"Howareya, Floss. Long-time no see! Are ya back for more punishment on the mats?" he asks, checking me out with a lingering look from head to toe. *No change there.*

"Hiya Des. No, definitely no training for me tonight. My body's still recovering from six months ago. I'm actually trying to find Tash, the Aikido instructor."

"She's not due in till seven bells. She takes the beginner's class at 7.30. Do you want me to let her know you were here?"

"No, no, not at all. I'll pop back in later. Thanks Des all the same."

I head back out the door with the bipolar feelings of serious disappointment and massive relief.

Here we go again.

I nip home to while away the hours, but being too restless to stay put, grab Leon's leash and try to keep up with him as he bounds out the door in his pre-walk enthusiasm. We have a few hours to kill so we head for our favourite trail, the South Wall. About halfway along the last stretch of the wall with the huge bumpy pavestones, where I'm always tripping up, I trip up.

"Shit, mothery fuck!" I say out loud, immediately receiving a judgemental look from a power-walking mum with buggy.

"Sorry!" *What a bitch!* She didn't even stop to see if I was ok.

Which I am, although the heels of my hands are badly grazed and my dignity has definitely taken a pounding. I sit down on a wooden bench to gather myself and pull a tissue from my bag to dab at the bleeding. I've managed to get a few tiny bits of grit stuck in there nicely and it stings like a fresh scald, but I keep my cursing inside my head this time. I sit there staring alternately at my hands and then the sea, feeling sorry for myself, when I hear behind me: "Seven stitches both hands, I would say, first glance."

I turn around, already knowing from the crisp, clipped English and the sudden pounding of my heart that it's Tash.

Leon, who has been busy chasing birds along the pier, also notices Tash and appears equally happy to see her as he comes tearing towards us. Christ, what is she, the Dog Whisperer or what? They only met once.

"Easy, boy" – but Tash is braced for impact as Leon launches his full, aerial love attack.

"He's ok. No problem," she says laughing as she is smothered by him.

"Down, Leon. Sit," and bless him, he does. But I can tell he is just itching to jump and slobber over her again. She must get this reaction from just about everyone she meets. Dogs, dykes, geezers young and old.

I turn to face Tash properly and am instantly reminded why I was infatuated with her all those months ago. She is totally windswept, in a scruffy pair of jeans, a tight-fitting black polo-neck sweater and a retro-style pair of Adidas runners. Not a hint of make-up and hair in a ponytail as before.

But simply stunning.

I realise with a jolt that I have to speak first. To acknowledge my ridiculous behaviour the last time we met.

"Listen, Tash. I'm really sorry about the last time when we …. well … went for that walk. I'm not sure what was going on, but I found it all really confusing and a bit overwhelming. You're a really great person and I think I owe you an apology for being so rude." This doesn't come out quite the way I'd quickly rehearsed it on the way to the club, but I think I'm getting the message across.

Tash has been looking straight into my eyes the entire time I was speaking, challenging me to break eye contact, but I hang in there, by a thread.

"I think," she says, after an agonising pause, "that the Aikido world is still crying for losing your talents."

I do a double-take, as I was expecting some form of admonishment, but quickly realise she is letting me off the hook with this quip. We crack up laughing at the thought of anyone missing my Aikido abilities.

"I think we both know that six months ago, the world of Aikido let out a collective sigh of relief," I say, instantly more comfortable making fun of myself than blabbing about feelings. "I was actually on my way to see you. I dropped in at the club earlier."

"I know, Des tells me, while staring at breasts," she chuckles. "I thought I might find you and The Bear out here and I had time before class. My curiosity gets the better of me."

"Hey, it's really lovely to see you again," I blurt out before I can stop myself. *Hello? Have you lost your mind, Floss?*

"That's really nice to hear for me," she says kindly.

"Well, I had this specific reason for coming to see you, but now I hardly even want to talk about it. How have you been for the last while?"

"Busy. And alone," she says with a mischievous look. "Why don't we head back and get your hands fixed?"

"My hands? Oh yeah, of course." I had completely forgotten about my stinging hands.

I call after Leon, who is showing an enthusiastic level of

interest in some poor Labradoodle's rear end. We head back along the pier with Leon pounding after us.

"So, I realised after our last walk together that you managed to keep everything about yourself nicely hidden, while I was spilling my guts. The complete Floss download. I know nothing about you. Like, what do you do for a living?"

"I do various contract work for the Lithuanian government."

"There you go again! I don't even know what that means. You could be an office cleaner or an assassin."

"Well, definitely not cleaner." She starts to laugh.

"OK, so none the wiser on your job. What about friends and family?"

"I am orphan, so no to family. Sorry. But I have some friends, honestly. I speak Lithuanian, Russian, Latvian, German and Arabic. I like long walks on the pier with giant hairy dogs, and I'm Aquarius."

"Ah, and Aquarian? That makes sense."

"Please, do not say you believe in star sign stuff?" she says incredulously.

"Believe? No, but I do think there is some commonality of traits across the signs. You, for instance. Big on learning. Good with the languages. Very adaptive to your environment. That suits you with all the moving around you've done. All classic Aquarian attributes."

"Kvatch!!! Absolute kvatch!!!"

"What in God's name does that mean?"

"It's the German for 'you're wrong' – q-u-a-t-c-h."

"But much cooler-sounding."

"So what is your star sign, Floss?"

"A fiery Sagittarius."

"Ah, idealistic and flighty. Often paired with Aquarius lovers, I think."

"Well, you sure can talk the talk for someone who thinks it's all a pile of quatch!" I laugh.

"I had Hindu friend once. When they arrange marriages, the couple's star signs must to be aligned."

"So I've heard, but I never bought it. Indian people seem so sensible and grounded."

"It's true, believe me," she says.

We have arrived back at my place and Leon is panting at the door, gasping for a drink.

"Can I interest you in a coffee?" I ask as we go through the door.

"That would be nice. I'll boil water if you go and get first-aid kit so we can fix scrapes."

"I might be a little light in the first-aid kit department but I'll see what I can do." I head into the bathroom, returning a few minutes later with cotton wool, stingy-looking antiseptic liquid and plasters with pictures of "The Incredibles" on them.

Tash looks at them quizzically.

"They're for my friends' kids. They never fail to hurt something when they're here."

Tash gently takes my hand. "Let's see what we have here."

Her closeness makes it difficult for me to breathe.

"Nasty. This is going to hurt a little." She dabs my hand with liquid fire. I try not to whimper. I imagine that she has an unlimited pain threshold.

"Is ok?" she asks.

"Lovely," I say through gritted teeth.

She cleans both hands until all the grit and dirt is removed, then places a couple of "The Incredibles" plasters on the worst grazes. When finished, she seems to reluctantly let go of my hands.

There is an awkward pause, so I jump up and say, "How about that coffee?" I bustle about in the kitchen, grinding and plunging coffee, and return with two mugs along with a carton of milk and packet of sugar. Mum would be horrified.

"So, you said you come to see me. What for?"

"Well, it's about a potential client or case of ours that I think you'd be able to help us with. We'd be prepared to pay you for your time, at whatever the going rate is."

"So you want me to assassinate someone?" she says, but fails to keep a straight face.

"Definitely not. It's hard to get the dead clients to pay! No, seriously, this Russian girl approached us about a friend of hers that's gone missing or 'been stolen', as she put it. We met to try and figure out how we could help, but her English is not great and my Russian is non-existent. It was a very short meeting."

"So, you need me translate?"

"Exactly. I'd like you to be our interpreter. And as I mentioned, we'll pay the going rate."

"There is no question of money. I'd like to help. It will be a welcome break from throwing bad students around the mat."

"That's fantastic. Her name is Nika and we're to meet her again tomorrow morning at nine in Café Kylemore on O'Connell Street. Does that work for you?"

"Actually, little later in morning is better. I have some early morning assassinations to take care of." Her crazy green eyes are glittering with mischief.

"Now who's the wise-ass? Will you be finished murdering innocent victims by eleven, say?"

"I never say they were innocent. And yes. Eleven is better for me." She's still smiling but a part of me begins to wonder what she really does in these government contracts.

"Great. It's a date … I mean a deal." Off goes the red flush from head to toe again. "I'll text Nika to let her know we've changed the time." I fire off a quick text to Nika.

A minute later, a text comes back:

OK …

A woman of few words.

"Would you like another coffee?" I ask, hoping to prolong her stay.

"I would like very much, but I must to give class now, so I need leave." She unfolds herself from the couch in that effortless feline way of hers.

"Of course, yeah. I totally forgot about your Aikido." I try to hide my disappointment. Exactly as before, the hours have just dissolved away. We just click, and there is a level of comfort mixed with excitement between us that both terrifies and fascinates me.

"Can I tempt you to come back to Aikido class? I promise to be nice." Again she is making fun of me.

"I think my spine just recovered its original alignment after a six-month resting period, so I'm not keen to open that door again, but thanks."

"No problem. So, I see you tomorrow at eleven o'clock?"

"Perfect. I look forward to it." *What?! Shut up, Floss.*

She raises an eyebrow with that I'm-up-to-no-good' look of hers and says quietly, "Me too, Floss. Me too." And then more glibly, "Look after those hands! No more walks along the pier with no supervision."

"I think we have another deal," I say while internally cringing at the utter cheese I've managed to dish out this afternoon.

She gives Leon, who's zonked out in his doggy bed, a quick caress before heading out the door with a wave to me. No hug this time. Disappointing but not surprising after the impact her last hug had on our friendship.

I close the door and lean back against it. I look at Leon as if to say "Well, what do you make of that then?" He looks back at me as if to say "I, too, am under her spell, but I'm really, really tired right now, so can you talk at me later?"

"You're useless," I say. But he's already asleep.

10

I spend the night tossing and turning, trying not to think about Tash and the palpable buzz that zings back and forth between us. So, of course, I do nothing but think about Tash. They're not sensible or logical thoughts, just random quick-fire questions with few useful answers. Is she gay? More importantly, am I? Why her? I've had one lezzer dream in my thirty-something years and now this? What is going on? Is there a helpline? My folks would kill me. My sister is going to have a bloody field day. What will my mates think? Surely they'll be sweet. But Penny? Queen of Conservative and the Tweed Ensemble? What about Conor? He'll be chuffed. He can get bragging rights with his buddies for the third wheel in their marriage being a potential threesome option. God, blokes! But I love blokes. What about Milo? The Ultimate Man … alpha male to his very toes. Or do I like alpha females?

And on and on it goes all night, with breaks for hot chocolate and finally a hot whiskey to try to knock myself out. I nod off around four-thirty, then thirty seconds later (or what seems like it) my alarm goes off - telling me in depressing 'Morning Ireland' terms that it's eight o'clock on Friday morning.

I drag myself out of bed and take Leon for a quick run, or rather medium-paced walk along Sandymount Strand. Back at the house shortly before nine o'clock. Extra strong coffee for me and the usual gloopy muck for Leon. My mobile rings. It's Penny. *Oh shit! Shit!*

"Either that's you disguised as a six-foot-four Nigerian guy in the corner, in which case, I'm impressed, or you slept it out this morning," says Penny, attempting to cover up her annoyance with humour.

"Pen! I'm so sorry. I had to delay the meeting until eleven as Tash can't make it till then. I completely forgot to text you. I'm sooooooooo sorry!"

"If you leave me here, I'm liable to eat my own body weight in cake, which I will be forced to charge CTB for. Who's Tash?"

"Look, I'll be there in twenty minutes tops. I'll give you a full run-down then."

"You better! See you shortly," she says briskly.

I hang up, wolf down my breakfast and throw the remainder of my coffee into my travel mug. I'm sitting next to Penny exactly twenty-three minutes later. She's in the same undercover outfit as yesterday.

"Morning Pen," I start. "Really sorry about my snafu this morning. Bad form on my part."

"Buy me a coffee slice and all is forgiven," she says, smiling. I get her a coffee slice and can't resist a pecan Danish for myself. A pot of tea for two and we are all sorted.

"Here ya go," I chirp as I bring the tray to the table.

"Lovely. Thanks, Floss. So, fill me in." This is an order.

"Not a huge amount to tell, really. Do you remember Dad made me do that Aikido class ages ago?"

She nods.

"Well, the teacher was a Lithuanian girl called Tash who happens to speak Russian. I spoke to her yesterday and she's agreed to give us a hand with translating for Nika … free of charge."

"That's great, Floss. But why all the secrecy and what's the catch? No such thing as a free lunch and all that." And just like that, she zeroes in, laser-sharp. God she really is the brains behind this operation.

"There's no secrecy and maybe she's just a good person who wants to help a geographical neighbour out. They do exist, you know ... good people. Why all the cynicism, Pen?" Right back at you. Attack really IS the best form of defence.

"I'm going to ignore the fact that you can't quite make eye contact with me right now, which indicates you're being a tad frugal with the truth. I'm going to move on. But for the record, know that *I know* that something fishy is going on."

"Whatever, Sherlock," I say, annoyed that she always sees right through me.

We while away the next hour sipping our tea and chatting about inane stuff. At ten to eleven, Penny takes up her position by the window and I start watching the door like a hawk. My heart has begun a slow, steady drumbeat and I know it's not Nika I'm excited about seeing.

At 10.55, Tash walks in the door, looking ready for battle. She is dressed from head to toe in black. Black fitted cargo pants, black merino liner and a sleeveless black vest jacket that makes it look as if she's about to start dismantling explosive devices.

She strides across the café, leaving a trail of wide eyes and open mouths in her wake. I close mine just in time to say hello.

"Good morning, Floss."

"Morning! Now just to be clear, did you in fact just kill someone this morning? I haven't watched the news yet. But you're certainly dressed for it." The old dear beside me nearly chokes on her cream bun.

"It has been very busy morning." I notice she hasn't answered the question.

Just then, Nika makes her appearance. I stand up quickly.

"Hi Nika. Thanks for coming. This is Natasha. She's going to help us talk through your problem."

Without missing a beat, Tash starts translating what I just said into what I assume is Russian. I can hear the word 'Tash' and they shake hands. Nika is visibly more relaxed and at ease. *Dogs? Russian girls? Me? Is there no end to her talents?*

"Can I get anyone anything to drink or eat?" I ask.

"Sparkling water for me," Tash says, then babbles to Nika in Russian. "And black coffee for Nika, please."

"Grand, so." I start to get up but Tash grabs my wrist with an alarmingly firm grip.

"Before we start, do you know person staring at us in reflection of window in grey sweatshirt?" she asks nodding subtly in the direction of our alleged stalker.

She's noticed Penny. "That," I say, "is my business partner, Penny Firth. She's here to keep an objective eye on things."

"Good. She need practice spying skills. Maybe ask her to join on way back?" says Tash.

Seriously. She IS a female James Bond. *Scary but God so attractive right now.*

I pop up to the counter and get the orders in. On my way back, I drop over to Penny.

"Apparently, you failed your Spooks test. Tash clocked you as soon as she arrived. You might as well come and join us rather than earwigging from over here."

"Holy shit. What did you say she does again? Aikido? She's good. I was doing my best bored, unemployed person impression."

"Honestly, I'm not sure what the hell she does and I'm a bit scared to ask, but she appears to speak Russian pretty well and Nika looks a little less stressed." I glance over at the two of them and they are chatting away. I feel a tiny pang of jealousy and have to reign myself in. *Focus on the job at hand, Floss.*

"Ok, let's go," says Penny, getting up and heading over to our table.

I introduce Penny to both Tash and Nika and we all sit down again. Once I've dished out the drinks I turn to Nika.

"Are you ok to get started with your story?" I ask her gently. Tash translates. Nika nods and those little worry lines reappear instantly. I want to give her a hug.

Nika starts to talk rapidly. Tash translates quickly.

Aoife Sheridan

11

What Tash translates goes something like this:

Anna and Nika grew up in Siversky, a small town roughly seventy kilometres to the south of St Petersburg. Siversky is mainly known for the red banks of the River Oredhezh nearby, and the fact that every kid growing up there dreams of escaping it, generally in the direction of St Petersburg. Anna and Nika dreamed and schemed together of one day opening up their own beauty salon on Nevsky Prospekt in the centre of St Petersburg.

The two girls were thick as thieves, spending as much time in the other's house as in their own (reminded me of Penny and myself as kids). When they graduated from high school, aged seventeen, Nika's parents paid her way through beauty school, but Anna's mother was a single mum of five children. Undaunted, Anna soon found a bartending job in a local bar. The pay wasn't great, but she could fend for herself and help her mum with the weekly bills.

This kept Anna content for a while, but the dream of her own business still burned away inside. She was constantly on the lookout for other jobs or ways to make a quick buck. Nika, in the meantime, was knuckling down with her studies.

Towards the end of their first year out of school, Anna came to Nika with what she perceived to be the answer to their prayers. She had seen an advertisement in the Derzhis Krepche newspaper for a fantastic job opportunity in Dublin, Ireland. The ad guaranteed pay of at least two thousand euros per week, including accommodation and visas. This was more money than either of the girls had ever imagined and Anna was ecstatic about the possibilities it would offer her and her family. Nika was not so sure. She had heard rumours of these types of 'dream jobs' and thought it was too good to be true.

Anna remained undeterred and applied. Nika made her promise not to make any decisions without consulting her first.

Things went quiet for a while. Nika hoped the whole thing had fizzled out, but in early July, when beauty school was wrapping up for the summer, Anna announced that she had been accepted for the job in Dublin. She would be a live-in nanny for a wealthy Irish family, looking after the children and doing basic housekeeping duties. She had even been put in touch with another Russian girl who had a similar job in Dublin. This girl was overjoyed with her job and strongly advised Anna to accept the offer.

Anna tried to persuade Nika to apply for one of the jobs too, but Nika was unwilling to sacrifice her beauty training and was also nervous about travelling to a foreign country without any guarantee that the job was real. They argued for a long time. Anna accused Nika of being jealous of her good fortune. This was the last time they had spoken.

At this point in the story, Nika gets quite upset and we agree to take a break. I organise more teas and coffees. I look at Penny. She shakes her head as if to say "I know exactly where this story is going".

When everyone is settled again and Nika has regained some of her composure, she starts to speak again, a little more hesitantly.

Nika was furious with Anna, but she secured a part-time job in a beauty salon and so was distracted and excited to be earning and learning her trade. But after a while, knowing that Anna was the stubborn one who would never give in and get in touch, she called around to Anna's house to try and patch up their friendship. Anna's mum told her that Anna had left for Dublin three days earlier. She had called her mum on arriving in Dublin, but nobody had heard from her since.

Nika went straight home and called Anna's mobile. The number was out of service. She convinced herself that Anna had gotten an Irish SIM card. She fired off an email to Anna apologising for not being in touch and asking her to reply immediately.

Days, then weeks passed with still no word from Anna. Nika was getting very worried. She tracked down the newspaper cutting with the ad that Anna had responded to. It included a mobile number. Nika tried the number. No response. She began to panic. She went to the local police station and reported her friend to be missing. They refused to file a report unless it was submitted by either an immediate family member or partner. Nika was reluctant to worry Anna's mother unnecessarily, but not sure what to do next.

At the end of September, Nika realised she would have to tell Anna's mother of her fears, so they could report her as missing and get a formal investigation under way. She called around first thing in the morning before Anna's mum started her shift work at the iron processing plant, and confirmed the lack of any contact by Anna. They went to the police station together and filed a missing person's report.

Days passed with no apparent progress although the local police were liaising with the Gardaí in Dublin. Nika was convinced that both the Russian and Irish police believed Anna was a straightforward runaway.

In early October, Nika decided she could no longer wait around. She contacted her brother, who worked for a Russian investment bank in London, and arranged for a loan to cover a short stay in Dublin. She had been in Dublin for one week. She was not sure where to start and was struggling with the language barrier.

At this point, I interrupt Nika and ask her how she had found CTB. Apparently, we were the only female investigators she could find online. She was determined to use female investigators.

Nika had spent her seven days in Dublin trawling bars and prostitute hangouts looking for Anna. She had shown Anna's photo to anyone who would look and listen, but to no avail.

"I'm really sorry to hear about your friend," I say. "I'd like to think she has met her Irish prince charming and has just forgotten to get in touch. But I suspect that is not the case."

"Will you help us?" asks Nika in accented English, looking imploringly at me.

I start shaking my head, saying "There are other more qualified investigative agencies who…" but notice Penny nodding her head furiously.

"Sidebar, McFarland," she says, using her full mammy tone.

"Excuse us for a second," I say to Tash and Nika. We head out the front door of the café.

"What the hell are you saying?" says Penny. "Are you completely out of your mind?"

"I could ask you the same thing! Do the words 'dangerours bad guys' mean anything to you? Or what about the phrase 'completely out of our depth'? Any alarm bells ringing?" My voice has taken on that squeaky stressed pitch, which makes me sound like a cartoon character. "And finally, my own personal favourite, pro bono! There is no way this girl is going to be able to pay us to risk life and limb tackling what I suspect is best case a kidnapping and worst case a full human trafficking outfit."

"You're thinking about it the wrong way, Floss. This could be CTB's greatest ever case, the big break we've always been waiting for."

"I like our tiny investigations of fraud and cockatoo porn. They're SAFE, Pen. If Conor found out I let you get involved with something like this, he would throw me out of your marriage permanently and I'm not sure I could handle that."

"Are you honestly saying you're not going to help that poor girl? She's only doing what you would do for me and vice versa. Try and put yourself in her shoes." Full guilt-tripping mode.

"I'm not saying we won't help her. We'll help her get someone more qualified to help her."

"How's about we get the case started and then hand it over to some other crowd when we start to feel the heat."

"The heat? Who are you now? Robert de Niro? I don't know Penny, this is pretty heavy stuff." I bite my lip.

"Let's give it one week and see what we turn up. Then I promise we'll hand it over to the heavyweights."

"Do you promise? Do you swear?"

She nods.

"On Dermo's grave?" I ask.

"Ouch, that's a tough one, but yes, I promise."

"OK, let's head back inside and let them know."

Tash and Nika are bent over, heads low, deep in conversation. Nika looks up hopefully.

"Well?" asks Tash, looking directly at me. If I had been about to say no, her look would have changed my mind.

"Look, I'm going to be honest with you. We are not qualified to do this job. We have never handled anything quite so serious or potentially dangerous." As Tash translates, Nika's face drops in disappointment. I quickly add "But ...!" Her face lifts up in hope.

"Penny and I have agreed to spend at least one week looking into Anna's disappearance. If, after a week, we find we're making no progress or are in too far over our heads, we will hand your case over to another agency that we can recommend. Does that sound fair?"

Nika nods and says "Da! Yes! Yes!" excitedly. Tash looks delighted, which makes me feel a full-body thrill at pleasing her. Penny gives me a sideways glance and I realise I had better cool my jets.

Tash says, "Nika will pay full rate and expenses. She has secured funding, so no problem."

"We couldn't possibly accept full daily rates for ...", I say. Penny interrupts: "What Floss is trying to say is, yes thanks. Full rate and expenses will be fine." I scowl at her.

"OK good," says Tash. She shakes Penny's hand. "Also, I would help out wherever I can. Interpreting, spying, killings ... what help you need."

"I'm not sure we could afford you, Tash."

"This will be free. I paid well enough for other jobs."

"Now I *am* fascinated," says Penny. I avoid making eye contact with Penny.

"So what's the plan?" asks Tash.

Fair question. "Yep, the plan ... ok ... Tash, I need you to translate the advertisement word for word. It's our only lead. Nika, I need you to write down a list of all the bars and streets you've visited looking for Anna, ok?" Nika nods.

"Penny and I will knock our heads together to come up with the rest of the plan. So, how about we meet back at our office at 5.30 this evening?" Penny is grinning from ear to ear. I haven't seen her this excited since we slipped an E into her drink on New Year's in 2005.

Tash breezes out of the café in much the same way as she breezed in. I can see tears welling up in the corners of Nika's eyes. She hugs me, whispering "Thanks. Thanks. Thanks" in my ear. She pats Penny on the arm and heads out the door.

That leaves just me and Penny, and I know I'm in for it.

"So what's with you and Russia's answer to Lara Croft there?" she asks.

"What? Nothing! I don't know what you mean. Who do you mean? Tash?" I stammer, pulling a complete redner.

"You know exactly what and who I mean, Florence McFarland. Miss Russia. What in God's name has gotten into you?" She's actually wagging her finger at me.

"Don't wag your finger at me. You're not the boss of me. And she's Lithuanian, not Russian, by the way".

"Mmmmm ... the defendant has refused to answer the question. Do you actually have the hots for a woman? For Tash? Well Peter, Paul, and all his humble saints. Would you credit that?" asks Penny, trotting along to keep up with me as we head towards my car.

"What's with all the questions?" I blurt out.

"GUILTY as charged!" shouts Penny triumphantly. And then, in gentler tones, "Jesus, don't feel bad about it, Floss. You and ninety-five per cent of the clientele and staff back there were having the same thoughts. As ladies go, she's a bit of a stunner."

"Look, Penny. I don't know what the hell is going on with me at the moment. One minute I'm about to hop in the sack with Milo McCarthy and the next minute I'm having sordid thoughts about a woman, for Christ's sake! I am not ready to talk about this yet. I need to figure it out myself before I can even think of trying to get into it with someone else."

"Alright, Floss, honey. Don't auto-combust on me. Let's park it for now, but can I just say one thing?"

I nod slowly, anticipating a reprimand.

"If it came to a showdown between Milo and Tash, my money would be on Tash. Every. Single. Time."

12

Penny and I drive separately back to the office. I feel emotionally exhausted after listening to Nika's account of Anna's disappearance. I keep asking myself how anyone could be so naïve these days? How could her mother have let her go? But as I'm asking these questions I know that the answer lies in desperation. Luckily for me, I've never been so broke that I couldn't make ends meet. No matter how bad my life could get, I could always slink back to Mum and Dad, to a refuge. I realise that I've always had the comfort of a safety net.

I pick up two lattes from Massimo and thank him for his help with Nika, letting him know that we eventually found each other. There's some flamboyant Italian hand waving and a "bueno" before the deal is done.

When I get to the office, Penny is already there, surfing human trafficking websites. I'm not sure I'm ready for that just yet, so I flop down behind my desk and start trying to formulate a plan of attack.

There are a couple of angles we can follow. The first is phone records. We need to try to find any information behind the mobile number that was included in the ad in the St Petersburg newspaper. It was an Irish number, so we should be able to track it down at this end. We could also try to find out if the last call that Anna made to her mother was from her mobile or another Irish number. The second avenue is to try to discover who placed the ad. They won't have used real names, but it's somewhere to start. Finally, we need to track down the flight that Anna took to Dublin. If we can establish whether she was travelling alone or in a group, we might be able to find other girls or, more importantly, a 'group leader'.

Ok, so that's the 'what' we need to do. Now I just need to figure out the 'how'.

"Can I interrupt your web surfing there briefly, Pen?" I ask.

"Sweet divine Mother of our Lord, please do. These trafficking sites don't make for happy reading, but I'm hoping they might be useful at a later date for support groups and networks."

I come out from behind my desk, saying, "I'm going to pop my thoughts so far up on the whiteboard. Partly to help gather them, but mainly to make me feel important." We are both feeling pretty sombre right now. I'm sure that Penny is projecting how she would feel if it were one of her kids in Anna's place.

I jump up to the whiteboard along the back wall and outline my three options for tracking Anna down. The caffeine has me completely reenergised. Penny is nodding furiously as I write and talk. When I've finished point three about the flights, she pipes up: "Good thinking, Floss. Like that one on the flights. I also think it's worth contacting one of these helplines to see if they have any further advice. There's a couple here I could try, to get the ball rolling."

"Agreed. I'll jot that down as point four. However, I want you to tackle number one first – to hit up your network at TelcoWeb and see what they can find on the phone number from the newspaper ad and that last call to Anna's mum." Penny used to work in telecommunications before she became a part-time mum/detective. She still has loads of contacts from that time.

"And look, Penny, I'm aware that we're running into a grey area on the legal front in terms of phone records, but see what you can do. If you don't get anywhere, we'll come up with another approach."

"Great. I'm on it. Anything I can offer in terms of sweeteners?" asks Penny.

"If you're talking to the geeks, let's promise them some of Zippy's gear. They would love all that stuff. If it's a normal human being, let's talk straight cash. But no more than a grand."

"I'm definitely going to start with the geeks. I'll need to dig out my Rolodex from the old days. These guys are so technical, they're far too paranoid to be on something as mainstream as LinkedIn or Facebook."

"OK," I say, rubbing my hands together, "that leaves me with the flights."

"What will we get Tash and Nika to work on?"

"Maybe number two on the board there. Tash could look into the ad and its origins," I suggest, averting my eyes from Penny's gaze at the mention of Tash.

"Good idea and while we're on the subject of said Tash, anything further you'd care to share with Assistant Private Investigator Penny?"

"Not a sausage. Get back to work."

"Slave driver," she snaps, but she is smiling to herself.

"I think you mean Employer of the Year." She chuckles.

I start with the flights (probably the easiest of the angles to tackle), looking online at possible routes between St Petersburg and Dublin. While it's possible that Anna was flown through London, it looks as if the Lufthansa option via Frankfurt is the cheapest and most regular route. If we're talking about a human trafficking network, they'll be doing everything on the cheap, so I'm going to risk assuming that she came through Germany with Lufthansa, and see where that takes us. Worst case, we can go back and widen the search net at a later date.

I make a quick call to Zippy, my gadgets guy.

"Yeah?" he answers with his usual charm assault.

"Hey Zippy. It's Floss here again at CTB. I need you to hook me up with a particular skillset."

"Uh huh …"

Not sure if that's his complete answer or indeed if it's a question but I plough ahead anyway. "I need a propeller head with questionable moral values, particularly in the area of accessing flight records."

"Mmm, I know just the guy but he's not cheap and I'll need to give you an introduction. He can't take direct calls."

"Does he have any form with the gardaí?"

"Clean as a whistle." He actually whistles – coming from Zippy, that is significant animation.

"Perfect. Where to next?"

"I'll drop you a text with details, when I have them. Oh, and a 10% cut for me in honour of the hook-up."

Cheeky bugger! "What is this? The Wire? 5%. Last chance."

"Deal. Laters." He hangs up before I can say another word.

Damn it, I should have started at 2%. As I'm rethinking my negotiations, the phone rings. I grab it quickly, assuming it's Zippy calling back, and say, "You're taking me for a complete ride."

"Well, just name the time and the place, McFarland, and I'll be there." I can feel the burning sensation flush through my face as I recognise the lazy drawl of Milo McCarthy.

"Not a shit show's chance, McCarthy. But apologies, I did think you were someone else."

"Some other lucky chap!" he says chuckling away to himself.

"To what do I owe the pleasure?" I ask, trying get back to business.

"I just wanted to let you know that I got a call from Janet at Trilby and I have my first meeting with the other three directors this afternoon at 3pm."

"Great stuff. That's a little quicker than I would have expected, but sounds like Janet must have done a good job on the hard sell."

"You know I'm an easy sell, McFarland."

"Not lacking in self-confidence, are we?"

"No, as a matter of fact, not at all," he says without a trace of modesty. It's exactly this type of cockiness that makes my blood boil with simultaneous annoyance and attraction. He infuriates me.

Penny's looking at me over the top of her giant rims. "Milo?" she mouths. I nod. She shakes her head and rolls her eyes at the same time, managing to look like a school principal.

"Well, thanks for calling to let me know. Can we have a chat after the meeting to get a full debrief?" I ask, again back to my best businesslike tone.

"My pleasure, McFarland. Wish me luck ..."

"Break a leg," I say, and ring off before he can get in the last word.

Penny laughs. "Well done, Floss. Didn't know you had it in you – where Milo's concerned. Things are really hotting up in your corner at the minute, aren't they?"

"It's like waiting for the 31B bus. None for half a lifetime and then two come along at once," I whine.

"Alleluia Jesus! This is progress. So you're admitting, in this little soap opera of yours, that Tash is, in fact, a bus." She can't help prying. It's one of the reasons I hired her.

"Please refer to my aforementioned communication about not engaging in any discussion about the matter," I say, focusing intently on my laptop.

"Suit yourself, Floss. But this has all the hallmarks of a complete train wreck in the making ... or should I say bus wreck?" she says with a wink.

I fling a whiteboard pen at her. It narrowly misses but she gets the message.

Many minutes later, as I'm still staring blankly at my monitor, my mobile emits its sonar blip. I snatch at it.

A text from Zippy:

> "Jeremy. 85 Strand Road, Sandymount. He knows ur comin. Z ..."

Very posh area and only a short drive away. I might as well head over before Nika and Tash arrive back at the office for our 5.30 catch-up.

"I'm heading off to catch up with one of Zippy's crew, hopefully to get a line on those flights," I tell Penny as I begin to gather my things.

"Need some company?" asks Penny, just dying to get out there again.

"No, I've got this one covered. You keep going on the phone records angle. I'll be back in time for five."

I jump in The Jalopy and cruise down by The Point. The traffic is light enough but they're digging up the north side of the quays. I smile in sympathy at the guy holding the stop/go sign.

While stuck at the road works, I send a text to Nika, asking her for the exact date when Anna flew out of St Petersburg.

Twenty minutes later, I pull up outside 85 Strand Road, after several attempts to find the right turn-off. The house is surprisingly well tended. I had been expecting some student rental digs with an overgrown garden, complete with couch as a centrepiece. But No 85 is a classic, white-painted terrace house with tall sash windows, a big, old Victorian-style door and an immaculately manicured garden.

I ring the bell. An apron-clad lady in her mid-50s opens the door. "Hello. Can I help you?" she asks politely but warily, peering at me through her bi-focals.

I can tell from her wary expression that she thinks I'm either selling something or on the scrounge.

"Hi there. Is Jeremy in?" I ask, feeling like I'm asking if my friend can come out to play – which turns out to be not far off the mark.

She shouts up the stairs: "Jeremy! You have a … visitor … what's your name, dear?"

"Florence McFarland," I say, increasingly self-conscious.

I can hear some movement upstairs and then a boy aged about 14 bounds half-way down the stairs, looks at me and says,

"Come on up."

I look at his mother. She manages to nod while also making it clear that she's less than thrilled at the thought of a 30-something woman visiting her son's bedroom.

"Thanks," I say sheepishly and rush to follow Jeremy up the stairs – and then up another set of stairs from this landing, as Jeremy's room is a converted attic space.

His room is a cross between NASA mission control and a shrine to Marvel comics, complete with a life-sized cardboard cut-out of Iron Man. The windows are blacked out; the only light comes from the five 20-inch monitors stacked on the bench-style desk and a broken lava lamp in the corner.

"Hi Jeremy. I'm Florence ... Floss."

"Yeah I know. Zippy told me you'd be dropping by," he says, staring at a screen containing multiple moving, wave-like green and black graphs.

I'd been expecting the clichéd 20-something geek, complete with ponytail, nerdy glasses and a pale, spotty complexion. But Jeremy exudes 'essence of jock', is dressed in smart chinos and a navy rugby jersey, and is well-built for his age. His fair hair is tidy in a clipped short-back-and-sides style and his sallow skin adds to his boyish look. I revise my estimate of his age to 15.

"First, are you sure it's ok with your mother for me to be here?" I ask, still mortified.

"I wouldn't say she's exactly happy about it, but we have come to an agreeable arrangement," he says, sounding like a middle-aged lawyer.

"Secondly, what age are you?"

"I'll be 16 in December," he says, with the conviction that this will finally make him a grown-up.

"I've got to be honest with you, Jeremy, I was expecting someone a little ..."

"Older?"

"Well, I was going to say 'experienced', but I guess it amounts to the same thing."

"This business is not about longevity, it's about natural ability and I was born for this. But if it helps, I hacked into the Irish prison systems inmate register when I was eight years old. It was either this or go to Cambridge, aged 14. I chose this."

"Wow, so you're some form of child genius?" I say, genuinely impressed.

"In a word, yes." He says this with straightforward honesty. I like him already.

"OK 'Rainman', I need help with tracking down some passengers on inbound flights. Think you can help with that?"

"Like taking candy from a baby," he smiles and cracks his knuckles. "Which airline?"

"Lufthansa, but that's a best guess. The route's from St Petersburg to Dublin, and Lufthansa seems to make the most sense."

"When?"

"I'm waiting for the exact dates." I check my mobile to see if Nika has come back to me. Nothing ... but there is a message from an unknown number:

We think Anna left 15th August ... Tash x

From Tash? Nika must have asked her to translate. And with a kiss? *Not now, Floss. Focus.*

"Ah, I have it. She left on the 15th of August."

"And the passenger name?" he says, fingers flying over the keyboard.

"Anna Durchenko."

"OK, what I'm doing here first is writing a quick script to assess all the optimum routes and then I'll have to kick something off a bit more substantial to trawl the various airline flight records."

"What I'm really after is not just how she came in, but who she came in with. Can you do that?"

"Embarrassingly easy. Leave it with me. I've another job on today but I can leave yours running in the background," he says, still typing furiously and oozing self-confidence.

"Great. Can we discuss your fee?" I ask, expecting pocket change.

"For a pretty lady like yourself, I'll do a discounted rate of five hundred euros."

"Sorry … that's your discounted rate for a day's work!? I'd have thought you'd still be living off your confirmation money," I splutter.

"Think of it as an introductory offer," he says without breaking his stride.

"Your generosity overwhelms me. Any chance of a receipt?" I ask hopefully.

"None … I'll call you as soon as I've anything to tell you."

With that, I guess, our meeting is over. I slink downstairs as quietly as I can, trying to avoid bumping into the mum. No such luck. Just as I'm opening the front door, I hear over my shoulder: "Was Jeremy able to help?"

I turn around, "I hope so. And it's for a very good cause." I say knowing that I'm really trying to assuage my own guilt for putting a fifteen year old kid on the payroll.

"That's what they all say. Just as long as you join the cause when I'm fighting to keep him out of prison. Goodbye Florence." The door is closed firmly behind me.

Well, that was an experience.

I jump back in the car, I spend ten minutes trying to compose a response to Tash.

Thanks Tash

Genius.

I've been neglecting Leon. I go home to get him before heading back to the office. I don't admit to myself that it's also to please Tash, who clearly adores him.

I feel the ground moving as he gallops to the front door I'm putting the key in. All that pent-up energy has to go somewhere. I hold off opening the door as I know what's coming. He skids and thumps into the door on the other side. He has never really learned to master braking on wooden floorboards. I open the door as he is gathering himself up off the floor.

"Alright, alright. That's my boy." He's up in my face in a nano second, wagging his tail so enthusiastically that his entire body is swaying from side to side.

"We're off to the office for a meeting with Tash, ok?" He keeps on wagging.

We hop into the car and I have to leave the window slightly ajar to provide some relief from Leon's dog breath. We're at the office just before five.

"How did you get on?" asks Penny as she ruffles the fur behind his hears. "How are ya, boy?" He loves the attention.

"Well, apart from the fact that CTB could now be accused of exploiting children for hard labour, just fine."

"What?" asks Penny, looking confused.

"The guy that Zippy put me onto for the flights is still living with his mother … mainly because he's only 15 years old."

"Oh, dear God."

"Yeah I know. He's basically a kid wired into the Internet from his upstairs bedroom. I had to go through his mum to get to him. I nearly died of embarrassment. I tried to comfort her with the theory of her son using his powers for good, but she wasn't having a bar of it."

"Don't blame her! If it was my Oscar, I'd have our connection to the Internet ripped out at home."

"I think you're pretty safe where Oscar's concerned. Consummate charmer he is, child genius, he is not." I say this knowing Penny can take it. She is under no allusions as to Oscar's IQ.

"I'll try not to take offense to that. From his Godmother of all people!" she says, pretending she's offended.

"Anyway, hacker-child Jeremy is on the job. He thinks it's a piece of cake. How are you getting on with the phone numbers?"

"Well, I managed to rule out the mobile number used in the newspaper ad. It's a pay-as-you-go jobby that's had no activity since early August. No outbound calls were made from it, only inbound. It's basically a disposable phone registered to a bogus profile, so there's not much point in trying to track that down."

"Bummer. But to be expected."

"The call that Anna made to her mum, that's going to take a little longer. Also, I need Anna's mum's mobile number for my guy to get started."

"Well, Nika should be here any minute, so we can get it then. Who are you using for this?"

"The less you know the better, but it's one of the database guys over at TelcoWeb."

"Ok good."

I do a quick check on my email. Nothing interesting and no new sex spam, so that's a positive.

Leon lets out a low growl followed by a loud bark.

"It's OK, big fella," I say, "we're expecting visitors."

I open the door. Tash, who was pushing the door inwards, falls in on top of me. I'm propelled backwards and down and we land with a crash, her splayed on top of me and me spread-eagled underneath on my back. We're almost nose to nose.

Tash smiles: "Perhaps another time?"

I can't help giggling. Penny cracks up in the background. Leon wags his tail.

 "Great one-liner, Tash!" says Penny, as we awkwardly extract ourselves from this. Nika steps into the room.

"Right, well ..." I stammer, rather shakily, "welcome to the headquarters of CTB Investigations."

13

Nika takes the spare seat at my desk and I get one of the spare fold-out chairs for Tash. Penny arranges teas and coffees. As Tash sits down, she hands me two pages of typed text.

"What's this?" I ask glancing down at the first page.

"It's the list of bars, clubs and streets Nika has covered in her search," she says. "Like you asked for?" Her Lithuanian-accented English gives her sentence an undercurrent of 'you better need this and not have been wasting my valuable kick-ass, assassin time'.

Quickly I say, "That's great, nice one," and after properly taking in the list, "you really have been busy this week". I'm looking at Nika and she just nods timidly.

"Ok," I say, "if everybody's happy, we'll get started." I look at Tash to make sure she's ready to start translating. "Right, we've come up with a couple of angles of investigation, if you'd all care to take a glance at the board." I spend the next few minutes taking them through our ideas and progress so far.

"So, how can I help?" asks Tash.

"Yep, I was just going to get to that. I'd like you to try to follow up on the newspaper ad. I know it's a total long shot, but I still think we have to cover it. But no killing anyone, ok?"

"I will try, but no promises."

Tash is looking at our plan on the whiteboard, concentrating hard. "I think there might be other option to follow on phone," she says.

"Go on," says Penny.

"OK," Tash says. "Nika says Anna speaks to other girl who already lives in Dublin. It should be possible track down this number from Anna's phone, no? She probably not receive many calls from Irish phone before leaving Russia. If we find Irish number, it might be interesting to us."

"You're absolutely right!" I say, both impressed with Tash and embarrassed at myself for not having picked up on it. "God, I'm such a numpty for missing that."

Nika shakes her head: "No problem."

"Don't worry about it, Floss" says Penny. "It's just combined girl power working its magic. Doesn't matter who has the idea, right girls?"

Tash winks at me: "Yes, it's just girl power, Floss. Nothing to be afraid of."

Hey presto, my face is bright red again.

Penny saves me: "Well, is everyone ok with the plan?"

We all nod. "Well, then I think this meeting is adjourned," I say. "Let's meet here same time Monday. Nika, can you give me Anna's mobile and her mother's phone number for the trace, please?"

Tash translates. Nika checks her mobile phone and writes down two numbers, then hands her note to Penny.

"OK," I say, "remember, let's do it to them before they do it to us." Everyone turns and looks at me with a 'what-the-what-now' look?

"Sorry, it's an old Hill Street Blues catchphrase. I've always wanted to use it and didn't really ever get the opportunity in my actuarial days. Now just seemed like the right time."

Another eye-roll from Penny.

"We will try, Floss," says Tash as she and Nika file out the door.

Penny turns to me: "Seriously, Floss, the heady mix of girl power, Hill Street Blues quotes and the heat off your face is enough to overpower a person. What in God's name is going on?"

"Can I plead the fifth?" I whimper.

"In a court of law in the United States of America maybe. In a prefab in a car park in Dublin's north city centre? I think not."

"Well … you see …"

"Oh God the suspense is killing me. Are you going to tell me you're gay? Because it's completely fine if you are, you know. Nobody will give a damn, least of all me."

"No, I'm not gay! At least I don't think I am. I'm just having this weird … reaction to Tash."

"Well by my superior powers of deduction, I'm going to hazard a guess that this has been going on for some time, given that Tash was your Aikido instructor six months ago. So, knowing you, my dear, you've been suppressing this little mind bomb down in your very core in an attempt to make it go away."

"Maybe," I say feeling like a 10-year-old who has just been caught stealing from her mother's purse.

"*Maybe* my behind. And how exactly is that working out for you?"

"Just peachy, as you can see. Just peachy."

"Dear God, what are we going to do with you, Floss? But the more important question is how are you going to tell your folks?"

"Mothery fuck, Pen, this is hard enough without trying to figure that one out!"

"OK, I hear you. I'm thinking baby steps, yeah?" she says gently.

"That's about all I can manage for the moment," I reply.

"Right, well, I'll go back to my phone guy and see what he can do about Tash's idea about the phone records."

Penny knows I need some quiet time.

"I'm going to head off," I say, grabbing Leon's leash.

"See you tomorrow, hon."

I drive over to Dollymount to take Leon for a spin, knowing that I'm avoiding the South Wall and Tash. We walk the wooden bridge, beautifully lit up in an eerie, orange dusk light. We go right to the end of the walkway. I can't help but strain my eyes along the South Wall for Tash's athletic shape. No sign.

I feel the need to do something while we're waiting for Jeremy and Pen's contact to come back on the flight and phone records and am wracking my brain for what that might be. Nothing is coming to mind so I try to park the case and enjoy the walk with Leon instead. Leon is in his element, chasing birds on the rocky side of the walkway. I'd love to see him actually catch a bird one day. He wouldn't have a clue what do with it if he did. Back at the car, I decide to drop in to my parents, who are just up the road. This is partly out of proximity and partly out of fear that someone would have spotted Leon and myself and reported it to Mum. She has a broad-reaching network of spies. If she found out we were this close and didn't drop in, I'd be in serious trouble.

She opens the front door. I see billowing smoke and smell burning meat.

"Hello! Do I need to call the fire brigade?" I ask, battling my way through the fog. Leon is whimpering beside me.

"What's going on," Mum informs me in top sarcasm mode, "is your father's Friday night dinner production, per our agreement. In revenge, he incinerates everything within a ten-mile radius. He's trying to wear me down, but mark my words, I'm not giving in."

In the kitchen, Dad is sweating like a bastard and the tears are running down his face from the smoke.

"Hello love, fancy some dinner?" he says, giving me a squeeze.

"Well, delicious as it smells, I think I have some leftover dog poo at home. So I'll probably go with that, thanks."

"Very funny," he says. "I just struggle to get the hang of this gas hob. It has a mind of its own."

"What was that before you gassed it to death?" I ask, pointing at the blackened mess in the wok.

"Pork chops with stir fried vegetables and noodles."

"I think we'll have to call in CSI to identify the remains."

"Get out of here," he says jokingly as he flicks a tea-towel at me. I retreat to the living-room with Mum. Leon is sticking to my side. He's slightly intimidated by my mother. Who isn't?

"How are you darling?" she asks as she flicks on the TV. The news.

"Grand. Busy, which is great. Dinner looks fantastic, I'm really sorry I can't stay."

"I think we'll have to get take-aways. I'm at my wits' end with your father."

"Oh don't be so dramatic. It's only some burned food. And at least he's making an effort. He looks like a coal miner in there, so even if he is trying to outfox you on the dinner rota, I don't think he's having any fun while doing it."

"I suppose you're right. I could have a philandering good-for-nothing husband like Des Connors. Mary rang this morning to say she thinks he's having an affair. Would you credit that?"

"First Des finds religion and now a new lady friend? He must be having a late life crisis. In fairness to Des, if I was married to Mary Connors, I'd be having an affair too, Mum. She is painful with a capital P. I don't know how you're friends with her."

"I'm not really friends with her. She's just in the bridge club, so you have to keep on the right side of these people. They're vicious if you break ranks."

"Sounds like a total blast." In the background as we chat, I hear the RTE news anchor hand over to a reporter on the ground in Vienna. He's talking about a United Nations initiative on intervention in Syria. Bing! I remember the husband of a college friend of mine who is now working for the UN, the Human Trafficking division. Why didn't I think of Padraig sooner?

I jump up, kiss mum goodbye, saying, "Thanks, you've been a great help!"

"What? What did I do?" she asks, flapping a tea towel to try to clear away the smoke.

Leon is already at the door trying to escape both the smoke and my mother.

"Seeya Dad! Bon appetite!"

I vaguely hear him saying "Are you sure you won't stay for a bite?" as we head out the door. Poor Dad, he tries to use me as a mediator between Mum and himself but I'm not having a bar of it.

I drive straight home and look up Emer's number. Emer and Padraig were university sweethearts who married in final year. We all thought they were completely mental, but 12 years and three gorgeous kids later, they've proven the doubters wrong. I text Emer:

> Hey Emer! Can you send me P's mobile number? Need some help with him on the work front. Hope all good with you and the kids? Flo xx

While I'm waiting to hear back from Emer, I feed Leon and scramble around in the fridge for something for me to munch on. It makes for pathetic eating. Two slices of toast and a half a tub of Ben & Jerry's Caramel Chew Chew ice cream. *Nutritious.*

A text comes back from Emer:

> Flo! Good to hear from you. Padraig is 085-2318765. He's in Vienna at the minute but you should catch him still. All good here at the madhouse. Jenny is making her communion this year. Can you believe it? Dinner soon? E xx

I flick back a quick text in thanks and then try calling Padraig. Straight to voicemail, so I leave a quick message asking him to call me.

I pour a glass of wine, turn on the TV and settle down on the couch with Leon for some trashy soaps. Lately I've become addicted to Shortland Street, a New Zealand show based loosely around a hospital. It's so bad it's good. You can miss as many as twelve episodes and still be in touch with the storyline.

At nine-thirty, my house phone rings. It's Declan from the poker club.

"I take it I should mark you down as an absentee this week?"

"Ah dumb balls. I've been completely slammed with work and totally forgot it was Friday night! Sorry Deckie. Who's there tonight?"

"The usuals and Julie from next door."

"Fresh meat! Damn it. I could have made a killing!"

"Well, we'll miss your company but not you fleecing us. Maybe catch you next week? It'll be at Harold's place."

"Definitely and let me know how tonight goes."

"Will do! See ya round," says Declan and rings off.

I've been playing Friday night poker for the last five years with pretty much the same group of codgers, mainly college friends from back in the day. My Dad taught me how to play when I was 12 and then had to stop playing with me because he said I was robbing him of his pride and manhood. When it comes to poker, I like to think I'm shit hot. I have an uncanny ability to read people. And something happens to me when I sit at that green felt table. It's as if an inner calm descends and an outer blank exterior locks into position, like the invisible shield from Star Trek. I become impenetrable.

Those Friday night poker games, with their hundred euro maximum bets, have sometimes been the only thing that stood between me and the breadline. I am sorry to be missing them.

At a quarter to eleven, I'm half way through the Graham Norton show, with the delicious Javier Bardem, when my mobile rings. It's Padraig.

"Hello is that Flo?"

"None other. How are you doing, Padraig?"

"To be honest, I'm completely locked. Just out at a leaving do for my boss. We're all fucking delighted he's leaving," he says, slurring every word.

Oh dear.

"I hope, for you, he's not within earshot."

"Oh jaysus, good point." And I can almost hear him checking over his shoulder.

"Coast is clear." It sounds something like 'coash ish clear'.

"Ok, well now is probably not a good time for this little chat. I need some help with your expertise on human trafficking."

"You're too old to be trafficked, Flo," he says, laughing to himself.

"Hilarious! Look, give me a call in the morning when you've had your first dose of Paracetamol. This is serious, Padraig," I say in my stern voice.

"Oh-oh. Righteo, Flo. Hey! That's a rhyme! You better call me, as I'm not going to remember this call in the morning."

"Sound. Will do. Enjoy the rest of the night!"

"You betcha ..."

Well, someone is obviously enjoying the work travel gig. Like most parents with kids, when they get the chance to go out on the town they make the most of it. Fair enough.

I hit the scratcher shortly afterwards with images of Javier Bardem, Milo and Tash vying for top spot in my dreams. Nobody wins and I have my recurring dream of being chased by my old parish priest and an army of altar boys. *Terrifying stuff.*

Aoife Sheridan

14

On Saturday morning, I wake up delighted not to have a hangover. There are benefits to skipping Friday night poker. It's a crisp, blue-sky, good-to-be-alive day in Dublin. I love these days. They put a spring in everyone's step.

I go for a quick run/walk with Leon in the park and then head into town to meet some old school friends for brunch. I gorge myself on a full Irish with home fries and two lattes. Afterwards, I'm fit for nothing but the couch. I head home and start tucking into an ancient James Bond movie with Sean Connery. It's the one where a tarantula climbs across his chest while he's in bed. I remember reading that Sean Connery is terrified of spiders, so the spider is actually crawling on a sheet of glass. As I look carefully, I can see clearly that the spider is kind of floating above his chest hair. *Classic!*

When the movie finishes and James Bond has got the bad guy and the hot girl, I call Padraig again, hoping that I've given him enough time to recover from his, no doubt, almighty hangover.

He answers with a very groggy hello.

"Hi Padraig. It's Floss again. Should I be speaking very quietly?" I ask in a mock whisper.

"You have no idea of the pain I'm going through. Did we talk last night? Something is vaguely ringing a bell."

"Yep, technically I talked and you slurred some rubbish down the phone. Suffice to say you were in flying form."

"Sorry about that. Hope it was all appropriate. What's up?"

"Quite a bit actually. I'm working a new case that involves the disappearance of a young Russian girl and we suspect she's been trafficked."

"I thought you dealt in the more corporate end of the market. People with their hands in the till, and the like."

"Normally, yeah, I do. But this case kind of fell into my lap and I really want to help this girl."

"First, Flo, be careful. The guys involved in these trafficking rings are not good corporate citizens. They're the parasites that live off the bacteria that feed off the scum of the earth. Know what I mean?"

"Yep, I know we're slightly out of our depth here. But I've only committed to getting the investigation started and if it gets too dodgy for us, we'll hand it over to somebody more qualified. At the moment, from what I can gather, her case is getting lost in limboland between the Russian and Irish police."

"Flo, you sound like you're already emotionally invested in this case. I know fuck all about investigative work, but I'm guessing that's a bad thing."

"Point taken. Are you all done dispensing the fatherly advice now?"

"Yep, I think that's the lot, but don't say you haven't been warned. I'm really only on the policy side of things in the UN. So I'm all about education rather than investigating. But give me the basic details and I'll see what I can find from my buddies here."

"Thanks Padraig. That'd be fantastic. Her name is Anna Durchenko, aged 18, from St Petersburg. She responded to an ad in a local newspaper promising new life and riches in Dublin. The usual sort of stuff. She took the job against her friend's advice and her last contact was a call, we think, from

Dublin saying she had landed and was fine. That was two months ago. Her best friend travelled here to find her and got in touch with us. And that's about the height of it."

"Classic trafficking scenario. Leave it with me and I'll see if I can find any useful information for you."

"Thanks Padraig. I'll owe you one."

"You can help me out by dropping into Emer at some stage. I'm away for another week and it can get a bit much with the three girls when she's on her own."

"I hear ya. Will do. Cheers Padraig. Hope the hangover subsides."

"No chance, this one's here for the long haul. See ya." We hang up.

I look at Leon: "Doesn't sound like good news for Anna, Leon." He dog-shrugs as if to say, "Honestly, this is outside my area of expertise."

"Fair enough, boy."

I'd heard an electronic blip while talking to Padraig so check my text messages. There's an update from Declan at the poker club to say that the new girl, Julie from next door, cleaned up. He was putting it down to beginner's luck. Maybe I saved some cash by not being there.

At five o'clock I change into my scruffy gear, torn old Diesel jeans and crusty grey hoodie, intent on doing a bit of a spring (but more accurately autumn) cleaning. I'm behind the couch, knee-deep in dust and horrified at what I'm finding there, when the doorbell rings.

Shit bums. I can't answer the door in this state. I dither, contemplating a quick change, but curiosity gets the better of me. I open the door to find Milo McCarthy looking outrageously scrumptious, with a promising brown bag, which, fingers crossed, contains cake!

"You didn't need to dress up on my account," he says for openers.

"Had I known you were coming, I would have dressed down even further," I reply. Not bad under the compromising circumstances.

"Is it possible to dress down any further than that?" he asks, giving me a slow once-over that practically tingles.

"I'm in belated autumn cleaning mode, if you must know," I say testily.

"So, what does a fella have to do to get invited into a gal's home around these parts?" he says in an affected John Wayne drawl.

"Giving some advanced warning of your approach would be a good start ... come on in, I suppose."

"Your enthusiastic welcome is touching." Sarcastic to the core.

I bring him through to the kitchen, the room least affected by my cleaning efforts. He slides smoothly onto one of the tall stools at the breakfast bar.

"Can I get you a cup of coffee? Tea?" I ask, slipping into hostess mode.

"Have you a beer by any chance? Or anything stronger?"

"You're probably out of luck on the beer front, but let me see what's hidden around here." I go out to the hall and look in my drinks stash. I shout back, "I have white wine, but it's warm, some Merlot, straight vodka and what appears to be 14-year-old sherry. I'm not sure I'd recommend the sherry, I don't think it's supposed to be aged."

"Sounds like an impressive drinks cabinet. I'll take a glass of the Merlot, but only if you'll join me."

"I can give you some nice cheddar and stale crackers with that, if you'd like?"

"Tempting, but I'll stick to the wine."

I pour us both a generous amount in oversized glasses.

"What do you say to a toast, McFarland?"

"Why not?" This should be interesting.

"To all future joint endeavours," he says with a wink and we clink glasses.

"I'll drink to that ... so what brings you to Irishtown on this fine Saturday afternoon, Milo?"

"I wanted to give you a heads-up on my meeting with Trilby & Co yesterday. Frankly, I'd have expected you to be chasing after me for an update."

"The only thing I can guarantee is that I will not be chasing after you." I'm feeling bolshie today.

"Fair enough," he says laughing. "I probably had that one coming to me. Look, do you want to hear how it went yesterday or not?"

"Of course, Milo. Please ... go ahead," I say making a dramatic, courtly gesture.

"Well, I met with Janet first of all for a pre-interview briefing. She is so old school. I bet if you looked up 'tweed' in the dictionary, you'd find a little picture of her there. But she's a strong old bird."

"Sorry to interrupt you, Milo, but I'd prefer if you could avoid calling my clients 'old bird' if at all possible. She is a mature, strong and successful woman and I'd like it if we treated her with the respect she deserves."

I'm really not sure where all this stroppiness is coming from!

"As always, I stand corrected," he says.

"And anyhow," I add, "my business partner Penny has the monopoly on tweed in the dictionary," trying to take the sting out of my earlier comment.

"You could be right. Janet Trilby is a formidable woman, don't let my casual description mislead you. If it was down to me and her good self in a scrap for survival, I know I would come out of it the worse for wear."

"Ha! You're not wrong. Go on ..."

"So, Janet briefed me along the same lines as you did. We went through my alias and profile to make sure she was comfortable with it and there were no risky areas. She seemed happy enough, so afterwards she brought me into the boardroom to meet her key players: the finance guy, James Kenny, the CEO Arlene Henderson and the IT guy ... let me check my notes ... really chatty and happy-go-lucky guy ... Paul Fitzsimons."

"Never met him. Strange he was in at board level," I comment, almost to myself.

"Well he's not actually on the board. Apparently he's been assisting with the investigation on the technical side. Fancies himself as a bit of a forensic technician, by all accounts. "

"He hasn't made much progress!" I scoff.

"Yeah, he could be one of those all talk and no action types. Anyway, we went through my CV together and I gave them the full 'Magnus Flynn" hard sell. I explained that business development was going to be my focus, particularly an expansion into the UK market where most of my contacts are. They were lapping up every word by the end of it."

"Any initial thoughts on potential suspicious cats among them?" I ask, curious to hear what his first impressions were.

"Well, it was very high-level and they were more focused on me than the other way round. But my money's on the head of finance. He's all twitchy and edgy. Plus, I just never trust bean counters. They know how to find money and they know how to hide it."

"He's an unsympathetic sort, but that doesn't make him guilty just yet," I say.

"Yeah, but I also took the IT geek, Fitzsimons, out for a few drinks yesterday. Once I got the first drink into him, I couldn't shut him up. He has big plans for the place, all IT related, you know "remote this" and "networked" that. Bored me to tears. Although, he wasn't willing to point the finger at anyone, I could tell he didn't like James Kenny either."

"Mmmm … ok, that's a bit more compelling, but let's keep an open mind. And don't get too chummy with anyone there. Magnus Flynn would tend to remain aloof."

"Yes, boss."

Grrrr. Must maintain composure.

"So, what's next?" I ask quickly, as I'm at risk of punching his handsome face.

"Well, the board meeting is on Wednesday. Janet has information she is going to leak at this which is actually fictitious, so if anything leaks after that we know where we stand. We'll do the bug sweeps, sound and video and see where we land after that."

"I'll line up the surveillance gear for Tuesday, so we've plenty of time to get everything in place in the boardroom."

"We've a van we use for this type of thing – Marney Carpet Cleaners. It comes with matching jump suits so nobody will suspect a thing. You're welcome to the use of it for the install."

"That would be perfect. One less thing for me to worry about."

"I have to say, Floss, you do look a little preoccupied around the edges. Is everything ok?"

This softer, caring side to Milo is something I've never seen before. I'm taken aback. I can feel the stress, which has quietly been building up: behind the furrowed brow, in the pit of my stomach and in my racing and confused mind. I have to summon every ounce of strength not to break down into a blubbering mess in front of him.

I take a minute.

"More wine, methinks," he says, delivering another generous pour.

"I have to admit, this has been a hell of a week."

"Tell uncle Milo ..."

"We landed another case this week ... one that's not really in our area of expertise and I'm terrified I'm going to make a total balls of it. The stakes are a lot higher than anything we've dealt with before. Not some shyster getting away with some minor penny-pinching ... there are lives at stake. I feel emotionally involved in more ways than I can explain."

"Look, Floss. No matter what I say here, it's going to sound condescending, but I'm going to go ahead anyhow. If you need some help from me and my crew, just say the word. We can shuffle things around to make it work."

"Remarkably for you, Milo, that did not actually sound condescending. I appreciate the offer and I'll seriously consider it. We have some outside help on contract already, but that may not be enough."

"Well, I'm just saying, I'd hate to see the cutest investigator in all of Ireland get maimed somehow."

"Now that was condescending," I say, lashing out with my hand to give him a playful dig in the shoulder.

Before my hand has connected, he's grabbed my wrist and pulled me to him, while his other hand is instantly at the back of my neck, tilting me towards him. Next thing I know his lips are on mine. I try briefly to push away, but he's holding firm and his tongue refuses to take no for an answer. My mouth is momentarily in shock as it's been out of commission for well over a year. Then it suddenly jumps into action and I'm in danger of devouring him. I hear a deep moan from him, which only serves to spur me on.

We find ourselves in an awkward clinch across the breakfast bar, grappling at each other across the divide. Milo pushes back his stool with a sudden jerk, pulls me up to my feet and presses himself against me. The stool topples with a crash. Then I scream "Noooooooooooooooooooooo, Leon!!" as my dutifully protective dog springs up, knocks us both over and pins Milo to the ground with his oversized paws.

He'd awoken from his nap, taken one look at the situation and obviously concluded that I was under attack. He is right up in Milo's face, growling and baring his teeth.

It's the first time I've seen Milo McCarthy caught off guard. He's petrified but trying hard to hide it.

"Leon, it's OK, down boy. Milo's one of the good guys," I say in my best doggy-soothing tones.

Leon pauses, looks at me as if to say "Really? This schmuck?"

"Yep, he's our friend. Up you come and sit, boy." With that Leon releases Milo and sits down by my side.

"And there I was thinking he was just a gentle giant," whispers Milo as he picks himself off the floor and dusts himself down. "You have him well trained."

"Honestly, I've never seen him do that before. I have this whole routine where I can get him to growl at people on demand, but I've never seen him go for someone quite so ... enthusiastically. Although, in his defence, he's never seen anyone go for me quite like you did just now either," I say, beginning to blush.

"You haven't seen anything yet, McFarland."

This comment nearly flips me back over the edge. I want to take another running jump at him, but I have to get it together.

"I think ... in the interest of .... professionalism and Leon's peace of mind, that we should ... maybe call it a day."

"Really, McFarland? Now that *is* a shame."

"I think it's for the best," I say quietly, feeling quite sheepish now.

"You're the boss. I'll make myself scarce. Thanks for the wine. See ya, Leon," he says, doffing an imaginary cap. Leon growls.

"Leon! Don't be so rude." He lies down and gives me the it's-not-my-fault look with his ears perked upwards but folded over.

"I'll call you next week about arrangements for the board meeting," says Milo.

"That'd be great."

"And I still owe you lunch," he says over his shoulder as he makes his way to his car. A racing red 2012 BMW 3 Series. I could have guessed.

I wave from the door as he skids off to impress me.

I close the door. My knees are still weak from that unbelievable kiss. If kisses could be x-rated, that one more than met the certification.

"What just happened, Leon?" He raises his doggy eyebrows and says, "I was just doing my job, but the guy's a douche bag, if you ask me."

"It's not what you did that's bothering me. It's me. I've just gone from celibate loner to skanky hoe in about three seconds flat." But Leon's not interested, he's padded softly back to his mutt bed.

I go into the bathroom and splash some cold water on my face, trying to erase the heat of Milo McCarthy from me. I stare into the mirror at this newly sex-crazed, confused, curly-haired mess and give myself a stern talking-to.

My mobile rings in the kitchen. I dash in but just miss the call. I check the number. It's marked 'Private'. *God, that's annoying.* How are you supposed to screen a call if they don't let you know who it is?

There's a little blip to indicate a voicemail. I dial immediately. It's Jeremy.

"Hi Miss McFarland. I think you're going to totally dig what I found. Call me on 01-8325465 … Oh and it's me. Jeremy. Boy genius."

15

I'm about to call the Whizz Kid back when my doorbell rings. A mystery caller on a Saturday evening. Intriguing. As I make my way to the front door, I'm hoping to the very tip of my toes that it's Milo who's come back because he finds me beyond irresistible.

Poo and snot.

It's my younger sister, dressed head to toe in spandex. She looks like she's just completed a serious workout that would have killed a mere mortal, but has hardly caused a blip on the nerdy heart rate monitor that is strapped to her shoulder.

"Hey sis! Really letting ourselves go are we? That outfit would get you the March slot in the Lezzer of the Month calendar, no problem," she says, breezing down my hallway towards the kitchen with a whiff of expensive perfume and not a hint of lady sweat.

I blush at the mere mention of the lezzer word, panic briefly that she has somehow telepathically figured out about my Tash issues, but then realise it's completely impossible. My sister is anything but astute. Her main skill in life is torturing me. There are two prongs to the pain she inflicts on me. First, she's known how to wind me up since we were knee-high to grasshoppers. Secondly, she inherited the premium set of genes from both of my parents. She is dark and exotic like Mum but with the body and athleticism of an Amazon. After completing a degree at University College Dublin in Psychology and Spanish, she made the wise decision to go into Personal Training. What, I hear you ask, is the connection between an

Arts degree and being a gym bunny? Excellent question. Answer … absolutely nothing.

During her studies, Sophie worked part-time at the UCD gym and developed nothing short of a fan club among the male clientele. There were actually waiting lists for people to get a session with her. Her group classes were packed to the rafters with drooling admirers, all trying desperately to impress her with their lunges and squats. She even negotiated a 50 per cent pay rise with her boss, who was not only a card-carrying member of the Sophie fan club, but also under no illusions as to the riots that would ensue if he let her go.

Sophie is a man's woman – resented by around 99 per cent of the female population.

I just remembered a third annoying prong to my sibling. Her name. My parents' ingenious idea for our names was based on the cities where we were conceived. This worked out pretty well for Sophie which is short for Sophia, as in the capital of Bulgaria. It even suits her with her dark, exotic looks. Me? I get Florence after the Italian city. I know it's a lovely place and all, but as a name? *Really?*

So she drives me nuts on three counts, but underneath it all I love her to bits. Two years younger than me, she's my baby sister at the end of the day.

By the time I've caught up with her in the kitchen, her head is already in my fridge doing a quick stocktake of the nutrient count per shelf.

"Jesus H Christ, Flojo, there's more nutrition in a radioactive Wham bar than in your fridge. How are you even standing up with this diet of yours?"

"The coffee. Take away the coffee and you'd be left with shell of Flojo."

"Or scrounging meals off Mum and Dad more like. Remind me to send you through that new eating programme I was talking about. The one with lots of protein and very little carbs. You won't know yourself. Head clear, bowels regular as clockwork."

"Yuck! No more bowel talk. Just so I know where I stand on this new diet of yours, do banoffee pie, pecan slices and donuts all fit in the carbs category? Coz if that's a yes, there's no chance of me signing up to that type of empty existence."

"You're a hopeless case, Flojo. What about exercise? Anything above a light walk with the beast?"

"My walks have been known to accelerate into a light trot at times. Sweat has been known to break out on my brow."

"Please let me help you. Come to my gym," Sophie begs.

"What! And have guys bumping into the machinery around us because they're so busy drooling over you? No thanks. The gym's a humiliating enough place without being out-babed by my baby sister."

"The ingratitude! Honestly!" she says, feigning a strop while chuffed at the compliment.

"Sorry, Soph, it's just not my bag, you know? All that testosterone and the constant staring at yourself in the mirror. A modern-day form of torture – and people actually pay for it! Give me the rack from back in the good old days, I say."

"I give up, then" Sophie says, exasperated.

"Please do. It would save a lot of energy on both sides."

"For the moment, maybe. Anyhow what's up with you? Mum tells me you've a scary new case?"

"It's not so much scary, it's TERRIFYING!"

I fill her in on Anna's disappearance and how we're trying to help Nika. I leave out the whole Tash sideline, as Sophie would not only shred me to pieces over it, but be instantly on the blower to Mum.

"How d'you fancy some take-away pizza from Il Fornaio and a nice drop of Merlot?" I ask hopefully.

"I'll have their chicken salad but with no dressing and maybe a half glass of wine."

I shake my head. "Remind me again, were we adopted?"

She does her little snorty laugh.

"Ok, so if I can't tempt you to pizza, how about some Dirty Dancing?"

Her gorgeous face lights up. "Sounds fab!"

Since we were kids we have a shared love of cheesy Eighties movies, but nothing tops Patrick Swayze and Dirty Dancing.

I call in the order for the pizza and salad and pour the wine. We settle down in front of the TV and crack into the movie. We both know all the words and mouth them as we go along.

When the guy arrives with the food, I remember I have to call Jeremy – before the wine begins to take hold. His Mum answers. I don't know her second name.

"Hello, this is Florence again. Is Jeremy there by any chance?"

"Yes, he hasn't left his room since you called around. This 'noble pursuit' of yours certainly has his attention. Please hold."

That last bit makes me feel like I'm talking to a call-centre rep. Very formal, but at least she's letting me talk to her son. I can hear him taking the stairs two at a time.

"Hiya Floss?" he says, slightly out of breath.

"Hi Jeremy. Did you manage to unplug yourself from the matrix?"

"Just about."

"So, you mentioned that you had some luck?"

"Luck has nothing to do with it. Sheer skill."

"Of course, Jeremy. How rude of me. Go on."

"Ok, well you gave me the date of travel as the 15th of August. I hunted on the Lufthansa flight via Berlin and couldn't find any Annas. I checked all possible routes via Heathrow. Still nothing. I was thinking they must have travelled under false identities. So I went back to an actual map of Europe to see if there was something I was missing. There was. St Petersburg is very close to Helsinki. It's an old smuggling route so I checked out the train from St Petersburg to Helsinki on the 15th – and whaddyaknow! Anna Durchenko and Piedr Korsak, both listed as Russian nationals, second-class tickets … one way."

"Bingo bongo! Brilliant work, Jeremy."

"It gets better. So I checked out flights from Helsinki to Dublin and sure enough, your friends Anna and Piedr were on the flight to Dublin on the same day. I decided to cast the net a bit wider. Nothing for the girl, but this guy Piedr is making regular trips on this route. He's always with one or more girls on the way out, but travels alone on the way back."

"Pure gold, Jeremy. Well done! I need to get a list of all the girls he has travelled with in the past year. Can you do that for me?"

"In my sleep. I have the code written now so I just need to

widen the date parameters."

"Great, whatever you just said, do that. " I'm not great on the technical front. "Will you email the results over to me at fmcfarland@ctb.ie."

"Will do."

"Actually, can you write something that also checks when he's going to be travelling in the future? Would be a great help in trying to get a step ahead of him. I appreciate it might be extra."

"Are you joking? This is fun stuff. My normal thing is to crack into a bully's Facebook account. BOR-ing?!"

"Oh and one last thing before you go, can you spell out the guy's name for me?"

He spells it out slowly and I write it down in my desk diary.

"Also, I'm presuming this is a cash job?"

"Correct."

"As soon as I have that list, I'll drop the cash over."

"Thanks Floss. I know you're good for it." We ring off.

I go back to the couch and flop down beside Sophie. She has paused the movie … you'd swear I'd have missed out on the plot or something.

"Who was that? A new man friend?" she asks.

"Boyfriend, if anything," I say with heavy emphasis on the 'boy'. "That was Doogie Howser of the computer world. I was worried about child labour laws until he just delivered the result of the week."

"Nice one. For a second I thought it might be a new love

interest." She is snooping for gossip now.

"Where were we in the movie?" I say to redirect her.

"We're just coming up to the 'Nobody puts baby in the corner' bit," she says. We're back to being two sisters enjoying a rubbish movie on a Saturday night. I really need this.

The following day, I get up early and take Leon for a long walk to Stephen's Green and back. I realise that the identification of Piedr Korsak, although a great leap forward, only serves to highlight how limited my investigative powers are. What am I going to do? If he was an Irish guy, I'd know where to start, but I've zero contacts in the Russian law enforcement network. I could ask Tash, but am reluctant to contact her on a Sunday. I have this illogical logic that if I am in touch with her during the week it is more professional and thus safer.

This debate keeps my head ticking over for the duration of the walk. When I get back, I realise I'm being an idiot. Anna has to be the priority. All emotional baggage must be stowed away for the duration of this case. I pull out my mobile, take a deep breath and dial Tash's number. She answers on the first ring.

"Hallo, Tash here." She sounds a little sleepy.

"Hi Tash, it's me Floss."

"I know. I see you on my phone." I see you ... *how cute is that?* "I'm in middle of thing here. Can I call you soon, please?" I hear what sounds like another female voice in the background. And some giggling.

"Yes absolutely. Talk to you later." I hang up.

My mind goes into overdrive. What is a 'thing'? Who was she with? Did I wake her? Them? Was she giggling at me? Oh *God.*

Listen to yourself, Florence Maria McFarland. Get a grip!

I turn on some music, get some breakfast for Leon and myself, try to distract myself with the Sunday newspapers, but my mind keeps going back to Tash. As I'm half way through a crossword, my mobile rings. *Think of the devil.*

"Hallo, Floss?" says Tash.

"Hi Tash. Thanks for returning my call," I say attempting to be all businesslike.

"No problems," followed by silence.

I realise she is waiting for me to explain why I called. She doesn't do small talk.

"Right, so … my hacker guy got a result on the airline records. We found the bozo that Anna travelled over to Dublin with. Only he didn't just travel with Anna. He's been travelling between Helsinki and Dublin quite regularly, with girls on the way here but always alone on the way back. So it's definitely our guy."

"This is good news."

"It is, isn't it? The only problem is I'm not sure what do with this information."

"Well, I think you have two options. Go to the police or give it to me and I'll see what I track down."

"What would you recommend?" I ask, hoping she doesn't go for the police option.

"At this stage, I think option number two is for sure the best. If you go to police now they want to know hacker friend and how you get hold of information. I am assuming he is secret friend, yes?"

"Absolutely, I've just discovered this guy and the last thing I'd want would be to get him into trouble. Mainly, I should add, because I'm scared of his mother."

"Ah I see. I think," she says bemused, "I am best for you. Do you want give me name and I will see what I find?"

"Sounds good. His name is Piedr Korsak, he is Russian and that's all I know."

"Good. I am still working with newspaper advertisement. I will communicate with you soon."

"Thanks Tash. Bye for now."

I stare at the phone. She was extremely businesslike, no hint of the previous flirtation and mischief. Maybe she's just not a phone person. Maybe it's the mysterious chick in the background. I'm torn. But lady friend would be simpler for me. A nice, tidy exit out of this quagmire I find myself in.

The walls of the house are caving in on me, so I decide to go out for a drive. I try to leave Leon behind but he is not having a bar of it. He's at the passenger car door as soon as I open the front door. While starting the car, a text comes from Jeremy:

> List of other travel dates and travel companions is in your Inbox now. J

Travel companions? Very Jane Austen.

I head to an ATM to get the cash for Jeremy. It only lets me withdraw 400 euros. I pop the notes in an envelope with a message saying I'll drop the rest over next week. I drive to his house and slip the envelope in the letter box to avoid having to face his mum again.

I drop a quick text to Jeremy, in case his mum intercepts the payment for her garden fund.

> Hi Jeremy. Just dropped €400 in an envelope in your letterbox. The ATM won't give me any more today. I'll fix you up next week. Great job by the way, thanks. Floss

He comes back before I've even started the car. How do kids these days type that fast on these tiny phone keyboards?

> Np. Call it quits. First time buyer's discount. + I like u. J

It appears that young Jeremy has developed a little crush on moi! Precisely what his mother was afraid of, no doubt. Well, far be it from me to discourage this sort of behaviour if it means discounts for CTB. Note to self: wear more revealing tops next time.

I text back a non-committal, but slightly flirtatious thanks:

> Thanks J. You're the bizzo … Floss

Leon and I have the full afternoon ahead of us, so we head to Grandad Dermo's grave in Glasnevin cemetery for a visit. On the way, I pick up some flowers and a bottle of single malt whisky from Islay in Scotland, his favourite. Glasnevin is an historic graveyard with a newly developed visitor centre. So it's not just a graveyard, but a tourist attraction, housing the remains of some key figures from Ireland's past but also with tree-lined walkways and old-style headstones – 1.1 million people buried here, not far off the current population of Dublin. We swing by Daniel O'Connell's crypt on the way through. I hated history in school, but he always came across as a bit of a stand-out guy.

At Dermo's grave, we do a bit of a tidy-up and place the flowers in the little vase attached to his tombstone. I chat away to him, have a small nip of whisky for myself and pour a generous measure on his grave. None for Leon, despite his obvious interest.

Before we leave, I pour an extra two shots onto his grave....for medicinal purposes.

We head back home for a quiet evening. Chinese take-away for me. Pedigree Chum for Leon. We pile onto the couch and I spend the evening sipping wine and reading a book on Ireland's Criminal Assets Bureau. I wake up at one in the morning, having passed out with Leon sprawled over my lap. My leg is dead. I crawl into bed and am out for the count before my head hits the pillow.

Aoife Sheridan

16

I'm up at sparrow's fart on Monday morning and in the office with latte in hand by eight, ready to fight the good fight. First, though, I have to do 'evil administration' – pay a few bills, mainly the essential ones like electricity, internet connectivity and our subscription to Hello magazine. Ok, maybe that last one is almost non-essential. Penny seriously frowns on this sort of 'gossipy fish-wrapping' as she calls it.

True to his promise, the email from Jeremy has come through with the list of Piedr Korsak's travel dates and the girls he has brought into Ireland. Nine girls in the past year, but I'm guessing that's only on the St Petersburg route. There could be others.

By the time Penny lands at nine o'clock on the dot, I'm over the whole administration bit and am dying for a catch-up.

"Morning Pen! How was your weekend?"

"Do not ask. I had to call around to my neighbour's house for some quiet time. It was either that or throttle my husband."

"You really are a walking advertisement for marital bliss."

"I know! I mean, I love Conor to bits, but when he's under the weather, I really begin to question what I see in him. Man flu doesn't even begin to describe it. He was in his 'royal chair' all weekend, to support his back, you understand. He was only short of ringing a bell at me for service at one stage."

"I know where I'd have put that bell."

"Not if I got there first. Anyway, enough about me and my woes. How was your weekend, hon?"

"Actually, I had a lovely, relaxing couple of days. Visited Dermo's grave and Sophie came around on Saturday night to criticise my diet."

"Let me guess. Wine and pizza for you, sparkling water and a salad for Soph and mmmmm ... and another wild guess ... mmm ... Footloose?"

"Almost bang on ... everything bar the movie. Dirty Dancing. But I also had a very productive weekend. Well, the Wunderkind did at least."

"Do tell."

"Jeremy came up trumps on the flight records. He got us a name for the guy who travels with the girls from St Petersburg. Piedr Korsak. I gave the name to Tash to see what she can find out via her network."

"That is serious progress. Good resource to have, this Jeremy chap."

"Yep and he even knocked 100 euro off the price, so happy days. Any word on the phone records?"

"I got word from my guy at TelcoWeb. The number that Anna made her last call from is one of the phone boxes in Arrivals at Dublin Airport. I guess they forced her to make that call as soon as she arrived. I told him to focus instead on the call from the mystery nanny who was allegedly already set up in Dublin. Unfortunately, he's at some nerdy data conference today but he'll be back on deck tomorrow and said he'd make it his number one priority."

"Shag. Two strikes on the phone records. Here's hoping something comes through on Mystery Girl. What are we paying this guy anyhow?"

"My undivided attention. I can bat my eyelids with the best of them."

"Don't I know it? You might be a niche player, but when they go for you, they go for you big time." We both laugh out loud, thinking about the broken hearts in Penny's past.

I check my email and see a message from Padraig's Gmail account rather than his normal UN address.

> Dear Flo
>
> Great to hear from you the other day. It's been ages. Sorry I was so hung over. I think I told you I was celebrating the departure of my boss, also known as The Prince of Darkness. Suffice to say it was a big one.
>
> I talked to some of my colleagues who work closely with the police here. They said that given the situation you described and the fact that nobody has heard from the girl in so long it is almost 100% guaranteed that she has been trafficked into the country and is more than likely being held against her will. They normally remove girls' passports, threaten families and friends and roughhouse them a bit to keep them in line. And it's pretty effective by all accounts as most girls can't see a way out, particularly if they don't speak the lingo.
>
> The other thing they said was not to take these guys lightly. They are typically violent types who would not think twice about extinguishing anyone who gets in the way of their little moneyspinners.
>
> I really think you should take this to the police, but if I know you and I think I do, you'll do a solo run.
>
> So, the only avenue they had for you was to get in touch with a local organisation called Turn Off the Red Light in Ireland. They are primarily educational and fund-raising focused, but will be clued into the scene in Dublin.
>
> Will have to get you over to dinner when I get back, but in the meantime, be careful.

Cheers

Padraig

P.S. You might drop in on Emer for me? She's not speaking to me at the minute as she called me on my drunken Friday night, way later than your call. You can imagine the rest ...

"Hey Pen. You might want to read this. It's from Padraig, you remember, Emer's husband who works at the UN in Vienna? It's only fair you're warned before we go much further on this thing." I forward the email to her.

"Got it," she says. She speed-reads the email and looks at me with a look of grim determination: "You know this type of stuff only makes me stronger. We may need help at some stage, but I'm not giving up just yet. We knew they were going to be proper bad guys, but all the more reason to try to get Anna out of their clutches."

I knew Penny would not be cowed by Padraig's warning words, but always worry she has a lot more to lose than me.

"That's my girl" I say and slam my hand on the table. "BRING IT ON, bad guys!"

At that exact moment, there's a loud knock on the door and both of us nearly jump out of our skins.

"Jesus, Mary, Samson and Delilah! My heart actually stopped beating there briefly, some heroes we are," Penny says getting up to go to the door.

She gently opens the door, aware of the slapstick routine that ensued the last time I answered the door.

It's Tash.

"Good morning, Penny. I was just passing and thought I

would give you latest update. Oh hello Floss!" she says with a beaming smile as she catches sight of me at my desk.

She looks outstanding. Today's outfit is all Nike-sponsored running garb. She's worked up a beautiful healthy glow. Her hair is in its standard ponytail format but she has a black Nike cap on.

"Morning Tash. Out for a run?"

"Yes. Something like this. Have you had coffee?"

"Yeah but I could squeeze in another one. I know just the place."

She turns to Penny "A coffee for you?"

Penny nods and begins to get up to come with us. "I will bring you back one," Tash says quickly. Penny blushes slightly as she quickly gets back behind her desk. Interesting. Maybe Tash wants to talk to me alone.

"Catch you in a few minutes, ok Pen?" I say, to try to ease the awkwardness of the moment.

She nods. Completely miffed.

"Let me just print something out for you before we go," I say to Tash. I print out Jeremy's list of Piedr Korsak's girls and travel dates.

We head out towards Massimo's cart. On the way we pass Whacker, who is leaning against the pillar by the gate to the car park. The match permanently stuck in his gob falls out as he stares open-mouthed at Tash.

"Howareya geerls!" he says, turning on the charm. "Are ya goin' t' introduce me to yer pal there Floss?"

"Not a chance, Whacker." I usher Tash quickly out the gate.

"Is he employee?" asks Tash after we're out of earshot.

"Ha! No. Unfortunately he comes with the car park. He's not the worst sort in the world and he makes a good watchdog when I need one. He's harmless enough and terrified of Leon, which keeps him in line most of the time. But put it this way, according to Whacker, if your car's not locked around here, it's fair game."

We cross the road to the van. I can see Massimo's eyes light up at the sight of Tash but shake my head to let him know he's barking up the wrong tree. He smiles and shrugs his shoulders as if to say, "I can't help it, I'm Italian!"

We order our coffees and Massimo throws in some free pastries "for special ladies". We sit down at one of the two tables set up by the cart.

"So, how are you getting on?" I ask.

"Good, thanks. No information just yet. Although I did speak to very helpful person in advertising department of Derzhis Krepche … St Petersburg newspaper?" she adds, as I look at her blankly. "The ad was run three times during summer by same company. She gives me company name but I investigate and company is false."

"Bummer. Although it would be amateur hour on the human trafficking front if they had been a real company, I suppose."

"I still have other angle for follow, so it is not over yet," she says in her Lithuanian staccato. I try to focus on what she's saying, but keep getting lost in her green eyes. They are almost opaque sometimes, so that it's like watching water flowing … mesmerising.

I shake myself back to my senses and hand her the printout.

"This is a list of names of girls brought into Ireland by Piedr Korsak via the St Petersburg-Helsinki route. Would you be able to check via your network if all of these girls have been reported missing?"

"No problem. I can do this for you, no problem."

"Good, good. And … is there any other reason you dropped by?"

"No," she says turning away, but she glances at me out of the corner of her eyes.

"Oh … oh right," I say not sure what to say next. It seems that Tash is here on a social call and I can feel how high that is making me feel. Then I remember the giggles of another female on the phone yesterday. "Sorry, I woke you up yesterday," I say, fishing for information.

"You did not wake me. I was in bed, but not sleeping."

My heart drops to my toes. *That does not sound good.*

"I have friend from Lithuania stay with me at moment."

I'm immediately trying to judge how she said the words 'my friend'. 'Buddy from the old country'? 'Old flame that is being rekindled'? *Please say it's the former, please!*

Everything I've been feeling must be showing on my face, because she looks at me and asks me if I'm ok. Where have my poker skills gone? This god-like woman sees right through me. I feel completely vulnerable and open with her and, worse still, I like it!

"Yeah, of course, I'm fine."

"Maybe you are little jealous of my friend?" she asks. Now I feel like a worm wriggling on a hook.

"Me? Jealous? No, no, no. Not at all. Possibly a little bit curious, but that's about it."

"Ask me any question you like." She stares right through me with her ice-green eyes.

I'm about to blurt out "Are you sleeping with this friend of yours?" when Massimo thankfully interrupts with "Your coffees ladies." I've never been so grateful to him. Sometimes I need speed bumps between my brain and mouth.

"Saved by the bell?" Tash says, looking at me with a knowing look. She gets up, pays for the coffees and turns as if ready to go. "I'll talk to you later or tomorrow." And with that she heads off over the Sean O'Casey Bridge.

"Sure. Thanks for the coffees," I shout after her. I can't help but keep watching her. She paces slowly, with the elegance of a panther.

I head back with Pens' coffee and pastry. As I pass Whacker he shouts "Who the fuck was tha'? Pussy Galore?"

"It's top secret, sorry Whacker. I could tell you but I'd have to kill you."

"Jaysus, she'd be wurth dyin' fer."

You're not the first to think that Whacker.

When I get back, it looks as if Penny is still in a snot with me.

"Here you go," I chirp, handing over her goodies. "That will cheer you up!"

"How's your girlfriend? …. Ah! Pain au chocolat! My favourite!"

"Well, I can confirm that Whacker has fallen in lust and Massimo is probably contemplating monogamy. When have we ever got free pastries from Massimo?" I ask.

"It must be terrible being that good-looking."

"Yep. Must be a total curse."

This gets Penny giggling too and as quick as that, she is over her strop.

I look up 'Stop the Red Light' online and locate their offices, just off Mountjoy Square.

"Well, Pen, how do you feel about visiting that crowd Padraig mentioned in his email?"

"In like Flynn. I'll drive," she says, picking up her coat and bag.

Getting in a car with Penny is like an adventure in itself. She's not a tall lady, so behind the wheel of their family Volvo, she looks like a five-year-old trying to drive a tank. But she drives like Ayrton Senna.

I strap myself into the passenger seat, cling on to all available hand-holds and say to Penny, "Now, we're not in any hurry. So …" but my next words are swallowed in the G-force as we exit the car park at warp speed, raining gravel on everything in sight.

Like everything with Penny, even her driving is bi-polar. When Conor or the kids are in the car with her, she potters around at a steady 35km per hour, but get her on her own or with little old me? A complete speed merchant.

What should be a 15-minute drive takes us four and a half minutes.

As we lurch to a stop, like at the end of a particularly jolting rollercoaster ride in a theme park, Penny says, "Right boss. So what's our plan of attack here?" All business.

"Jeezus, let me just gather myself. I think my stomach is somewhere back there on Lower Gardiner Street." I take a few deep breaths before I'm fit to continue.

"There's no real plan and we're definitely not attacking ..."

"It's just a turn of phrase. You know what I meant, Floss!"

"These people will see the trafficking world through Anna's eyes. They try to help them to escape their captors via immigration assistance, lobbying, fund-raising, the whole kit and caboodle. So, I think we just rock in there and tell them about Anna and Nika."

"Right, so free-wheeling. I can do that," Penny says with that determined look of hers.

Sometimes I regret taking Penny out on these so-called adventures. She can be a bit more 'gung ho' than a situation demands.

"Easy does it there, Starsky. A nice, friendly chat is all we're after."

We hop out of the car and walk toward 59 Mountjoy Square West, one of Dublin's five Georgian squares and one of my favourite spots in Dublin. The buildings are four storeys high, imperious red-brick with brightly coloured, oversized doors and giant sash windows. In the middle of the square is a green park with a children's playground. The square is steeped in Dublin's history and its modern-day inhabitants are a cross-section of the Dublin's new ethnic population. Modern Mountjoy Square is as colourful as its famous Georgian doors.

We climb the four wide steps to the red door of No 59, although I struggle a bit as my legs are still wobbly after the whirlwind ride. Penny hits the buzzer beside T.O.T.R.L. and a few seconds later we hear a muffled "Hello".

"Hi. We're from CTB Investigations. Can we come up, please?" says Penny, sounding like an FBI agent. Complete silence from the other end of the intercom. I punch her in the shoulder.

"Ouch!"

"What are you doing? They'll think we're from Revenue or something."

We buzz again. No response. I'm about ready to beat the crap out of Penny, when the giant door opens slowly, just an inch. A large lady peeps out with a look of dread in her eyes.

"Is there something the matter?" she asks in a booming, earthy voice with a slight Scottish twang. She should be on radio.

I push my way in front of Penny.

"Not at all. Sorry if we gave you that impression," I say giving Penny a scathing look. "We're from a private investigators firm and we're looking into a suspected case of trafficking. A friend of mine from the UN said you might be a good place to start."

Relief floods through her face. She actually says "Phew-eee!" and starts laughing. "In that case, come on in and brace yourselves for a wee climb."

We follow her in through the hall and up four flights of stairs to the top. The T.O.T.R.L. office is at the end of the hall. The lower ceilings of the top floor make their space feel even more cramped than it is. The place is wall-to-wall posters campaigning against human trafficking, the kind that have you reaching for your cheque book on the spot. Beside the window on the wall, there's a large target and running total for fund-raising for 2012. It appears they are on track for this year's goal.

In the corner, there's a guy talking quietly on the phone. He has that student look about him, with skinny jeans, a trendy scarf and cool, oversized glasses. I wasn't expecting a guy to be involved for some reason, so I'm happy to see him there.

"Well, I should introduce myself. My name is Sheila Brennan and I'm the founder of Turn Off the Red Light."

"Thanks for seeing us. My name is Florence McFarland and this is my colleague, Penny Firth. As Penny mentioned, we are from CTB Investigations. To be honest, we normally specialise in corporate crime so I don't mind telling you we're slightly out of our depth here. But, we agreed to try to help."

"Well, how about I make us some tea and you tell me the whole thing from the beginning," Sheila says in her gorgeous voice that's like a warm welcome home. If I was left on my own with this lady I could picture myself spilling my guts within seconds.

Two large mugs of tea and around five Chocolate Kimberlys later, we've filled Sheila in on the case so far. She's spent the entire time nodding encouragingly and saying soothing things like "Oh dear" and "the poor wee tyke". I want her to hug me to her ample bosom, so she can pat my head and tell me everything will indeed be all right.

"First of all," she begins, "given what you have found out about Anna's travel companion, you should be under no misguided illusions. She has most certainly been trafficked into this country."

She is definitely not going to pat my head. *Pity*.

"What is unusual is the source of the girls. This is the first time I've heard about girls being brought in from St Petersburg. We normally deal with south-east Asians, Indian girls ... more impoverished countries. Some of them are drawn by the lure of a better life for themselves and their families while others are kidnapped, drugged and trafficked before they know what's hit them."

"God that's so awful. It makes me totally livid," I say through gritted teeth.

"I know, I know," she replies in her soothing manner. "I've learned to channel my anger for good. We try to target the guys who buy the services from girls that are clearly trafficked. It's a hard sell though and, frankly, sometimes I feel we're pissing in the wind, if you'll excuse my French. But we have to fight the good fight for the Annas of this world. One lobby at a time." She breaks for a sip of tea and continues on:

"My advice is similar to what your friend at the UN said to you. Tread very carefully. The types that move in these circles are prone to extreme violence, both towards the girls themselves when they step out of line and to anyone who tries to mess with what they see as their cash cows."

"If you were us and trying to find Anna, where would you start?" asks Penny.

"It's like looking for a needle in a haystack. These girls don't work the streets as that would make them much harder to control. They are kept in locked apartments and housing with heavy and normally armed security. The girls have their passports, money and ultimately their dignity stripped off them. They don't see the light of day and are constantly being threatened. Not just them but their families back home.

"I think the approach you're taking is the right one. Follow the paper trail. But once you have enough information, take it straight to the police. Everyone loves to slag the Garda

Síochána, but in this area, they are very well regarded in Europe. In some countries, the girls themselves are treated like criminals, so they end up being victimised twice. The gardaí are well trained in how to handle the girls and are much more focused on the guys that run them and rent them."

"OK, if we do find Anna and I hope to God we do, will you help us help her?" I ask.

"You just try and stop me!"

We gather our things and thank Sheila. We're halfway down the first flight of stairs when I stop suddenly. "Hold on a second, Pen."

I run back up and knock gently. Sheila is at her computer frowning and her colleague is still on the phone.

"I was just wondering if I could make a bit of a donation?" I ask, nodding towards the chart by the window.

"All donations gratefully received, as they say. You can do it with your credit card on our website www.turnofftheredlight.ie."

"Great … thanks, will do …" I pause then in some inexplicable but definitely needy way. Sheila doesn't let me down and gently enquires:

"Everything ok with you, Florence? Apart from the obvious concern for Anna's safety, you seem somewhat torn to me. You are being pulled in several directions."

A lump develops in my throat but I rally quickly.

"After hearing what you've told us about these poor girls, I realise I haven't a care in the world … but thanks … for asking."

"Suit yourself, lovey. And best of luck with your quest."

I nod and head down to catch up with Penny.

"Everything ok, Floss?" Penny asks with a concerned look.

"Nope. Not at all. Not until we find Anna."

Aoife Sheridan

17

The rest of the day passes in a blur of boring administration and waiting for the phone to ring. It doesn't. I call Zippy to double-check that the surveillance gear is all ready to go for the Trilby board meeting on Wednesday. He assures me that it's sitting, hot to trot at his place.

I ring Milo's office to check when we can pick up the undercover van. He's not there but he has left a message with his secretary that we can swing by and pick it up anytime. I arrange to pick it up at 8.30 in the morning. I also arrange to pick up Penny on the way to Milo's. I cannot handle another spin in the 'Vehicle of Terror'.

I call it a day and head home for a quiet night of Doritos, salsa and sour cream. Leon tries to diss me for leaving him at home today, but as soon as he hears the crackle of the crisp packet, his head is in my lap. I give him some Taytos instead, as the Doritos play havoc with his intestines.

I wake up early the next morning with nervous excitement. The idea of working the corporate gig is a welcome relief after the pressure of the trafficking case. I pop Leon in the car and we head over to Penny's in Marino. When I ring the doorbell at Penny's end-of-terrace two-up two-down, I can hear the bedlam inside.

Penny answers the door almost before I've finished pressing the bell. She slips outside, pulls the door to and starts whispering conspiratorially: "Just so you know, Conor thinks we're on a day off. We're off to the Dundrum Shopping Centre on a retail therapy mission. Got it?"

"Yep, and just so you know, I'm really not comfortable being dragged into your wicked web of marital lies and deception."

"On the deception side of things, it could be a lot worse."

She opens the door but I remain on the doorstep. I can see Sean and Oscar running amok while Conor is propped up on the couch like the Queen of Sheeba.

"Hiya Conor!" I say, waving. "Hey lads. Go easy on your father today!" They glance up from their game and shout "Auntie Floss!" in unison. They drop their guns and run full tilt towards me. One hug and they're back to their game, but for that brief moment they made me feel super-special.

"You girls have a great day," says Conor. "Penny needs a break. They've been working her so hard at the gallery."

"I know," I say, shaking my head in sympathy. "Damn those slave drivers." I have to turn my head away as I'm about to start laughing.

Penny flies around in a whirlwind of kisses and hugs and then we're out the door.

"Seriously, Penny. At some stage you're going to have to come clean with Conor. It's not fair."

"I know, I know. Can I drive?"

"Not on your Nelly, sweetheart."

We jump into the car and head for the resplendent offices of McCarthy & Co in Dublin's swanky Grand Canal Dock area. Milo's office is on Grand Canal Quay, a beautiful cobble-stoned street with a mixture of old and new buildings. His building is all glass and chrome, macho from the foundations upward.

What I presume to be our van is parked across the road. It

looks perfect for the job, filthy dirty once-was-white with branding boasting the fantastic cleaning services on offer. We go inside to reception and ask the young twenty-something with giant boobs, French manicure and back-combed bouffant if we can speak to Milo.

"He's not here at the minute but he said two older ladies would be calling around for the keys to the van. Here ya go!" she says chirpily.

Older? If I get a hold of that Milo, I'll …

"Well, if it isn't my two favourite lady PIs!" says the mocking voice of Milo McCarthy behind us. "I was afraid I'd miss you."

"We were just leaving," I say, turning on my heels. "Thanks for the van and the flattery." I say, attempting my best acidic tone.

"I used the word 'older' as a frame of reference for Crystal," he shouts in explanation as we storm out the door.

"Whatever!" I say, fuming at him and my lack of a witty comeback.

I turn to Penny: "I'll take the van and pick up the gear from Zippy's. You take my car and I'll meet you back at the office in forty minutes or so."

"The cheek of that upstart!" Penny is about to go ape-shit.

"Penny … focus. It's undercover day. Forget about Milo and Brainfree-Giant-Boobs, ok?"

She laughs. "Ok, see you shortly."

As I head towards the van I can feel Milo still looking at us. I'm not going to give him the satisfaction of looking back. *Shit, he gets under my skin.*

I check the back of the van to make sure we have everything

we need. The overalls look oversized but will do the job and there's a couple of dirty old caps we can use to cover our hair. The carpet-cleaning machinery looks fit for purpose (i.e. decoy). I attempt to start up the van. It stutters a bit. The gear box is clunky at best, but I get the hang of it quickly enough. I head straight for Zippy's place in Pearse Street, ringing ahead to ask him to meet me on the street with the goods. He's not happy, but agrees.

When I pull up outside his apartment block, he's standing there in his full winter woollies with the expression of a smacked bulldog's arse.

"Hi Zippy. You're a darling for sorting this. What's the damage all up?"

"Six hundred and fifty yo-yos, but you'll have this stuff for life. It's fully warrantied for three years."

"I'll have to write you a cheque. Who should I make it out to?" I ask, fishing for my cheque book in my purse.

"Just make it out to Zippy Cosmetics Ltd," he says sheepishly.

I raise my eyebrows.

"Some of the more delicate stuff doesn't go through the official books, let's say."

"Right, so you're the new Avon lady. I don't want to know any more. Anything tricky in the set-up that I need to know about?"

"The cameras are the ones you've used before. The ears are more or less plug and play. They're radio-based so you can just use one of those iPod radio tuners to pick up the signal. Should be crystal-clear."

"Sounds good. I'll give you a shout if we have any trouble."

"Bombs away," he says waving as he retreats out of the cold.

I put the stuff in the rear of the van and head back to the office for my rendezvous with Pen. When I get there, she's got her laptop and two lattes in hand. Just what the doctor ordered. We get dressed up in our overalls and caps and put a bit of gravel from the car park under our nails to make us look more 'real'.

"I'm so excited, I'm in danger of wetting myself," says Penny.

"Lovely, Pen. My stomach's in flithers." I make a quick dash to our Portaloo in the corner of the car park before we head off. Not pleasant but necessary.

Just as I'm putting the final touches to my hair, i.e. stuffing it under a cap, I hear a wolf whistle from behind.

"Lookin' very fine today, ladies," says Whacker.

"Get a job!" I shout, and hop in to the driver seat of the van before Penny can ask to drive. She slips reluctantly into the passenger seat.

"Go go gadget!" Penny shouts as we pull out of the car park.

We reach the Trilby offices on Fitzwilliam Square at 9am on the buzzer. Before we head in I turn to Penny. "Ok, so we're in full undercover mode now. If we meet Janet or anyone else we know, keep your head down and blank them. For today, you're Jacintha and I'm Violet."

"Got it. Let's go, Violet!" says Penny.

Penny grabs the carpet-cleaning machine and I take the surveillance gear (in unmarked brown boxes). We walk into reception. The matronly lady we've met before doesn't give us a second glance.

"We've been expecting you. Boardroom is the third floor, the door at the end of the hallway."

Dublin's Georgian buildings often lack lifts. The Trilby offices are no exception. We slowly haul the gear up three flights of stairs. "Holy shit! That was a serious workout," I say as I catch my breath outside the boardroom. In we go. I close the boardroom door firmly and put a chair in front of it to make sure nobody can surprise us. First things first: a full bug sweep of the room. Nothing found, which is a bit of a disappointment. I was hoping it was going to be a slam dunk.

Penny sets up the three cameras to give good views of all board members wherever they sit, while I set up the listening devices. One in the conference call phone, one in the Internet socket and one at the top end of the boardroom. The cameras will pick up some sound but the quality is never that reliable.

I begin doing some actual carpet-cleaning to avoid suspicion while Penny sets up the laptop to make sure she is getting both visuals and sound. There is a slight problem with one of the cameras; the lens cap had not been removed.

I turn off the carpet-cleaner briefly so we can do a quick sound check. Penny dons her DJ-style oversized headphones. I sit at the table in all the seats, using the following rap as a sound test:

> "She's MC Penny,
>
> she'll kill fo'a twenny
>
> She likes her tweed,
>
> when she be on speed."

She's not amused. I am. I'm cracking myself up.

Everything is ready to go for the board meeting at ten o'clock tomorrow morning. We can record all visuals and sound directly onto the laptop, which means we can keep it for more detailed analysis and posterity.

I've done a bit of a half-assed job at the carpet cleaning, so we spray some cleaning detergent around the room to give it the just-cleaned smell. On our way out, the matriarchal receptionist, Margaret, I think, asks us for the invoice. We tell her it'll be in the post. We almost skip to the van, happy with our work and glad we have not bumped into anyone we know. We pick up tandoori chicken sandwiches and soup from O'Brien's on Baggot Street and head back to the office.

In the afternoon, I update our accounting package for the various outgoings this week for both the Trilby and Anna cases. We could do with a good result on the Trilby job. There's a success clause in the contract which would swell our take by 30 per cent so we're extra keen to catch the leak this time around.

I ring Milo to let him know the boardroom has been set up in preparation for tomorrow.

"Is that Floss McFarland of Marney Carpet Cleaners? I really hope you got some pictures of yourself in that gear. I do love a lady in overalls."

"Might I remind you that I'm still not speaking to you over that 'older ladies' jibe from Boobtastic at your front desk," I say testily.

"Did it ever occur to you I might have done that to get a rise out of you? Very effective it would seem," he chuckles.

"It's definitely a skill of yours … annoying the shit out of me, I mean."

"Any reaction is a good reaction, Floss."

"Well, I need a serious response from you now," I say, turning coldly professional. "The boardroom is fully wired for audio and visual tomorrow." I give him the exact locations of each device so, if need be, he can adjust them on the fly during the meeting. "We'll be listening from outside and we've held on to the van for that reason. We'll also record everything. What time is it on?"

"Starts at ten o'clock sharp."

"Please ensure there's nobody in the boardroom between 9.30 and 10? Reschedule meetings if you have to. Penny or I will need to do another quick bug sweep before the meeting. Oh and can you arrange to do a full bug sweep afterwards? I presume you have all the necessary kit."

"Oh I assure you I am very well equipped." he says with that double-entendre thing he has going on.

"Great to hear you're so focused."

"I have you, I mean, the target in my sights, don't you worry, Floss," he says. Somehow that little slip up of his sounded deliberate. I wouldn't put it past him.

"Whatever. Well … good luck for tomorrow. Keep your eyes peeled."

"Now seriously, what is that expression about, McFarland? I've never really understood it and it sounds really sore … your eyes peeled?!"

"GOODBYE, Milo," I say, hanging up in frustration.

"How is our undercover director?" asks Penny.

"Infuriating as ever."

"You just hold onto that feeling, Floss. Angry at Milo is probably a safer place for you."

Five minutes later, I hear my mobile do its little ping – a message from Milo:

> "Eyes peeled: From about the 17th century on, pill was commonly spelt peel and took on the sense of 'to remove or strip' an outer covering, such as a fruit. The figurative sense of keeping alert, by removing any covering of the eye that might impede vision, seems to have appeared in the US about 1850." Keeping eyes peeled still sounds odd to me. Now peeling off an item of clothing, that'd make sense! M

I can't help but smile. He is such a chancer, but I'm loving the flirt text.

Penny looks at me: "From angry to happy so soon?"

"Oh shag off!"

"Elegant retort."

We both go back to trying to look busy. I take a call from Janet Trilby wishing us good luck for tomorrow and making sure we have everything we need. I assure her we do. She makes a point of letting me know she is very happy with Milo so far and could I pass that feedback along. I tell her I will and make a mental note not to.

Around half four that afternoon, Penny gets an email from her geek at TelcoWeb. It's the break in the case we've been waiting for.

18

I know it's good news almost immediately. Penny lets out a little yelp that a chihuahua would be proud of.

"What?" I ask.

No reply.

"Eh, hello? What … is … the … story?"

"Sorry, just trying to read to the end to get the full story … I think my guy has hit the jackpot … two secs."

"What has he written? A novel? Don't leave me hanging," I beg.

"Alright, alright Floss McPatience. To be honest, there's not a whole lot of content. Some initial key stuff and then he's warning that nobody must ever find out that he gave us this information, coz he'd be fired on the spot if his bosses got wind of it."

"His fears are fascinating, but what's the meat? Out with it!" I whine.

Penny loves to draw out any big announcements: it took her nearly twenty minutes to get to the point when Conor and herself got engaged. Painful with a capital 'P'.

"It would seem," Penny continues, "that Tash is an investigative genius. The call that Anna received from the alleged other Russian nanny in Dublin originates from one Larisa Markov. Her current registered address, according to her phone records, is 2 Castlecourt, Clontarf, Dublin 3. I also have her mobile number here and it looks to be still active."

"Bingo bongo!" I say, thumping the table with excitement. "Never mind batting your eyelashes, you owe your contact guys some significant sexual favours."

"No problem, as long as CTB will foot my legal bill when Conor and I are going through the divorce court."

"Ok, here's what we're going to do. We'll google her and see if we can get any pictures. Then we'll set up camp outside her house in Milo's undercover van and follow her to see where she works. When we've got a handle on her movements, we'll confront her. This is where we'll need your mobile source again. After we talk to her, we hope and pray she contacts the guys who asked her to make the call and we go from there. What do you think?"

"Sounds like a plan, Floss. Jesus, Mary and Joseph, cometh the hour, cometh the woman! I am soooooooooooooo excited!"

"Before we have complete lift-off, don't forget we have the Trilby board meeting tomorrow morning. I might get Tash to do the morning shift on our new target. If Larisa really is a nanny, she's more than likely going to be up and at it first thing."

"Makes sense. Tash might need to use her own wheels while we're using the van."

"I'm not even sure she has wheels, but I'll check. She can use my car if not."

Penny's already started furiously typing. "I'm just searching for pictures of her online. Google images has loads of Larisa Markovs, mostly of some scary-looking guy. A few Facebook profiles match the name, none with geographical location specified. I'll print out the best photos and we can see if any of them match the person living in Castlecourt."

"Great stuff! Email me through the links to those photos. I'll need to fire them across to Tash for the morning."

"Done."

I then realise that I don't have an email address for Tash. I decide to give her a quick call to check if she's free to do a stakeout tomorrow morning. I whip out my mobile and use Speed Dial Six. I know, I know. It's equally sad that I have her on speed dial and that I have only five other speed dials in my phone.

She answers on the second ring.

"Good afternoon, Floss." she says having caller ID'ed me.

"Hi Tash. How are you?"

"I am fine, thank you. Busy, but good. And you?" she asks in her formal way.

"Great. Look, we caught a bit of a break on the Anna case." I give her a brief synopsis of Penny's result.

"This is very great news."

"I was wondering if you would have time to watch Larisa's address tomorrow morning from 6.30? Penny and I have a conflict with another case. It's going to have us tied up until mid-morning at the earliest."

"Tied up? Interesting. Yes, I can definitely do this."

I am blushing at her 'tied up' comment. It's hard to know with Tash's deadpan Lithuanian delivery if she is teasing me or not. If it were Milo, there'd be no question.

"OK, I'll need to send you through the address and some photos we've managed to source. We're not sure if any of them are the right lady, but it's a start. Can you give me your email address?"

"Not problem: natasha@corecontracts.com," she says, spelling it out for me.

"Perfect, that should be with you in the next couple of minutes. I'll talk to you tomorrow morning. Give me a shout on the mobile if you have any trouble. Cheers Tash!"

"Goodbye Floss."

The second I've disconnected I'm typing in www.corecontracts.com into Internet Explorer to check out Tash's website. I'm severely disappointed. The website is just a black screen with two white, text entry boxes for a customer login and password. Nothing else. She remains an enigma wrapped in a puzzle.

I flick the links to the three photos and the address for Larisa to Tash's email address.

"Well, Penny, seeing as I have to drop you home, do you have any interest in doing a drive by 2 Castlecourt?"

"You don't have to ask twice. Let's go," says Penny, gathering her jacket and handbag.

On the way over to Clontarf, Penny tries to quiz me about Tash. I'm having none of it. I tell her I have to stay focused on the job or I'll go out of my mind.

There's still a bit of light in the sky when we arrive in the small development of Castlecourt. Although Clontarf is an expensive area for real estate, the houses in Castlecourt are quite understated. White-painted brick, uniform houses with well-kept gardens – except number No 2. It screams 'rental property' –unkempt lawn in an otherwise well-groomed neighbourhood.

We drive past the house, do a U-turn and park on the opposite side about three doors down under a large oak-tree. It gives us some degree of cover.

"Quite a salubrious area for a childcare worker to be shacked up, don't you think?" I suggest to Penny.

"Yeah, definitely a bit more than the average rental. Of course there could be 25 of them living in there for all we know, in which case it would be a total bargain."

"No activity or cars around the house, I'm guessing it's not over-occupied."

"Early days yet. How long can you stay?"

"I told Conor we'd be back by 6pm but I'll drop him a text to say we're stuck in traffic on the M50 on the way back from Dundrum."

"Oh yeah, I totally forgot we were 'shopping' today. You can't go back empty-handed …"

"I'll just say that we focused on you. He'll be delighted I didn't go to town on the credit card."

"Alright, so. We'll sit tight for a while."

At seven o'clock, we get really excited as a woman pulls up in a silver Ford Focus in front of Larisa's place. She heads straight for No 4. We relax back into the wait.

At 7.15pm sharp, the front door to No 2 opens and we try not to react too dramatically. The lady who exits is a short, Asian woman, possibly Japanese but I'm not sure. She doesn't look like a Larisa.

That's it. Penny has to get home. I drop her in front of her house but refuse to go in. I can't face lying to Conor about the imaginary items I bought for myself today. It's been a long day and I'm too tired to be creative. We agree to meet at the office at 8.30 before heading across in the van to Trilby's for the bug sweep and board meeting surveillance.

When I get home, Leon runs amok with excitement and then makes an emergency exit to do some damage to the back lawn. At least he prioritised me first.

I look hopefully, but in vain, at the contents of the fridge and realise there is no nutrition to be had there. I settle for beans on toast with an extra dash of tomato ketchup for good measure. Leon has the usual culinary dog fare.

We go for a short walk after dinner to brush off the cobwebs, just a couple of laps of the park. It's a crazily windy evening so we are blown up one end of the park and then have to battle our way back in the other direction. I'm feeling pretty self-righteous by the time we make it back home.

An early, wine-free night for me in preparation for what promises to be an even bigger day for CTB tomorrow. Well, if I'm honest, wine-free because I've run out of the stuff and am too lazy to stroll to the village to replenish my supplies.

The next day I'm up early. I buy some poppy seed bagels and coffee in the Ringsend deli and pick up a grateful Penny on the way to the office.

When we get to the car park, we hop into the van but this time only I get dressed up in overalls. I'll do the second bug sweep while Penny will be the technology lead.

We get to the Trilby offices at exactly nine o'clock. Penny gets the laptop running and double-checks all the cameras. The visuals all look good. Carrying a work bag, I check in at reception, explaining I need to do follow-up treatment on the carpets as agreed. She hardly casts a glance in my direction.

I climb to the boardroom just as Milo is leaving with the Director of Finance, James Kenny. They're laughing at something Milo has just said, looking like the best of mates. Milo politely asks if he can help me. As I explain about applying a protective coat to the newly cleaned carpets, he waves me away with the air of someone who is too busy to concern himself with such trivialities. I can't help but feel both impressed and slighted. But no time for that now.

I close the door behind me and do the sound check. Penny texts me on her mobile to let me know that all bugs are fine, bar the one at the head of the table. I take a quick look at that and see that it's been turned upside down somehow. I turn it back around and do another check. Penny texts back:

"All systems go!"

At 9.45am, I do another bug sweep. Nothing, apart from our own bugs. Whoever is smuggling secrets is not doing it via a listening device. The finger's pointing at one of the directors.

I leave at 9.50am, having sent Penny a "Start recording" text. I don't meet anyone else I know on the way out. I make a quick stop at the Spar shop on the corner for some Maltesers and bottled water, then jump into the back of the van with Penny. The van is set up with a desk and chair for monitoring surveillance footage. There's only one chair, which is a bit of an oversight on our part. I make do by sitting on a pile of overalls on a wooden crate. Not exactly ergonomic, but it'll have to do.

The directors begin to file into the boardroom at around 10.05. The mood is buoyant but efficient. All directors present and accounted for. Penny and I are bursting with excitement, like two kids at the circus for the first time.

Our anticipation is somewhat unjustified, because what follows has to be the most boring hour and a half of our entire lives. Each director drones on about the progress and challenges "going forward" in each of their respective business units: expedite this and leverage that, touch base and think outside the box, proactive synergy, win-win paradigm shift ... The lowlight is the reading-out of monthly numbers; the highlight is Milo's uber-confident delivery of his plans for business development at Trilby. Ambitious and exciting, to the other directors at least. Half way through the receptionist brings in a tray of tea, coffee and biscuits. Old school.

After the short break, Janet gives her forecast for the next quarter, which is to include the item of information she wants leaked to the press by our rogue director.

"Ten per cent lower profit margins than forecast ..." That's it – exactly the type of thing to get the share market agitated.

Just before 11.30, I send a text to Milo with the location of the three listening devices so he can discount them from his final bug sweep. The meeting finishes just after 11.30. On screen, we see Milo hanging back. When everyone's gone, he closes the door and takes a compact bug-sweeper from his briefcase. As he passes each camera, he stares at it and executes his should-be-patented double wink.

"Oh God, not the double wink," moans Penny. "Be strong, Floss, be strong."

Once he's done, he gives us a quick 'thumbs down' and exits the boardroom.

Penny turns off all the footage and starts checking that everything has recorded ok. My mobile pings with a text.

"Sorry, McFarland. No sign. Back to the drawing board? Will call you later ... M"

I reply:

You did a great job. Anyone behaving 'hinkily'? (if that's a word ☺)

A few minutes later, he texts back:

I still like the Finance guy ... M

Penny and I are gutted. We were both convinced we'd find a bug somewhere in the boardroom and had sold Janet Trilby our pitch based on this hunch. If that's gone south, then so might the contract. Our almost-banked windfall might be swept from underneath our feet.

"How's it looking?" I ask Penny, nodding at the laptop.

"Quality looks perfect and I think we got everything but am just fast-forwarding to make sure all's good."

"Can you do that while I drive?" I say getting ready to jump into the front seat of the van. My back's aching from sitting on the crate.

"I'll manage, but I'll come through to the front so I can belt up." Good old Penny, always the wise one.

"Safety first," I chirp, scrambling into the driver's seat.

We head back towards the office.

"Pants. I was sure either the sweeper or Milo would pick up something ... God, what now?" I ask.

"No panic yet, Floss. I need to review the recordings thoroughly, there could be something in there we missed. I'm sure I nodded off a few times during the meeting. Plus, we're not even sure that there's going to be a leak. The problem might have gone away."

"Unlikely Penny, but I'm loving your optimism! And it's true, I nearly died of boredom during the meeting. You're going to need speed or something similar to keep you going when you're reviewing the footage."

"You're not wrong," Penny replies giggling.

"And speaking of things to keep us going, we need some serious cake-age to get over the disappointment. What say you?"

"Sold."

19

When we've stuffed ourselves full of carrot cake and made our way back to the office, I call Janet Trilby to let her know that nothing jumped out at us from what we saw of this morning's meeting, but that we still have a lot of analysis to do. She reminds me to keep an eye out in tomorrow's papers and confirms that the lower profit forecast is the item she expects to make the business headlines.

Penny goes into analysis mode. I leave her to it and call Tash.

"Afternoon Tash."

"Hello Floss."

"How's the stakeout going?"

"A young man leave house at 7.30 this morning but since this time nothing."

"Would you like some company? I'm a little bit stuck workwise, so could give you some help?" I ask tentatively. I feel like I'm asking her to come to my Debutantes Ball.

"This would be very nice, I think."

As I'm puzzling over her ambiguous reply, I walk to the car. Did she mean it would be very nice if I joined her or, she's not sure if it would be nice? I go with the former and stop to pick up two lattes from Massimo and head over towards Clontarf. At Castlecourt, Tash is parked in a flashy red, Eighties boy-racer Toyota, complete with tinted windows, giant spoiler and speed stripes. *OK, not what I would have expected.*

The beaming smile on Tash's face as I jump in assures me I needn't have worried. She looks genuinely happy to see me.

"Well, I have to say that if I was going to imagine the car you might drive, this particular hoon machine would not spring to mind. I had you pegged for a Ute or Range Rover type of gal."

"This not my car. This on loan and good for cover. It looks cheap and irrelevant and we need this."

"Right, got it. So what do you drive?"

"A Volvo XK90. I like it for the roll bars."

"So I wasn't too far off with my Range Rover. "

"Yes but very much East of the UK, in Sweden."

"So, no movement I assume?"

"Nothing. We will require patience, I think."

"Not my strongpoint. I'll try my best."

We sit in comfortable silence, eyes trained on the house. I get so comfortable I nod off into a delicious sleep. Some detective I am. I'm woken suddenly. Tash is sitting up ramrod straight. I glance at the house and see a girl locking the front door of No 2. Tash scans our Facebook pix. As the girl turns around, she says: "I think this is girl. Picture number three." What you think?" she asks.

"It's her!"

Larisa Markov is walking rapidly down the road. .

"Is she going on foot do you think?" I ask turning to Tash.

"Yes. It looks like this. Let's go. Today we are two young lady power walkers."

We jump out and follow her, our only link in the chain of Anna's disappearance. Larisa sets quite a high tempo. We walk along the Howth Road for at least twenty minutes. I'm huffing and puffing and blowing steam, while Tash is breathing normally.

I size up our target. No more than 22. Petite, elegant frame. Dark blonde hair, pulled back into a severe bun. Short grey skirt, thick woollen tights, black duffle coat. No hint of being involved somehow in human trafficking. She does not look guiltily over her shoulder and appears not to have a care in the world.

In Killester she turns left onto Collins Avenue and keeps up her power walk. We remain in hot pursuit.

Five minutes later she turns into a terraced house with a sign out front which reads "Little Munchkins – Creche & Montessori". The house is painted baby-blue, and there are murals of the sun, stars, rainbows and a large munchkin, beside the front door. The munchkin reminds me of the flying monkeys in The Wizard of Oz, so must be pretty spooky for the kids. It certainly freaks me out. I am staring so much that I nearly come to a stop, but Tash grabs me firmly at the waist and steers me onwards to walk by the house. Her touch sends an electric shock through me.

"She works there," says Tash as we leave the house behind. "This is new place to watch. Where she lives is no longer important."

"Why don't we check if it is definitely Larisa that works there?" I say taking out my mobile. Tash nods. I dial 11890 for directory inquiries and get the number for the crèche.

"Good afternoon, Little Munchkins, this is Aisling speaking," says a bright and cheery voice.

"Ah, good morning. May I speak to Larisa Markov please?"

"Yeah, hold on a sec, she just came in, I think. She should be upstairs in the yellow room."

I hang up immediately. "That's definitely our girl."

"I'll get someone from my team to watch this place and girl. I need follow-up on advert and see if can find information on this Larisa."

Tash has a team? I thought she was a one woman band. She's like a triple skinned onion with the amount of layers to her.

"OK great. I'll look into the crèche and see if it's all above board," I pipe up.

"There might be another problem," Tash says with a serious tone.

"Oh yeah?"

"I have not heard from Nika for two days. Could be nothing, could be problem. No texts. No answering. Normally she replies quickly."

"That doesn't sound good. I haven't heard from her either, but I haven't being trying to get in touch. Let's give it one more day. If we don't hear from her, I'll go straight to the police."

"I agree. Are you hungry?" asks Tash.

"Are you kidding? That rumbling you're hearing is my stomach protesting at the lack of action."

"Yes, I am finding it difficult to hear my thoughts over the noise." We both laugh out loud at this.

"How about soup and sandwich at my home?" Tash asks quietly.

"Let's go," I say. My heart has begun a low but palpable drumbeat inside my chest. *Easy does it, Floss.*

We flag down a taxi to get back to our cars in Castlecourt. When Tash starts her car, it roars to life with a growl, its souped-up engine dying to cut loose. It's amusing to think of Tash booming around town in this thing, given she's normally so stealth like.

I follow her back into town, over the breath-taking Samuel Beckett Bridge (or harp bridge as I call it) and we pull up outside a tall glass apartment block on the corner of Grand Canal Quay and Pearse Street. For some reason I was expecting Tash to live in a crusty bedsit off the North Circular Road, but she lives in one of the most sought-after apartment buildings in the city.

We pass through an opulent lobby and step into the lift. Tash presses the top button 'P', which I assume is for penthouse. I'm not wrong.

Her apartment, or should I say mega-gaff, is like something out of a designer magazine, but without any icy austerity. Its living space is open-plan, with three steps up to the kitchen. The furnishings are minimal and Scandinavian, but not your cheap, put-it-together-yourself IKEA gear. This is the real deal. The walls are all tinted glass, affording a 360 degree view of Dublin city and the bay area. Tash is living in my dream home.

"Sit down. Be comfortable. Is miso soup and chicken avocado sandwich ok for you?" she asks.

"Sounds delicious," I reply, sinking down into the corner of the soft, L-shaped couch, but resisting the temptation to put my feet up on the ottoman. "Should I take my shoes off?" I ask, realising that is often 'a thing' in foreign circles and that Tash is already barefoot.

"Only if make you more comfortable," she says as she

effortlessly puts together our lunch. I don't even know what miso soup is made of and to attempt soup and a sandwich at the same time would result in a kitchen disaster for me.

I remove my shoes and stretch out on the couch. I could get used to this.

"So, how do you put up with such awful living conditions?" I ask.

She giggles. "Very tough at first, but now I am used to it."

"And is your Lithuanian friend gone back home?" I ask, failing to avoid sounding nosey.

"Yes." Nothing more.

"Well I hope she brought you loads of Lithuanian treats from home," I say to fill the gap.

"Yes. Enough smoked meat for winter feed. Feel free to look around."

I wander around in awe. Four extra rooms and a bathroom off the living space. An office with high-tech gear, fully equipped gym, master bedroom and guest bedroom. I wonder to myself why her Lithuanian buddy wasn't sleeping in here.

All tastefully decorated in the same sophisticated Nordic style.

Tash shouts, "Food is ready". We sit on the couch and start into our food.

"Wow, that soup is delicious. It tastes just like in Yamamori! How do you do it?"

"It is the easiest soup in the world to make. Miso paste and dashi stock mainly."

"Ah, miso paste! So that's what it's made of. I wasn't quite sure."

She laughs at this and says, "Really, Floss. What are we going to do with you?" and she stares unflinchingly at me with a sly smile.

I, on the other hand, flinch. I look away embarrassed.

"I know. I'm a bit useless."

"Ach, quatch!" and we both laugh at this which releases the sudden tension that had built up around us. "I'll make green tea."

While she's doing this, I fall into a delicious sleep on the couch. I wake up to find a down comforter has been tucked around me and my head is resting in pillow heaven.

Tash is at the other end of the couch, staring at me with an amused look. "Hello sleepy head!" she says smiling.

"God, I'm so sorry. How embarrassing! I have not been sleeping well lately …" I say in an attempt to apologise. I check my watch.

"Jesus! It's a quarter to five!" But I'm so comfortable I'm not that willing to move.

"I do acupuncture and can help you with your sleep if you would like?" Tash says.

"Eh … despite my heroic exterior, I'm a complete girl when it comes to needles. I'd pass out … again."

"I don't have to use needles. I can just use touch and it will work the same. I will relieve you of stress and anxiety, you will be calm for night-time."

"OK. I guess it's worth a shot."

She unfolds her lithe form in one smooth movement, dims the lights and puts on some Sigur Ros in the background.

"I love these guys," I say. "I wish I knew what they were singing about."

"I am trying to learn Icelandic," says Tash. "This song is about desire and loss, I think."

She comes back to the couch and sits very close beside me. "I need your head," she says, and gently places my head in her lap. My heart begins to race, my breathing speeds up.

"I'm not sure this is helping my anxiety, Tash," I say, trying to keep my tone light.

"Trust me," she says. I do. She spends the next hour applying gentle but firm pressure on various points around my head and neck. The tension oozes out of me. I'm like a relaxed jelly fish.

"This last pressure point," says Tash, almost whispering, "is the most important. Do not be scared."

I nod. Her fingers move to a point midway between my belly button and the bottom of my chest bone. It feels overwhelmingly intimate. Although it's relieving the tension, it starts a raging fire further down. I hear a soft moaning sound. It has come from deep within me. I'm about to take hold of Tash's hand and put it where I want it but my mobile phone jerks me to attention.

Stupid phone. But I'm already feeling the severe guilts at not having done much in the area of investigating this afternoon. I struggle into a seated position and answer.

Milo McCarthy of all people. *Is this God trying to mess with me? If so, it's over Rover.*

"Hello, Floss here," I say somewhat breathlessly.

"McFarland? What's up? You sound a little ... squeaky."

"Sorry. I was just in the middle of ... something."

"Something nice I hope?"

"You could say that." I clear my throat: "How can I help?"

I glance over at Tash who is watching me like a hawk.

"Always down to business with you, McFarland. Just wanted to talk through this morning's meeting."

"Oh yep, right. What did you think?" I ask, still struggling to get my heartrate down after that close encounter with Tash.

"Well, there was no digital device other than yours. Nobody really flinched when Janet went through the forecasted figures. It didn't look like it was news to any of them. I don't like the finance guy, but he'd have helped to put those figures together for Janet. And it hasn't made it to the papers yet, so I'm not so sure anymore. But most importantly, they really liked my business expansion plan!" he says laughing away at his own joke.

"Well, at least you got an ego boost out of the meeting!"

"How did it look at your end?"

Tash gets up and heads into her office, presumably to give me some privacy. Talk about losing the moment!

"We got the same impression at our end. Nothing out of place or twitchy and sadly nobody ear-wigging. All in all, pretty disappointing."

"I was thinking we could watch the footage of the meeting over a bottle of wine at your place?" he sneakily offers. Cheeky monkey.

"Well, you really do know how to sweep a lady off her feet with the romantic suggestions. Re-watching a board meeting? Even wine couldn't save such a date! Besides, I have Penny going over everything with a fine-tooth comb as we speak."

"That's a shame. Could you get Penny to send over the footage on disc before end of day?"

"I'll see what I can do," I say, annoyed at receiving orders.

"I'm trying to help, McFarland."

"And it's much appreciated. Sorry if I'm a little snippy. I'm just a little frustrated." Frustrated on many different levels.

"I'll let you know how I get on," he says and hangs up.

I hate it when I don't get the last word in.

I sidle over to Tash's office door and gently knock although the door is slightly ajar. "Come in."

She is sitting in front of four 25-inch flat-screen monitors. Everything's in Cyrillic script.

"Sorry about that," I say sheepishly. "That was one of my sub-contractors."

"Cheeky boy, by the sounds of it."

"He's a good guy, in the main. Look, I better get going. Penny will think *I've* been trafficked. Thanks for everything, the food, the acupuncture, the …. hospitality." Awkward!

"My pleasure, Floss. But can I ask you personal question?" she asks mischievously.

"Ye-es" I say. I hate being put on the spot.

"Am I dog at wrong tree?" she asks and instantly I flush bright red.

"No, I don't think so. But … well … this tree you're barking at … it seems to have half its roots in one field and the rest in another field, way over on the other side of the fence … if you know what I mean."

She gets up from her desk and gives me a light, non-committal hug. She has learned that over-hugging can send me fleeing.

"I understand. I'll just keep watching tree for moment."

"Thanks Tash. Talk tomorrow."

As I leave her apartment building, I feel how relaxed and at ease my entire body is. *I'll be damned. That acupuncture mumbo jumbo might just have done the trick.*

Aoife Sheridan

20

I head back to the office to find Penny has left for the day, but she's left a note on my desk for me:

Dear Floss

It's hard running this company single handed ☺

I've watched the footage twice over now and nothing is jumping out at me, but eyes are wrecked. I'll give it another go tomorrow. I sent the footage over to Milo, hope that was ok.

See you in the morning.

PI Penny

I feel a bit guilty about my relaxing afternoon on the couch, but at least we made progress on finding Larisa. I send Penny a text:

> Thx for holding the fort today. We found Larisa! She's working at a crèche in Killester. We'll talk through next steps tomorrow. Floss x

I check my email. There's one there from Janet Trilby to say the Irish Independent newspaper called to ask her if she wanted to comment on the fact that they would be printing an article on the poor forecasts for Q4. Must remember to get the Independent in the morning.

Sonar ping. A reply from Penny:

> Good result on Larisa! Very jealous I missed some proper action. Talk tomorrow. Penny

OK, she's sounds miffed, but not too miffed.

I start researching the Little Munchkins crèche online. I start
with the Companies Registration website. Nothing out of the
ordinary jumps out at me, although in truth, I'm hoping to find
'Mr Really Bad – Director of Human Trafficking'. No such
luck. The crèche was set up in 2002 by a partnership of an
individual and another company. So, they've been in business
for twelve years and some of that through some severe
recessionary times. The individual is the owner operator,
Martina Keevney. I check her out online. All looks pretty legit.
Started out as a nanny in France, then back to Ireland where
she learned her trade working in various crèches before going
out on her own.

The company that owns the other half of the crèche is called
Funtimes & Co. They appear to part-own a number of crèches
and children's play centres across Dublin. Their ownership
structure is similar to Little Munchkins. One individual and
one company. The owner is a guy called John Shaw and he
appears to be your average entrepreneur type, who dabbles in
lots of different businesses. Finances look solid. The other
company involved is called Freedom Holdings Ltd. Nothing
obviously untoward. Looks like they file their accounts on time
and have been in operation and profitable since 2007.

Might be a dead-end. But I make a note to look into both
Freedom Holdings and Funtimes & Co at a later date.

I look at our investigation planning board for a quick review.
We've actually made a bit of progress in the few days we've
been trying to trace Anna's whereabouts. Our best lead is still
Larisa, but I'm hoping Jeremy comes through with the next
travel date of Piedr Korsak. That would be solid gold.

It's after 7.30 when I head home. Leon almost bowls me over
as I come through the door. I'm feeling guilt at leaving him at

home so much, so we go for a long walk along Sandymount Strand and out as far as Blackrock. We stop for a pint and dinner in Jack O'Rourkes pub. The best pint of Carlsberg in Dublin and they always give Leon some nice scraps.

We get home just after ten o'clock. I flop onto the couch to watch some mindless TV and fall asleep for the third time in the day.

Just after midnight, my quality couch-time is interrupted by the shrill ringing of my doorbell. Leon's draped over my legs so it takes me awhile to extricate myself and make it to the front door.

I look through the peephole. Milo McCarthy! *Oh buggery-do.* I look like a complete shambles in my tracksuit and UGGS, hair completely out of control. He, on the other hand, looks scrumptious in some form of grey teenage hoody and jeans.

The doorbell rings again insistently. I nearly jump out of my skin. Leon finally pads his way into the hall. Some guard dog!

"I know you're in there McFarland. I can hear your hair moving around in there."

Damn him and his bionic hearing. I check in the hallway mirror – hopeless case! – then open the door.

Milo is grinning from ear to ear. "Well aren't you a sight for sore eyes, or to make eyes sore, not sure which."

I'm about to slam the door in his face, but he blocks it with his foot. I hope it hurts.

"Not so fast, McFarland. You look fine … in a kind of Scary Spice meets Sporty Spice kind of way."

I roll my eyes to heaven and open the door to let him in.

"What in God's name are you doing here at this unearthly

hour?" I ask as I traipse back into the kitchen.

"I think I might have figured out what's going on at Trilby," he says triumphantly.

"Nice one," I say yawning. "I'm going to need tea if we're going to have a semi-decent go at a conversation at this hour. Any interest?"

"Coffee for me, if you have it."

I begin faffing in the kitchen. Leon comes in to check on who's here and lets out a low growl to inform Milo he's got his eye on him.

"Easy, Leon. Milo is a workmate … Is instant ok? I know it's sacrilegious but I can't be bothered making the real deal at the minute."

"Fine for me," he says amiably.

He's brought a laptop and starts setting it up on the breakfast bar. I start thinking of us being in a clinch at that very spot and already my blood begins to circulate faster around my body. His hair is slightly tossed as if he's been rubbing his hand through it constantly and he has a five o'clock shadow that adds to his overall ruggedness.

When I have the hot drinks ready, he pats the tall stool beside him, indicating I should sit there. I sit down one stool beyond just to make a point. Leon growls quietly in the corner.

"Suit yourself," he says and turns the laptop around so we can both see.

"You're going to fall head over heels in love with me … again, after you've seen what I think I've found."

"Again? Eh hello?"

"Never mind. Just watch this." He fast-forwards to a spot he's bookmarked (or video-marked if that's possible).

"The meeting looks a lot more interesting like that – fast and soundless," I quip.

"Right here. Watch the door," he says and hits play.

James Kenny is talking and his hands are gesticulating wildly, the most animated I've seen him. Over his shoulder, I see the door slowly opening. The middle-aged receptionist comes in with a tray of tea and coffee.

"You see it?" Milo asks.

"You can't seriously think that old dear is the mastermind behind all these press leaks? She wouldn't even understand what they're talking about half the time. A pretty efficient receptionist but criminal genius? I can't see it."

"Hold on, watch again." He fast-forwards to another point just before the meeting is about to break up. We see the receptionist come in again and clear away the tray as everyone is getting up to leave.

"I should have thought about it during the meeting," Milo says with a hint of embarrassment, "but these receptionist types operate on an almost invisible level. They just make things mysteriously happen in the background."

"For you board-level types, you mean?"

"Something like that. I bet there's a listening device in that tray or in the stuff sitting on top of it."

"I still don't buy Margaret as the corporate fraud type. She reminds me of Penny's Mum for Christ's sake! So, what next?"

"I think you need to do a swoop on their office and check out the coffee and tea gear. They probably use the good stuff for the board meetings so it should be easy to spot. If you find something, then you need to have a little chat with Margaret."

"God, that should be interesting. I'm slightly scared of her. I'll bring Penny. She's better at handling this type of beast."

"So, McFarland, have I earned my keep?" he asks, looking confidently at me with one eyebrow cocked.

"I hate to say it, but yes ... yes you have."

"YES!" he says, punching the air triumphantly. "Why do you always give me such a hard time? I'm not that bad a bloke, you know."

"I've known worse, I suppose."

"Oh, be still my beating heart. 'Not the worst' is the highest of compliments coming from you."

"It's the best I can do at this time of night. Listen, I have to go to bed."

"Want some company?" he asks chancing his arm.

"No thanks, I have Leon," I say punching his arm lightly.

"Well, that's the closest I've got to affection coming from you. Lucky Leon is all I'll say." He gets up to leave and I pad after him to the hall.

"Thanks, Milo, for the video work. It was a good spot."

He clearly takes this as a come-on. In one fluid movement, he closes the door to the hall with his leg to block Leon from following, grabs my hips and moves in for the kill. His lips are on mine before I can let out a surprised yelp. I make a very lame attempt at pushing him away but his mouth is rapidly weakening my defences. Where did this guy learn to kiss? Probably lots of practice. Exactly the type of guy my Mum warned me about. His hands move around from my hips to my behind and he is pressing me firmly against him. I'm under no illusions as to how he's reacting to our embrace.

Just as suddenly, he pulls away.

"Let me know how you get on at Trilby tomorrow!" he says breezily as if that snog had not just happened – and he's gone.

I manage a half-wave, concentrating on my knees not buckling before I close the front door after him. I wobble back into the kitchen. Leon is looking at me as if to say, "So what just happened there?"

"I'm not exactly sure, but I think body won over brain for once."

I head to bed and spend a restless night thinking about Tash's hands gently pressing my stomach, Milo's 'smash and grab' and what the hell we're going to say to Margaret the receptionist tomorrow.

The next morning, I'm up at seven on the dot. Leon and I go for a walk and pick up a copy of the Independent and some emergency snacks on the way back. Over breakfast of the strongest coffee possible and two Nutrigrain bars, I find the article about Trilby Wealth Management:

Shareholders nervous as profit forecast slumps for third quarter running

Our mysterious saboteur is still in operation, but at least we're getting hotter.

I land at work at 8.30. Penny has got in ahead of me.

"Hey Floss. You look wrecked, you poor thing."

"Thanks for that Penny. You really know how to boost a girl's ego first thing in the morning."

"Oh I'm sorry, honey. But you *do* look tired."

"You're starting to sound like my mother!"

"Bound to happen. Once I had the kids, things started popping out of me that were my mother all over. It's horrific but there's no avoiding it. Anyway, I'd better get back to the video footage."

"You can hold off on that."

"Oh really? Why? What's up?"

"I'd a late-night visit from Milo McCarthy last night."

"Oooooh! So that goes a long way to explaining why you look so tired this morning. Business or pleasure?" she asks, doing a scary porn-star voice on the word 'pleasure'.

"Very humorous. Not that type of late night call. It was strictly business-ish."

Penny just looks at me with an 'I-told-you-so' look.

"He'd gone over the footage and spotted something interesting. At their half-time break, Margaret, the receptionist, brought in a tray of teas and coffees and then, just as the meeting was breaking up, she came in and whipped it away again. That's the only way a listening device could have been brought into the room without our sweeps picking it up."

"Matronly Margaret? I'd never have pegged her for this."

"That's exactly what I said, Pen, but first things first. This morning, we're going to go over there and figure out if Milo was right. I'm going to need you for that. You're better at the gadgets and old, scary lady side of things than I am."

"Like it! Now?" she asks enthusiastically.

"Why not? And before you ask, no, I'll drive."

Aoife Sheridan

21

When we arrive in the reception at Trilby's, Margaret is manning the desk and on a call. She politely gestures for us to take a seat. Wearing proper business garb as opposed to cleaning service overalls makes quite a difference! Apparently the clothes really do make the woman.

Margaret wraps up her call, and comes straight over to us. "Hello again ladies. Are you looking for Janet?"

"Yes, if she's about, that would be great, thanks," I say.

"Unfortunately, you just missed her - she's gone to some meeting at the solicitors and I don't expect her back until after lunch. Is there anything I can help you with?"

"Well, actually, there might be. I wonder if you could take us to your kitchen or wherever the tea and coffee pots and cups are for the more formal meetings - like say, the monthly board meeting," I say, watching Margaret like a hawk for any sign of alarm.

She shows slight bemusement and curiosity but no outward sign of tension or nerves. If it were me and I were guilty, I would have crumpled into a blubbering mess of guilty confessions.

"Absolutely, follow me this way. The facilities are actually on the ground floor, which is a bit tedious when meetings are up on the third floor. More carpets have been ruined by spilled teas and coffees than I'd care to mention."

She shows us into a large kitchen-cum-cafeteria with five stylish, brightly coloured tables with matching chairs. This is where staff must come when they bring their own lunch, so is obviously open to everyone. Margaret points to a cupboard in the top left-hand corner: "This is where the good crockery is kept. Staff are strictly forbidden from using it for their own purposes. It's put up there to make it awkward to get at but it doesn't stop them from trying."

"Right. Thanks for that, Margaret. We'll take it from here. Are you around for a while in case we need you?" I ask.

"Absolutely, dear. And if you wish you can call me on the internal phone on the wall there. Just dial 001 and you'll get directly through."

We wait for her to leave before saying anything.

"Well, either she's the world's calmest corporate fraudster or she's completely clueless as to what's going on. I don't know about you but I reckon it's the latter. What do you think, Pen?"

"Nobody could be that cool if they were about to be caught red-handed."

As I'm reaching for a chair to stand on to reach the top shelf, my phone blips:

> I have some developments. I will visit your office today after 2. Is it ok? Tash

I text a 'yes'.

"Wow, all our cases are breaking wide open!" Penny says excitedly.

"Relax, Columbo. And will you please hold this chair steady while I get the stuff!"

I jump up on the chair and pass down two coffeepots, a large teapot and a full set of eight cups and saucers. It's all top of the range Denby. No wonder they don't let the riffraff at it.

Penny starts sifting through the pots. I start on the cups and saucers but they all look pretty normal to me.

"I can't see anything here, Floss. I mean I'm looking for some type of compartment and without smashing the thing open completely, I'm not sure there's anything here."

"Pants. I was sure we were on to something ... hold on a second. What about the tray?"

We look around the kitchen and find three trays behind the microwave, but they are all quite flimsy and don't look like they could conceal a listening device.

"They don't even look like the tray that was used at the board meeting. It was more sturdy than those ones," says Penny.

"Double pants," I say, feeling deflated.

I'm about to dial 001 to get hold of Margaret when I see Penny's eyes drawn to the top surface of the fridge. Peeking out slightly is the corner of a silver tray. Penny's up on the chair like a flash and catches hold of it. She flips it over, lets out a yelp, wobbles and nearly falls. I rush in to steady the chair. When she's stabilised, she shows me the underside of the tray.

"How many trays do you own with what looks like a battery compartment?" she asks, glowing with pride.

"Amazeballs! Bring it down here so we can have a look."

She jumps off the chair and whips a Leatherman out of her purse. Ever the girl scout. She unscrews the two tiny screws on the small compartment and opens the latch, being careful not to leave any fingerprints.

Inside is just the sucker we've been looking for. A bug. I hug Penny with the sheer excitement of it all. Finally, we did something right! And although we still haven't found the culprit, we've gone a long way towards it.

"I think we should have a little chat with Lady Margaret. What do you think?" I ask.

"Yep, let's get her in the boardroom. Returning to the scene of the crime, if you like."

"Very Hercule Poirot. I like it, Pen."

I call Margaret's number and ask her to meet us in the boardroom in five minutes. She asks if she can bring some tea and coffee. If she is the leak, the irony of this offer is not lost on the two of us. We head straight up to the third floor, bringing the tray with us.

Two minutes after we've settled into our seats, there's a quiet knock on the door. Margaret comes in and stands there, waiting for us to make some administrative request of her.

"Actually, Margaret," I say, "we'd like a quiet word, if you can spare us some time."

She's clearly surprised, but not ruffled in any way. She takes a seat beside Penny at the table.

I start: "Margaret, I'm sure you are aware that Trilby Wealth Management has been receiving some negative and suspiciously timed bad press in the media of late."

"Yes, I know. It's been an awful strain for Janet," she says sympathetically.

"These leaks always happen immediately after the monthly board meetings. Janet employed CTB Investigations, our company, to look into the affair, because she was convinced it had to be an insider. We've been stumped for nearly a year. That is, until we found this tray."

With those words, I turn the tray over dramatically, expecting a guilty 'You've got me' reaction. Nothing. Margaret merely shows puzzlement: "I'm not following you," she says politely. "What role has the tray in all this?"

She's either as innocent as the driven snow or somebody capable of beating a lie-detector test. She should be in the CIA or in my poker circle!

"Well, you see this little compartment here?" I ask.

She nods.

"This is a hiding place for a listening device or bug, as they are commonly called in American TV shows. This explains how someone other than a director is gaining access to the confidential information shared during board meetings."

Suddenly, Margaret raises her eyebrows and opens her mouth wide: "Am I to understand that … that … you think I'm the person responsible for the leaked information?"

"What else are we to think, Margaret?" I say gently. "We have footage of you bringing in this tray and clearing it away before the end of the meeting."

"Be that as it may, might I remind you of several items of relevant information?" she replies, very formally and in total control of herself. "First, I've been a loyal employee of Trilby Wealth Management for 17 years and watched it grow from a two-person operation to a 70-plus team. Secondly, as reward for my loyalty, Janet gifted me a small sum of shares. I don't know how they work, but I do know that it's better for me if the share value goes up, not down. Thirdly" – she takes a breath here, allowing the intensity of her words to build – "I would not know useful information to leak if it fell over and hit me in the face. Finally, the idea of me setting up a listening device is utterly laughable – I wouldn't know a bug from a ladybird!"

Triple pants. That is the best defensive construction I've ever heard in my life. I would have lost it completely after the second point. I look to Penny for assistance.

"Let's take a step backwards. Do you accept that it looks as if this tray is the means by which the information is leaked?" Penny begins.

"Well, I'm no expert, but it certainly looks that way," she says, arms folded, in full defensive mode now.

"So, if you say you are not involved in any way, we need your help finding out who is. For example, does somebody else prepare the tea and coffee tray and you just deliver it?"

"No, I do the lot from start to finish. Janet insists on it as she's quite fussy about her coffee and some of the younger girls make it too weak for her tastes."

"Ok," Penny continues patiently, "what about before you go in, do you have to leave the tray somewhere for a short time? Somewhere where someone else might have an opportunity to tamper with it, maybe?"

"No, I just go straight from the kitchen up to here."

"Ok, can you think of any other way that this tray might be interfered with?"

"None at all."

I can tell that Penny's line of questioning has put Margaret at ease and she's now starting to think about the possibilities rather than just defend herself. I'm about to jump in with another question when Margaret unfolds her arms and puts one hand to her lips as if she's just done something embarrassing.

"What is it?" I ask. "Something's just occurred to you."

"Well, I'm not one to accuse anybody else and it could be absolutely nothing … in fact I'm sure it is."

"Margaret, can I assure you," Penny says calmly, "that whatever you say here is completely confidential? Also, it's probably important to bear in mind that we are trying to help Trilby, your shares and Janet. Whoever is behind these leaks is thoroughly unscrupulous and deserves none of your hard-earned loyalty."

Margaret visibly softens. *Brilliant, Penny*. She has just managed to zero in on matters dearest to Margaret's heart. She's ready to talk openly now.

"Well, it's just that I didn't buy that tray for the office and I've pretty much sourced everything for this office from the outset."

"Where did it come from?" I ask a little abruptly. I'm chomping at the bit, feeling we're seconds away from finding our culprit.

"Well, I remember thinking that it was a little strange at the time, but the tray was a gift of sorts from our head of IT, Paul Fitzsimons."

"Well, bugger me senseless!" I exclaim. "Excuse my French, Margaret!"

She blushes, and says, "I'm not Paul's greatest admirer around here but he's always so personable and chatty. More working and less chatting is what I like to see around the office. But I'd never have thought him capable of this and I certainly don't want to be the one pointing the finger at him."

"Don't worry, Margaret" I say. "Nobody's accusing anyone yet. What will happen now is we'll get the police involved, in as discreet a manner as possible. They'll fingerprint the tray and more than likely search Paul's office and take away his computer for forensic analysis. I'll talk to Janet and I'm guessing Paul will more than likely have to go on forced leave of absence. Either way I think you can look forward to hiring a more hardworking IT head in the near future."

"What should I do?" she asks.

"Absolutely nothing. Keep this to yourself. We don't want to alert Mr Fitzsimons before the police get here. So just go about your business as if this morning never happened. However, I will ask one thing, can we put this tray somewhere safe so nobody else can get to it? And then you can give it to the police when they get here?"

"Not a problem. You can put it in my stationery press. Everybody in the office knows it's strictly off limits."

I imagine poor young interns thinking of asking her for a pen or some post-its, but immediately chickening out. Every office has one like her. But she's a good old skin.

"I expect someone from the Garda Fraud Squad will be here this afternoon. In the meantime, we'll get out of your hair."

"I'll see you both out."

As we leave the building, we rush to get around the corner, and then do high fives and a chest pump.

"We're investigative geniuses!!" shouts Penny. Passers-by look at us as if we are escapees from John of Gods.

"Let's celebrate with cake!" I say. We head straight for Fallon & Byrne for some of the best carrot cake in town – and two bowl-sized lattes.

When we get back to the office, it's almost 12 noon. I call Janet and give her a synopsis of this morning's discovery.

"I don't know what I'm more horrified at," she says. "The fact that you thought Margaret might be involved or the fact that Paul possibly could be. He's my nephew and I hired him as a favour to my sister. He'd been struggling to find a job after he and his wife came back from the UK. I could kick myself."

"Don't beat yourself up over it. If he's been doing a good job on the IT side of things, you never would have had cause to question him. And we haven't proved anything yet."

"I suppose so, but if it is him, it's mortifying, as I had him helping me initially, trying to figure this thing out. He kept pointing me back at the directors, which makes more sense now. I feel incredibly stupid."

"Well don't. This is good news, even if it hurts."

"I suppose you're right. But I don't want any more scandal from this. Any more bad press will just hurt the share price further."

"I've already thought of that. I've an old college friend, Derek Keogh, who works in the Garda Fraud Squad. I've been making him look good for years. In return for slam dunk cases, he guarantees discretion, so nobody will be any the wiser."

"I'd appreciate that, Florence."

"Derek will be in touch shortly and, in the interim, avoid talking to Paul."

I feel sorry for Janet. The greatest challenge of running any company is managing people. Somebody is always letting you down, whether it be complaining that the free coffee is not up to scratch or stealing from the till. But this one is more personal, not only an attack from within her company but also, it seems, from within her family. A roundhouse kick to the boobs.

I text Milo McCarthy quickly to let him know he was on the money:

> Trilby case in the bag. Bug in the tray. Head of IT in the frame. Well done! Floss

I call Derek .

"Detective Inspector Keogh speaking," he sings in his lilting Cork accent.

"Is that the slack-arse who spends his time waiting for CTB Investigations to deliver a gift-wrapped case into his lap?" I say chirpily.

"Well, if it isn't my favourite, curly-haired, boobless wonder. How the hell are ya, girl?"

"Top form, Derek. What's shaking in the Phoenix Park?"

"Me mickey at the moment and dat's about it. Got anytin' juicy for me?"

"I think Christmas might have come early for you." I talk him through the case from start to finish. He's delighted and agrees to take a small, plainclothes team over to Trilby for an afternoon raid on the office of Paul Fitzsimons, former head of IT.

When I ring off, I have another hour and a half before Tash gets here for our catch-up. I'm relieved to get the Trilby case wrapped up as it not only gives us an extra cash injection, but also means we can refocus all our energies on Anna's case.

I spend the next ninety minutes or so writing up the notes for the Trilby case file. I will send a copy to Janet for her records but it's mostly for us. With a strong sense of achievement, I type up the final invoice with additional success bonus, but I resolve to hold off sending it until I get absolute confirmation from Derek. I do, however, file the Trilby case in our 'Closed Cases' section.

At exactly two o'clock, there's a firm knock on the door. I check my appearance in the tiny mirror by the door before I open it. Penny gives me a well-well-now look. I shake my head.

Tash is there on the steps of the prefab, in all her glory. Today she's sacrificed the killer spy gear for a smart tailored business suit with kick-ass heels, and is carrying a slim leather lady briefcase.

"Are you coming for an interview?" I joke.

"Ha! Well, it actually feels like I already work here."

"Fair point," I concede.

"I had another job this morning."

"Dare I ask?"

"No."

"Point taken. Come on in. Coffee or tea?"

"No. I'm not thirsty. Thank you. Oh, hello Penny!"

"Hi Tash. Looking sharp today," she says cheerfully.

"Thanks. It's not my choice. It's not comfortable for me."

"Penny," I say, "would give her left arm to have that suit, I'd imagine."

"Actually, it's your physique, Tash," say Penny. "If I had your body, I'd just go through life naked."

This is extra funny since Penny can be such a prude. She practically wears a burkini by the pool on holidays. It's one of her other bi-polarisms. Adventure hound meets coy nun.

"Well, let's all be grateful for the moment that you don't have Tash's bod," I say, rather ambiguously.

"I think I'm offended by that, Floss," says Penny.

"Alright, back to bizzo." I turn to Tash. "You have some news?" I'm determined to remain focused on the case today. This is proving difficult given that Tash looks like a complete Bond Bad Ass lady. I'm half expecting blades to flick out the top of her expensive shoes.

"Yes, I've news on many things. First is bad news. I still have not had any reply from Nika. I think she's generally pretty good, so it makes me very worried for her. I think it's time for police."

"Shit bums! This is not good," I say. Sometimes when I'm stressed, I develop a form of Tourette's, or at least that's my excuse, though I'm sure genuine Tourette's sufferers would be horrified at my lack of creativity.

"No, not good," echoes Tash, with a mildness that is possibly intended to rap my knuckles.

"Right, we'll go straight to the police station. What else? Any good news?"

"Yes, I think so. I've been looking at few things. The first is easy. Piedr Korsak." She takes a couple of printouts out of her briefcase and hands a copy to Penny and me. The printout shows what I take to be the Russian driver's licence of our chief suspect. He has a skinny, elfish look, sporting shorty mousy hair and a groomed goatee. He's looking at the camera with a bored expression. There's nothing threatening or extraordinary about him. Disappointing. I was expecting a picture of the Devil himself. Of course, if he looked suspect, the girls would hardly agree to travel with him in the first place.

"Is this our guy?" I ask Tash.

"Yes. That's a photo of Piedr from two years ago," says Tash. "As bad guys go, not worst bad guy. But not good guy. He has many convictions for robbery, assault and drugs. In and out of prison four times since 18 years old. Finished his last visit in prison exactly one year ago. Did not take long for him to get new job in transport of girls."

"This is solid gold, Tash. Well done."

"So, for Piedr, I think plan is get your airline friend to check when he plans to travel again. Now we know what he looks like we can follow him from airport and see what happens. No problem."

"Gung ho, Tash. I like your style," says Penny, all riled up.

"Hold it there, Cagney and Lacey. Let's cool our collective jets," I say.

Tash looks confused. "Who is this Cagney and Lacey?"

"Oh sorry, it's a brilliant cop show from the Eighties. Sometimes Penny and I joke around that we're them. It's stupid. Never mind. I just think we don't need to rush into anything. Penny has a tendency to get over-excited at the prospect of some actual action."

"Be that as it may, it still sounds like a bloody good plan to me," says Penny.

"Alright, alright. I actually have Jeremy already scanning the ether for airline bookings for Piedr Korsak, but I haven't checked with him for a while. I'll give him another nudge just in case he got distracted on some other geeky mission. So Tash, is that everything on Piedr?"

"Yep," she nods.

"You mentioned some other developments?"

"Yes. The next thing is watching this girl, Larisa. My team have been watching for one day now only, but there is nothing suspicious. She goes to work, comes home, watches TV with flatmates. No problem. She seems to work hard, is liked by her colleagues and parents at crèche."

"Sorry, was this surveillance or a 360 review?" Penny asks, impressed.

"We have our little methods."

"That eerily reminds me of a KGB torturer from the movies," I say.

"It was supposed to!" she says laughing and her whole face and shoulder crumple into it. Her giggles are infectious.

"Well, we're only one day in. I presume we keep it up ... the surveillance, I mean?" I ask, not hiding how new I am to all this. It's kind of exhilarating to think of Tash having a surveillance team and I'm really just trying to keep up.

"Normally, I would say yes. But with Nika now missing also, I think we need to follow more urgent path," Tash says returning to serious mode.

"Storm the house?" asks Penny, on the edge of her seat, keen to go into combat mode.

"Again, not so much," says Tash patiently. "I think we have first talk with Larisa. She is only direct contact and we could set cat among birds, as you say. First we try nice friendly chat. Next we do 'lift and shift'."

"Oooh, let's go straight to plan B!" says Penny. "What's a lift and shift? Another one of your little methods?" asks Penny, positively buzzing with where this is going.

"Yes. We lift her straight off street in broad daytime. She then thinks she is in big trouble, which shifts her perspective. Then we have more chat."

"Sorry to be boring old Florence, but it sounds on the wrong side of the legal fence, no?" I ask.

"You are correct, Floss. It is not strictly legal. But if Larisa makes bad call to Anna in very beginning, then we know she is connected to bad people, which leaves her on the illegal side, as you say. My experience, with these people is police will not be first person they call."

"Still, I feel a little uncomfortable about it."

"I will handle the second chat if need. This way your, how do you say, uncomfort, will be little less."

"Discomfort," I say.

"Ah yes, discomfort. Thanks. Also, after we have first chat, we get Penny's phone friend to monitor calls Larisa makes. She will go running to bad guys. I am sure."

"Well, apart from the fact that we might all end up in Mountjoy Prison at the end of this, I can't tell you how happy I am that we've you on our side, Tash. Without you, I think Anna and Nika's chances would be seriously poked."

"Hear! Hear!" cheers Penny.

"I happy too," says Tash, but her ice-green eyes have zeroed in on me. My insides start that familiar fluttering.

"Right, well, that all sounds like a great step forward," I say trying to change the subject.

"Lastly," Tash adds, "I was looking into company that made newspaper ad. As I said before, this company does not exist, but make big mistake. They did not pay cash! I applied some pressure to one of staff who sent name of company that payment comes from. It is holding company called Veeva Sporting Company. I'm still looking into who is behind it. It is slow because complex. I will let you know how this goes."

"Well, it feels as if you're doing the work of three people, Tash. Thank you so much."

"You're welcome, Floss," again with that disquieting stare.

I launch into action. "Ok, I'll have a chat with Jeremy. Penny, can you get your TelcoWeb guy lined up for monitoring Larisa's mobile number?"

She nods eagerly.

"When should we have the chat with Larisa?" I ask, looking to Tash for guidance.

"I think soon. You and Penny have first talk and then we see what happens."

"Ladies," I say excitedly, "sounds like we have the beginnings of a plan."

22

With our plan more or less agreed, we all start making calls. Penny is onto TelcoWeb. Tash is talking to somebody in Lithuanian or Russian. I call Derek Keogh to see how the afternoon raid at Trilby went.

"How're they hangin', Floss?" he answers, knowing it's me.

"They're not hangin' at all, Derek." He has always given me a hard time about my lack of anything vaguely resembling cleavage.

"Two calls in the one day? Sure yer spoilin' me now at this stage."

"I know. I'm too good to you. But I'm mainly calling for a favour. First I want to check on how everything went over at Trilby this avo?"

"Ah sure, grand. I think we scared the living shite out of yer man Fitzsimons. An awful chatty bollox if you ask me. We've got his prints and the lads are running them through the gizmo now to check if there's a match to the bug."

"Gizmo? Have they managed to get you to use a computer yet?" He's still very old school. The Garda have gone uber-tech but he's struggled with the changes.

"Sure why would I need one o' them computers when I've it all in me noggin, eh?" he says laughing.

"Anyways, we lifted his computer, two external drivey things and something called a local server that didn't appear to be connected to their network thingamajig. The forensic lads from IT are looking at it now, but they won't have anything till tomorrow at the earliest."

"Ok grand, thanks for that," I say.

"So what's this favour yer after? Nuttin' of a sexual nature, I hope?"

"No, you muppet!"

"Pity. Go on, so ..."

"I've a missing person in one of my cases. I want to report this, but not to any young pup straight out of Templemore Garda College. I want a seasoned old fart who knows his or her way around the traps. Would you have anyone that fits the bill?"

"Sure, yer spoilt for choice there, Floss. Go over to Pearse Street and ask for Mick Daly. He's far too fond o' the jar but fifty per cent of that fella is worth two of any other fucker. Tell 'im I sent you over. I'm not sayin' that'll help, but it's better than walkin' in off the street. How does that sound, Mrs?"

"You're a doll, Derek. Give me a shout on the fingerprints. I'll keep my fingers crossed."

"Good on ya, girl. Bye, bye, bye, bye now, bye." We swap another few bye-byes between us in the true Irish phone ritual and finally ring off.

I send a quick text to Jeremy:

> Hey Wunderkind. Any progress on booked flights for our buddy? Floss

About 0.02 nanoseconds later:

> Nada. Sorry. But the bot I wrote is still looking. If he books a flight into Dublin, we'll find him. J

"Right," I announce to the group, "I'm going to head over to the garda station on Pearse Street. Derek gave me some dodgy old drunk geezer to talk to about Nika."

"I'll come with you," says Tash. My heart skips a beat. I haven't been alone with her since that blissful afternoon in her penthouse.

"Ok, great. Penny, you ok with that?" I ask. She gives me a thumbs-up as she's still on the phone.

We head outside and Tash asks if it's ok to go in her car. We hop into her steel grey Volvo estate. It feels like a dream driving machine and Tash handles it like a pro. I wish we were off for a spin in the country together on a warm summer's day rather than taking a stop-start trip through the wet and windy streets.

"What's this music we're listening to?" I ask. The car is filled with beautifully serene but deeply sad piano music.

"This is Arvo Part. Spiegel Im Spiegel. 'Mirror in the mirror' in English. Estonia's greatest export. You like?"

"Haunting. Reminds me a bit of Gloomy Sunday, that Hungarian song that was supposed to have caused all the suicides. I'd never have figured you for a classical music lover – more Daft Punk." Even as I say this, I realise the music suits Tash to a tee. Almost disconcertingly calm.

"Really? No, this is the absolute music for me. When there is chaos all around, this music stops it from getting inside my head."

"Well, I'll have to get me some of this, because I've got a serious shit storm going on inside my head."

She smiles. "But now we're here."

Disappointing. I could stay in this insulated bubble of peace and quiet for a lot longer.

The 'here' Tash referred to is a parking spot in the middle of the spaces reserved for gardaí. "Are we ok here?" I ask.

"Check my registration plates. We'll be fine."

So much for my detection skills. I hadn't noticed that Tash has diplomatic plates. So she is on government business, of some form or other.

We head into the police station, a big old austere grey building across from Trinity College and probably one of the busiest stations in the country. Thankfully it's a quiet Thursday afternoon. As we walk through the main entrance, I notice that all the gardaí, girls and guys, are saying hi to Tash by name, although most refer to her as Natasha. They're also obviously checking her out.

"Have you done a few stretches in the Big House?" I ask.

"What?" she says, looking totally confused.

"It's just everyone seems to know you here, which means you're either working with the good guys or you are, in fact, one of the bad guys."

"I'm definitely not one of the bad guys," she says laughing, while continuing to acknowledge her friends and admirers.

"You really are going to have to tell me what you actually do for a living one of these days."

We reach the front desk. Tash actually high-fives (no I'm not kidding, actually old school high fives) the young buck on duty. He's operating out of an old-fashioned wooden hatch from the 1960s.

"Long time no see, Natasha. How are you?" he asks, eyes drinking in the sight of her. I'm apparently invisible. All eyes are on Tash (including mine).

"Very good, thanks James. How it goes in real Garda world?" she asks.

"Haven't a clue. I've been stuck behind this desk since I passed my exams. Hey, we still have to have that drink, remember?"

I've had quite enough: "Sorry to interrupt your little tête-à-tête here with some actual police business, but I was wondering if you could put me in touch with Mick Daly in Missing Persons?"

The young Garda is taken aback by my interruption and Tash just raises both eyebrows with an amused look in my direction.

"Alright, alright, keep your hair on, madam," says Garda James.

Madam? I mouth at Tash, horrified. She laughs at this but covers it up so James can't hear.

"Mick Daly is more often than not a missing person himself around here", says the young policeman. "I'll check if he's in the building."

"Thanks James," I say with my most winning smile, trying to make up for my earlier rudeness.

We potter around the reception area looking at the notices. Loads of flyers about missing people, of all ages, shapes and sizes. Depressing.

"Ladies!" we hear from James behind us.

We turn around and go back up to the hatch.

"Mick's left the building. If I was a betting man, which I'm strictly not," he says looking at Tash, and then almost whispering, "I'd say you'd have a good shot of finding him around the corner in Mulligans on Poolbeg Street. His second office, so to speak."

"Brilliant. Thanks James," and I go to high five him as Tash did but he looks at me as if I'm demented and leaves me completely hanging. Morto.

"Goodbye, James," says Tash as she pulls me out the door. I can hear him shouting after Tash not to forget about that drink. God loves a trier.

We head off on foot for Mulligans, which is only five minutes away.

"So, do you also know Mick Daly?" I ask.

"By reputation only," Tash replies. "I think he's one of older guys so have not meet him yet. I expect him to be … colourful person"

Colourful is right. Mick Daly, alleged Great Finder of Missing Persons, is propped up at the public bar with a half empty pint of Guinness, what looks like a whiskey chaser and today's racing pages in front of him. He has cop written all over him. Drunk cop.

"Detective Mick Daly, I presume?" I say.

"Lemygesh," he says, turning, "you must be the infamoush Flosh McFarland."

Not just drunk cop. Langered cop. *This should be interesting.*

He notices Tash. "And who might you be, my Lithuanian prinshesh?"

"Wow. Impressive. Most people guess Russian. My name is Natasha. Pleased to meet you, Mick," she says politely.

"Natasha the Lithuanian. That rings a bell somewhere in the

alcohol-sodden brain cells up here," he says, attempting to point at his head but missing and pointing instead at somewhere in mid-air.

I think 'lost cause' for a moment, but then remind myself that Derek would never put me wrong. "I take it Derek warned you I'd be seeking you out?" I ask him.

"He sent me one of those dreadful text message things this morning. With smiley faces and all! Now, ladies, can I interest you in a drink this pleasant afternoon?"

"Not for me thanks, Mick" I say. Tash shakes her head gently.

"Ah the sorry plight of a solo run," Mick says, staring into his pint. He must be around six foot three at least, from the time when all gardaí applicants had to be six-footers from the counties along the Shannon. Now they'll let any old short-arse through the door. He's built like a burly bear, with giant spades for hands and a ruddy complexion that would do the best whiskey drinker proud.

We grab two tall stools and prop ourselves up beside him at the bar.

"Look Mick, I'm not sure how much Derek said to you, but we've a bit of a situation on our hands."

"A situation no less? Sounds deadly serious," he says in his mocking Dublin tones.

Mick Daly is your classic detective. A unique blend of toughness, genuine caring and a lonely air, covered with a thin icing of humour and self-deprecation. You couldn't but warm to him.

"To be honest with you, Mick, we think it is deadly serious," I say. He straightens slightly.

I take this as encouragement to go on.

"Tash and myself are involved in a human trafficking case. The usual stuff – girl promised a great escape, girl leaves home country for the promised land, girl never seen again."

"I sympathise with your plight and theirs, Floss, but it's not really my department," he says, in a joking union-rep-type way.

"You're right. The trafficking bit isn't, but missing persons are. This case landed in our laps because a brave young Russian girl called Nika came to Dublin looking for a friend who, she believes, was trafficked into Dublin and …"

"Let me guess," Mick interrupts, "now she's gone missing."

I nod. "We haven't heard from her for three days. Before that she replied to texts in under a minute."

"Any chance she's run out of credit or done a legger with some local lad?" asks Mick.

"We don't think so. She had enough funding for two weeks in Dublin and we're only just over half way through that. Plus, she's a tiny, determined wee thing. If she'd run out of credit, she'd have walked barefoot to get in touch with us. Dropping off the radar just doesn't fit."

"Do you know how many missing persons I have in my caseload?" Mick asks us.

"I'm sure it's a scary number, but I do know that sitting in this pub getting shitfaced isn't getting you any closer to finding any of them," I say, allowing my frustration to seep through.

"Fuck you, Floss McFarland!" Anger flashes through him. "I lost one this morning. A 14-year-old girl, never came home after the youth club disco. She was found this morning and it wasn't pretty. So, if you'll excuse me, I've an appointment with oblivion." He turns back to the barman and signals for another round.

"Michael," Tash says, speaking for the first time since we entered. He turns in response to her quiet insistence. "I know the pain of the missing ones. I have many, many in here," she says, pointing at her heart. "Perhaps I handle it a different way, but I understand. This girl, Nika, is fresh one. If you help us now, we have chance of finding her. The longer we wait, statistically, the chance…it goes smaller all the time."

Mick stares at Tash, then turns back slowly to his freshly poured drinks.

I'm about to say something but Tash shakes her head. She takes hold of my arm and propels me towards the exit. As we open the door, Mick shouts after us, "File a report at the station. I can't work on it unless it's in a fucking file. Fucking bureaucrash …" and some more slurred mumblings that we can't quite make out.

He's looking at Tash in the mirror behind the barman.

Tash nods her thanks to him and we take our leave.

Once outside I turn to Tash.

"Jesus, I don't know what you did," I say, "but you're going to have to teach me."

She laughs: "I think Michael and I have an unspoken connection. He may not look like it, but he's Nika's best chance of being found alive."

Aoife Sheridan

23

We go straight back to Pearse Street station and file a missing persons report with James, per Mick's instructions. He's delighted to see us, or rather Tash, again. We include some Facebook photos that Tash downloaded and provide a description of Nika's last known movements. We ask James to make sure the report gets to the top of Mick Daly's in-tray. He's happy to oblige.

"You know you're going to have to put that poor fella out of his misery and go out for a drink with him at some stage," I joke, as we're leaving the station.

"He's not my type," she says simply. This brings an involuntary smile to my lips.

Tash drops me back at the office and heads off to "take care of stuff". I'd love to be a fly on the wall in a day in the life of Natasha … but I realise I don't even know her second name.

A text blips on my mobile as I go through the door:

Just spoke to Janet. The IT guy? Who would have thunk it? Solid result. "Team" celebrations sometime soon? … Milo

I send back a quick text saying the cheque is in the post, and add a smiley face, but only at the last minute.

Not long after, there's another text from Milo:

You didn't answer the question? M

He's persistent. I reply:

Team celebrations sound great. Penny very excited. Floss

That should shut him up.

"How did you get on?" asks Penny as I plop myself down on the couch.

"Well, I think we've enlisted the help of an apparently very competent, but decidedly alcoholic missing persons specialist, Mick Daly, and Milo McCarthy is keen to have a team celebration in honour of solving the Trilby case."

"I know what kind of celebrations that Milo McCarthy has in mind and they definitely don't involve me – and probably not your clothes," she says, wagging her finger at me.

I laugh at this and say, "God, it's a sorry state of affairs when you've resorted to finger wagging."

"You may laugh but you know I'm right!" Penny replies with a smile.

"And what if you are? What if he wants to 'clean my pipes'? Somebody has to. Nobody's been near them in a century. I'm at risk of closing up for business down there, due to lack of activity."

"It's not the sex I'm worried about. You know I'd love you to have a good seeing to. I'm married for God's sake! I'm supposed to live my sex life through you. So far this year, even my vicarious sex life is a disaster."

"Well, what are you worried about then?"

"The mess a guy like Milo McCarthy could make of you. I've seen it all before. Remember Ranelagh Romeo?"

"Oh pl-eee-ase. That was five years ago. Let it go already." The train crash she's referring to was my last big love. He was a handsome architect from a well-to-do family in Ranelagh and I was sure he was the man I was destined to marry until I found him in bed with a blonde intern. His intern. My bed. The fallout could have been described as supersonic. In fairness to Penny, herself and Conor bore the brunt of it.

"Be that as it may, it's trust that's the problem. Look at Conor and myself. Rock solid."

"Ehem" I cough dramatically, "might I just ask where Conor thinks you are today?"

"That's different. That's work-life stuff, not relationship stuff."

"Objection, the witness is floundering, your Honour. The prosecution rests."

"You do know what I mean, hon." she asks. "I'm only watching out for your mental health."

"Then help me find Anna! That would go a long way towards making me sane again. Fancy making a house call?"

"I thought you'd never ask."

We drive back to Castlecourt to the house of Larisa Markov and park right out front. No need to play hide and seek today.

"So, how do you want to handle this?" I ask Penny.

"I think we just tell her who we are, but act nice and friendly like she can really help us. Innocent until proven guilty and all that."

"Agreed. Let's go."

We stroll up the overgrown pathway to the front door and ring the bell. We hear footsteps coming down the stairs and a shout of "I'll get it" in a distinctly American twang, before the door is opened by the Asian girl we saw leaving the house yesterday.

"Hi there. We'd like to speak to Larisa Markov," I say in as friendly and polite a manner as I can muster.

"Ok, but if you're selling, we ain't buying," she says cheerfully and opens the door so we can follow her. She directs us into the living-room.

"LARISA! You've got company!" she shouts at the top of her lungs, then leaves us to it. The living-room is a classic shared rental, with a mixture of the cheapest IKEA gear and very old second hand furniture. The TV is the only expensive item in the place. Someone splashed out on it, probably a guy living here.

We hear somebody descending the stairs two at a time. Larisa Markov walks in. She must have been expecting someone else. Her expression changes from eager anticipation to confusion as she catches sight of us. "Who are you?" she asks in a brusque, Russian accent.

"My name is Florence McFarland and this is my colleague, Penny Firth. We are from a company called CTB and we're trying to locate a Russian friend of ours. We think you might be able to help us."

She's instantly on guard, arms folded, in a defensive stance. "I was expecting my boyfriend. I don't know who you are and I think you should leave now."

"Hold on a second, don't you even want to hear who it is we're looking for?" I ask in surprise.

"No. It's none of my business. I would like you to leave now." She extends her arm towards the door like we've forgotten where it is.

"Ok. We're going to leave now like you ask. But the person we're looking for is Anna Durchenko and we believe you spoke to her before she left Russia."

"Please leave now," Larisa says firmly.

Penny and I head towards the door but in the hall I stop: "I'm going to leave my business card here on the hall table. If you think of anything that could help us, please let us know."

She doesn't say a word so we continue on out the door. Penny and I don't speak until we get back to the car.

"Well, what do you think?" I ask Penny.

"Less than helpful!"

"Same. But I'll tell you another thing. She was terrified."

I drop Penny back to her car and head for home, exhausted after an eventful day. I'm too tired to take Leon for a walk, but he seems to have had a rough day himself and is happy to just follow me around the kitchen as I prepare my Supernoodles and his dog gloop. Once he's fed he joins me on the couch. I send a quick reminder text to Penny to get her phone guy to keep an eye on Larisa's mobile for outbound calls after 7pm. If Tash is right, she'll have panicked after our visit and called someone.

At 8pm, my mum calls: "How was your day, dear?"

"Long but good, I think. How about you?"

"Painful. Your Aunt Bridget called around and overstayed her welcome as usual. Plus she had the absolute nerve to comment on my scones not having risen enough. The cheek of her! I'd a good mind to squash one into her face."

"I'd love to see that. I can picture bits of scone hanging off her moustache."

"Don't be unpleasant, darling. You too will understand the vagaries of uncontrollable facial hair one day. It's in our genes."

"Well that's something to look forward to." I say laughing.

"Did you have something nice to eat?"

"Chicken and vegetables," I lie.

"I don't believe it for a second. You wouldn't know where to buy vegetables never mind how to cook them."

"What can I say, it's how you raised me … How's Dad?"

"He's out at mass again in the convent. So peace and quiet reigns here for a short while."

"I'm worried about him and his new religious zealousness."

"I don't know what's come over him but I'm not complaining. It gives me a bit of 'me' time. He's been totally lost since he retired, you know."

"Well, it is tough, Mum. Give him time to come round. In the meantime, enjoy mass time!"

"Oh I will, don't you worry. Night, night, love."

"Night, Mum."

By nine, I'm tucked up in bed. A minute later, I'm fast asleep.

In the morning, I take Leon with me to work. We walk from Irishtown to the quays … 25 minutes at least. At the office car park, I can tell immediately that something isn't quite right. The prefab door looks slightly out of kilter with the frame. Leon bends his ears fully back and tucks his tail between his legs. He's growling to try and make himself look tougher than he's feeling.

I open the door, wishing that Tash, or even Penny, was with me. The door is barely hanging on by the bottom hinge. But that's the least of it: our office has been completely ransacked. Papers everywhere, furniture strewn around – and a disturbing smell of urine. On the back wall, my beautiful Eithne Jordan print has been cast to the floor and in its place are the words, sprayed in huge red letters, Watch your fucking back.

Succinct and punchy.

Leon is still growling, outside the door.

I'm trying to get my mobile out of my purse when I hear a strained moan from behind my desk. I nearly fall over. Leon starts to bark like crazy.

"Who's there? This dog is a trained killer and I'm about to cut him loose," I say, my voice holding up quite well considering I'm planking it.

"Floss?"

It's moaned in a weak, male and distinctively Dublin voice.

I move around the desk. Lying in a crumpled mess behind it is none other than Whacker.

"Holy shit bums! Whacker? What in Christ's name happened to you?" I say trying to help him up.

"Ouch! Fuck. I tink one o' me ribs is brokens. Those fuckers," he says, and he spits blood and saliva onto the floor.

"Less spitting, more talking dude. What happened?"

"Here, help me onto the couch, will ya?"

I lift and drag him slowly to the sofa, and then flick on the kettle, which is thankfully intact. Leon is still growling intermittently.

"Leon, it's ok," I say. "Whacker has just had the shite beaten out of him, so go easy on him, please." Leon comes in and lies on Whacker's feet.

Whacker's just about to start the story when Penny arrives.

"What? … what the hell? …. oh my God!" She staggers around, open-mouthed, then sits on the edge of her desk, in silence.

"Whacker was just about to fill me in. Pull up a pew if you can find a non-smashed one."

I make tea while Whacker starts his story.

"I was on me way home from me girlfriend's. I'd a few jars, but not too many, mind. As I was passin' the car park, I saw the light was on. I thought someone was either acting the maggot or yous two were workin' late. I could hear loads o' noise and smashin', ya know, as I came up to the door, like. I didn't see yer man comin'. Smashed me from behind. I didn't have a chance. He pummelled the shite out of me and then told me to pass on a message to yous."

"What did he say?"

"He said Ms McFarland should read the writing on the wall and stay outta his business."

"Did you see what he looked like?"

"He was the biggest, ugliest fucker I've ever laid eyes on."

"Any more detail?"

"He looked a bit like that guy Jaws out of the Bond movies … Octopussy? Nah … You Only Live Twice?"

"It's bloody Moonraker," I shout, "but I'm not sure that takes us very far."

"Oh, Floss, there's one other thing."

"Yeah?"

"I'm after pissin' meself."

Aoife Sheridan

24

I'm relieved to discover that the stench of urine comes from Whacker rather than the thug who broke in. There's something deeply disturbing and aggressively personal about a person territorially pissing on someone's property.

I make tea, because in Ireland that's what we do in times of crisis. Despite the wrecked office and raging 'eau de Whacker', it does cheer us all up a bit.

"We need to get you to a hospital," I say to Whacker, who is wincing in pain every time he takes a breath.

"Nah, yer alright. They can't do anytin' fer broken ribs and besides, me private insurance isn't exactly up to date, if ya know what I mean."

"We'll foot the bill and they'll give you painkillers at the least. It looks very painful."

"Floss, when it comes to drugs, over or under the counter, Whacker's yer man. I don't need a hospital to get sorted on that front. But ta, all the same."

Penny is looking through the mess: "They didn't take anything from what I can see. Even the petty cash is still sitting in the box. What type of thief leaves laptops and the petty cash?" she asks.

"They weren't thieves, Penny. They just wanted to scare the shite out of us. That sprayed message is a shot across our bows and I'd bet my miniature boobs that it's as a direct result of our house call to Larisa last night. Do you think it's time we handed this case over to the police?" I ask looking at Penny.

"No bloody way. I'm angry now and I really want to nail these guys. Plus, this just confirms we're on the right track, so why stop now?"

"I don't know … safety maybe? You're supposed to be the sensible one, with a family to consider?"

"As far as I'm concerned, if we nab these guys, the streets of Dublin will be a safer place for my kids."

"Ok, but I think I should let Mick Daly know, so that someone in the Garda knows what we're up to."

"Agreed," says Penny.

I text Tash about the break-in and stress its link to our meeting with Larisa. She responds to say she'll be over in fifteen minutes.

Then I call Mick Daly.

"Morning Mick. It's Florence McFarland here. How's the head this morning?"

"Fair to middlin'. I got your missing persons report, if you're ringing to nag."

"That's not why I'm calling. I just wanted to let you know that we had a break-in at our office. It appears to be related to our trafficking investigation. Given that Nika missing might be related to that, I thought you'd want to know."

"Right, right. Where are your offices again?" he asks, sounding decidedly groggy.

I give him the address and he says he'll be over in half an hour.

A few moments later, there's a knock on the door. Leon, who has made a new best friend, stops licking Whacker's hand and starts a low growl.

"Easy tiger," I say to calm him, expecting it to be Tash.

But it's not. It's Milo McCarthy – with lattes and what looks like cake treats.

"Holy shit. What the hell happened here, McFarland?"

"An unhappy client."

"Really?" he asks, incredulous.

"Let's just say we must have set the cat among the pigeons in one of our cases yesterday, and this mess is the result."

"This does not look good, Floss," he says, handing out lattes to Penny and myself. "And who are you, buddy?" he asks, looking distastefully at Whacker.

"A friend o' the family," says Whacker aggressively, probably smelling 'cop' all over Milo.

"Whacker's fine. He's a local. He interrupted them and got the crap beaten out of him."

"Very noble, I'm sure," says Milo, not really taking to Whacker.

"I'll be on my way," says Whacker, slowly raising himself off the couch.

"I'll drop you home," Penny offers.

I'm not sure whether to warn Whacker about Penny's driving. He's been through so much already today.

Once they're gone, Milo says with a twinkle in his eye, "Alone at last." And then: "Is it my imagination or has the stench of piss around here just left the building?"

"Don't be so mean, the poor guy took a serious hiding on our behalf. And he's not a bad sort."

"I bet if I checked his juvy record, it would be as long as my arm."

"He keeps an eye out for me. Look, he's an okay kid and he is just that, a kid."

"I'll take your word for it. So what have you got yourself mixed up in, McFarland?"

I give him a three-minute synopsis of Anna's story. His face takes on a deadly serious expression and his brow is furrowed in thought.

"You've got to let me help you with this. This is not some namby-pamby IT guy stealing a few bits of data. This is proper, violent crime and I don't think you and your partner, no disrespect, are cut out for this type of thing."

"Well, maybe we're branching out!" I say petulantly, my blood beginning to boil. "And besides, we already have outside help on this."

"Oh really? Who? Some hairdresser who has decided to dabble in serious crime investigations?"

There's a knock on the door. Perfect timing! I know it's Tash because Leon is already wagging his tail at the door.

"Speak of the devil," I say to Milo quietly, and then call out: "Come on in."

In walks Tash, looking like a blonde version of Angelina on the set of Tomb Raider. My breath is momentarily caught in my throat. So, it would appear, is Milo's.

Oh here we go, I think to myself. They're going to run off together in alpha male and female heaven and live happily ever after.

"Hey Tash. This is Milo McCarthy. He was helping us on a corporate case."

"Hello again, Natasha," says Milo to my surprise. *Again?*

"Hello, Milo," she says gently.

"Right, you guys know each other?" I ask. *This can't be good.*

"So, this is your outside help?" Milo asks.

"One and the same."

"Well, you're in good hands then. I'd better get going", he says stiffly. Is it my imagination or is Milo struggling to make eye contact with Tash? Not good, possible doubly bad.

"See you, Floss ... Natasha." Another awkward nod.

And Milo McCarthy, man of men, charmer of women and surely not immune to the power of Tash, walks sheepishly out the door.

"Wow, very messy here," says Tash. "I know some specialist cleaners ... they could fix it up in a few hours."

"That would be great. Maybe after Mick Daly's seen it. But back to that little reunion that just happened here a minute ago. ... how do you know Milo McCarthy?"

"We met on a case some years ago. It ended up in big mess."

"What was messy? Your relationship?" I ask, not able to disguise my curiosity and jealousy, yes jealousy. Of both of them. What a match made in heaven they would make. What was I thinking when I thought I could compete at their levels. Tens meet tens, leaving us sevens to scramble around for six to eights.

"No," she laughs. "Not relationship. The case. It was messy. I helped a little. But Milo ... it was difficult for him to be helped by woman. You understand?" she asks looking intently into my eyes.

"Yes. I think so. Well, no actually."

"I think he was bit confused. It was tough time for him."

"A bit more detail?"

"No, it's not for me to say. Maybe Milo will tell you. I see he cares for you."

I laugh. "All Milo McCarthy cares about is which young nymphet he's going to nail next."

"I don't know. He is good guy, I think."

"Whatever you say, Tash. But just be careful that he doesn't have you in his sights."

"I think this is more for you to worry about," she says with a knowing smile.

Penny bursts in: "Dropped Whacker home, but not before we made a stop off at his 'pharmacy'. Looked like enough narcotics to take down an elephant."

"Wow, Pen. You've just done an illicit drug pick-up. The Drug Squad will be scoping out your house."

"That would be one way for Conor to find out about my day job."

Tash turns to me with a questioning look.

"Penny's husband thinks she works at a gallery," I say by way of explanation. Tash just shakes her head and giggles softly.

I hear a car outside and head out to see who it is. It's Mick Daly in an unmarked police car, with a young uniformed garda with him.

"Morning, McFarland," Mick says in his gravelly voice.

"Hiya Mick. Thanks for coming. Who's your friend – and

should he be out without parental supervision?"

The young garda blushes angrily.

"This fine young gentleman is Garda Noel Flynn. Graduated top of his class but, sadly for him, assigned to my care. Noel, meet Floss McFarland."

"Sorry, Noel," I say, "It's been a rough morning so excuse my manners." I offer my hand and he shakes it firmly.

"Noel is going to take some fingerprints and photos," says Mick. You might want to clear out while we're working. And you'll need some industrial cleaners lined up."

"Tash has that sorted. We'll get out of your way."

"Before you go, I'm worried that you're out of your depth here," he says with genuine concern – quite the softie underneath the gruff exterior.

"We've another few leads to pursue before we hand everything over. Plus we have Lithuania's answer to Bruce Lee on our side."

"Ok, but you've been warned."

We take our laptops and head over to my place in our own cars. My lovely, cosy cottage is a welcome relief after the wrecked trailer. I make more tea and scrounge around for something to go with it. Pen and Tash get settled in the lounge. I find some custard creams, whose sell-by date might be questionable, but we give them a shot.

"So, ladies. Where to next?" I ask.

"I thought we were going to do Tash's 'lift and shift' on Larisa?" pipes up Penny.

"After break-in, not a good plan," says Tash. "We need to go quietly. Very quietly. They are angry. We need to let them think they scared us."

"I wouldn't have to pretend too much to convince them," I say. "So, we leave Larisa for the moment. We keep going on Piedr Korsak and the company trail behind the ad?"

"This is all we can do for moment," says Tash.

My mobile rings. It's Derek Keogh.

"Hey Floss. Heard you had a break-in," he says for openers.

"My, my, word does travel fast."

"We're a tight-knit bunch. Listen, I'm calling about the Trilby leaks. Some good news. We've pretty much got the IT guy's hand in the biscuit jar. There was another server where he had a separate email account. There's a full record there of emails to Jane Lord at the Independent. Plus we got a match on the fingerprints on the tray and the bug. We hardly even needed those but it all helps. He's going to be arrested at home this afternoon."

"Well that is good news. Great stuff. Were you in touch with Janet?"

"Yep, she knows where everything stands."

"Ok, great. Thanks, Derek."

"No, thank you, Floss. You make me look good around here. So I owe you one, girl."

"You do indeed, sir. Bye Derek."

The girls are staring intently at Tash's laptop screen.

"Found something?" I ask.

"Just our next step," say Penny, hitting the table dramatically.

"Fill me in."

"You remember the company Tash found in St Petersburg? The one that paid for the newspaper ad?"

"Yeah, it began with a V ...something,"

"That's it," says Tash. Veeva Sporting Company. I've been untangling their web of holding companies, trying to find a link to Dublin. Five layers back is company in Holland called Ootban Holdings. That company owns other Irish company. This company is called Freedom Holdings."

"Bingo fucking bongo!" I shout.

"You know this outfit, Floss?" asks Penny.

"I don't know them, but I do know of them. You've just found a direct link to Little Munchkins crèche!" I pull up the file on my laptop and show them the trail.

"Now that is proper progress," says Penny.

"Good work, Floss," says Tash. I'm beaming.

"Do we have an address for these mofos?" I ask.

We check the Company Registrations Office and only find a PO box, but it's a start. The PO box is in the mail delivery centre on James's Street in the heart of Dublin's Liberties.

Penny gets a call on her mobile. I can tell by her breathless voice that it's good news. She's furiously writing something down. It's all happening today.

She hangs up: "That was my buddy at TelcoWeb. Larisa made two calls straight after our little visit. The first to a Russian mobile number. It didn't connect. The second to the mobile phone of Cecil Reid."

Penny's about to burst with the excitement of it.

"Guess where Cecil Reid works?"

"Freedom fucking Holdings!" I shout.

Penny nods. Tash smiles.

All roads, it seems, lead to Freedom Holdings.

25

The buzz in my lounge is electric. CTB has come of age. It's a real detective agency! No girlie-pretend stuff! Real crime with proper bad guys! And, at last, a few pieces of the puzzle are falling into place. I look over at Penny and I know she's feeling the same thing.

We're both excited. And petrified. Tash on the other hand is her usual, calm self. Whatever she does for a living, she has obviously seen all of this before.

"Ok," I say, "two biggies to follow up: Cecil Reid and Freedom Holdings. Freedom Holdings, like hell!"

"If they are the traffickers, they've got some nerve using that name," says Penny.

"I am not sure that these guys care very much about irony," says Tash quietly.

"Ok," I say, brimming with confidence. "I'm going to check out this Cecil guy and see if he has form as they say in The Wire. Then, we need to start camping outside this PO box on James's Street. Somebody probably picks up postage on a daily basis."

The girls nod. Tash's mobile phone rings. She answers "Da" and then listens intently. Finally, she says "Spasibo, dasvidaniya" and hangs up. "That is my team lead who is watching Larisa's house. She not leave house for two days. They have not seen her at all."

"I hope she's ok," says Penny, ever the mother. "She was scared when we spoke to her. Her call to Cecil Reid might have landed her in trouble."

"My team will keep watching."

"OK, good," I add.

Penny pipes up, "I've done a couple of searches for Cecil Reid. I can see quite a few Cecils on LinkedIn but none of them match up to our guy. I'm guessing he keeps a pretty low profile."

"Let me call Derek," I say, already dialling his mobile. He answers on the first ring.

"Floss! Don't tell me you're calling in your favour already. That would be the quickest turnaround in favour history!"

"I am, but it's a smallie. I need you to check a guy's record. I'd like to know if he's ever popped up on the gardaí's radar."

"No problem, I can whack that into PULSE while we're talking. What's the name?" PULSE stands for Police Using Leading Systems Effectively, the software system that retains all Garda intelligence.

"Cecil Reid. R-E-I-D," I say.

"Okey dokey. Let me see what we've got on him…"

"Yeah, fingers crossed …"

"Right well he has a clean bill of health … no run-ins with the law, not even a parking ticket. Let me just check his known associations … ah, not so squeaky clean here … a known associate of one Vlad Mursky. Let me just check Vlad … whoa! Vlad has been a very bad boy. A list of offences as long as a very long arm. Mainly violent. Assault, robbery and assault, drugs with intent to supply, prostitution … you name it, he's done it. I wonder how this charmer got into the country in the first place."

"Got any mug shots of Comrade Vlad?" I ask.

"Yep. They're not pretty. I'll email them over now."

"Any photos of Cecil Reid?" I ask hopefully.

"Nothing. Sorry Floss."

"Not to worry. Thanks Derek. Love your work!" pleased with the call, I hang up.

Around five minutes later, an email comes through from Derek with two mug shots attached.

I open the files: "Gather round ladies, we could have our first 'staff photo' for Freedom Holdings."

"Holy mother of the sweet divine Jesus. Would you look at the state of this guy," Penny says in horror.

Derek was right. Vlad Mursky is the stuff that horror stories are made of. One ugly son of a very ugly minger. All head and shoulders, no trace of a neck. A Slavic Mike Tyson. His nose has been broken so many times it now sits off to one side of his face. A jagged scar runs down the side of his left eye, leaving a gap in his left eyebrow, adding considerably to the 'full freak' this guy has on the go. Most menacing of all are his blank, lifeless eyes. The human equivalent of a man-eating shark.

"Just the type you'd want to bring home to your mum!" I say, trying to lighten the fear I'm feeling just looking at a picture of this guy.

"Give me a copy," says Penny. "I'm going to run it by Whacker to see if Vlad was the guy that beat the crap out of him."

"Good idea, Pen," I say. "Tash, can I interest you in a stakeout of a Post Office box in the Liberties?"

"Yes, but we will need equipment. I'll drive."

"See you later, Penny. Stay in touch."

I say farewell to Leon and start to lock up but Tash interrupts: "No, bring him. We need him for our cover story when watching the post office." Leon bounds out the door towards my car but quickly redirects when he sees us heading for Tash's Volvo.

As we're pulling out of my driveway, my mobile rings. It's Mick Daly. I put him on speaker phone.

"Howareya, Floss. Mick here."

"Hi Mick. I'm in the car here with Tash. How's it going over there? Anything interesting?"

"Well, apart from the smell of piss, we've got a pile of prints off the usual places like door handles, keyboards, mugs and arms of chairs, but I suspect your guys were wearing gloves. But we also found two listening devices, one in your office phone and the other under your kettle, which would pretty much cover sound for both ends of the trailer. They're not yours by any chance?"

"No."

"Hello Mick. It's Tash here. Can you leave the bugs in their places? We can use them to make guys think we have stopped search because of fear."

"Yes, of course, Tash. But you need to be careful. These guys probably wouldn't think twice about hospitalising three pretty ladies. You know what I mean?" he asks.

"I understand. But I don't mind putting bad guys in hospital either." Tash replies and giggles quietly.

"Ah Tash. For a lovely lookin' young one, you really are quite the bad ass. Just go carefully, the pair o' yis, is all I'm saying."

"Message understood, Mick," I say genuinely. "And thanks for your help. Say thanks to the teenager you have working for you too."

"Ha! The teenager found the bugs. I wouldn't have even thought to look!" he says laughing. "Cheerio, ladies."

"Cheers, Mick," I say and ring off.

I call Penny and explain the plan, telling her to go back to the office after seeing Whacker and call us from the landline, sending a clear message to the bad guys that we've given up the chase.

She's super enthusiastic about our clever ruse.

We're driving along the Grand Canal, just past the Dock. We pull in to a gravel driveway in front of a stylish mock-Georgian mews that blends in with the surrounding houses. Tash jumps out and unlocks the front door. Inside, it resembles a dusty storage facility.

"Wow," I say, "this must be the most expensive storage facility in all of Dublin. Did you never consider some of those rental places off the M50? A lot more cost-effective."

"This is much easier and nearby. Also, some day, I'd like to live here. You haven't seen the best bit."

She beckons me out towards the back through a wide hallway and opens a door on to a beautiful, spacious garden oasis, with red-brick walls covered in thick ivy on three sides. The back wall has a huge archway with a large wooden gate, which presumably opens onto the canal. The garden is completely wild and overrun but even in winter, its potential as a secret hideaway is plain to see.

"Holy shit! This is amazing. You should just buy a tent and live out here. It's stunning. "

"You like it?" she asks shyly.

"Like it? Are you kidding? It's amaze-balls. I mean, I love the penthouse and everything. But this, this is so….alive. It would be such a beautiful place to escape to. Right here in the middle of all the mayhem of Dublin."

"Yes. My penthouse has its own silence and peace, overlooking the city. This is my other escape place."

"Why do you need to escape, Tash?"

"To escape from questions like that," she says laughing. "Now, let's get the stuff."

We gather a small desk, two chairs, some IDs and a bucket for collecting money. She pulls out an iPad and seconds later a printer starts humming behind some free-standing wooden shelves. I go over to pick up the documents. Two of them. One is a Garda permit to make collections at the post office. The second is a sheet of lines where we can take people's names for an alleged raffle. The top prize is a weekend in the presidential suite at the Ritz Carlton in the Powerscourt Gardens in Co Wicklow. We are collecting on behalf of Guide Dogs for the Blind. That, clearly, is why Leon has joined the team. Genius.

By the time we've everything sorted, it's nearly four o'clock. I wonder aloud if it's worth setting up the stake-out at this late stage.

Tash agrees, adding: "Are you hungry?"

"I'm always hungry," I reply. "I spend my life trying to bludge food off other people due to the void that is my fridge."

"I will get us something in good place nearby. You can relax in the side room."

I'm a bit nervous about staying by myself in this dusty old place, even with Leon by my side, but Tash leads me into the side room. It's a loft-style conversion. The back 'wall' is all glass and opens onto the lush garden. It must be a 12-foot high ceiling and there's a mezzanine with double bed, up a wide wooden staircase. The space underneath the mezzanine is occupied by a huge couch and a square foot-rest pouffe. The far wall is lined with bookshelves from top to bottom, except for a small break where there's a kitchenette. The near wall has a table that could just about sit two people.

Compared to Tash's penthouse, this is cosy comfort. Gone are the open spaces and harsher angles. This has 'home' written all over it. A revelation after the front storage area.

"You really are full of surprises and secrets, aren't you, Tash?"

"Part of it is my work. Part of it is me."

"The plot thickens."

"They are both necessary places for me to stay sane. The penthouse is my fortress above city. I feel safe and in control up there, looking down on Dublin. Here is where I truly escape. If I need to lie low, this is where I come. It my bear's den," she says pensively.

"I think I like this space more, although I could probably struggle to survive in the penthouse."

Tash laughs: "Make yourself some tea and I will return with food."

"Yes, ma'am." I give a mock salute. Tash heads out through the front.

I make a cup of tea, then flop onto the couch per Tash's instructions. Leon hops up beside me. I shove him back down.

Just as I'm settling down, I get a text from Penny:

> Whacker says Vlad is the guy who pummelled him. He says he wants another crack at the title … bless him. P

I text back to ask her to call me from the office when she arrives, so we can have our fake call for the benefit of whoever is listening via the bugs. Five minutes later, she rings me.

"Hi Floss, it's me. I just got back to the office."

"Hey Pen, how's it looking over there?"

"Well, everything's trashed and covered in fingerprint powder. Tidiness is not the gardaí's forte."

"God, it'll never be the same," I say. "I feel violated and more than a little scared."

"Me too. I want to talk to you about that, Floss," she says hesitantly.

"Yeah? What's up?" I ask, as if I don't know.

"I think we should probably park this case and go back to the comfortable world of corporate crime. We're in over our heads on this one."

"I'm with you, Pen. I'm over trying to be brave."

Penny whistles a sigh of relief. "Phew, it's a relief to hear you say that." She's very convincing.

"Why don't you head off and have a nice evening with Conor and the nippers? We'll pick up the pieces at the trailer tomorrow."

"Sounds great, Floss. Where are you by the way?"

"I'm over at ..." – I start making noises – "cchhggghhhh ... I think the line's breaking up. See you in the morning."

I hang up before she can reply.

I'm still lolling on the couch when I hear Tash's key in the front door.

Leon bounds over to greet her. I resist the impulse to do the same, aided by the distraction of the delicious scent of Japanese food.

"Yamamori ... Yum! My favourite. You remembered."

"Yes," Tash is the definition of no frills.

"I get some good sake to go with," says Tash.

"Sounds fab, I'll get some plates organised. I'm afraid I'll have to skip the chop sticks. Me in action with them is not a pretty sight. A good solid knife and fork for me all the way," I say rambling away.

We chow down on the most delicious sushi, sashimi and selection of gyoza, washed down with a delicate sake. By the time we're finished, I'm so relaxed I start nodding off.

Tash nudges me: "Why are you always falling asleep on me, Floss? Should I be worried?"

"No, in my case, it's more of a compliment that I feel so relaxed in your company."

"Honestly?"

"I promise, cross my heart and all that."

"Ok. I'll put on some music." She plugs in her iPod. Lykke Li.

"That music is not going to help me with the sleepiness," I say laughing.

"Sorry. Should I change it?" she asks.

"No, no, not at all. I really like her stuff."

We relax for a while, appreciating the ambient music and our full stomachs.

"What do you think our chances are of finding Anna and Nika?" I ask.

"I think for Anna, we are on right track. For Nika, not so sure. I am hoping she has not crossed path of Freedom Holdings."

"Yeah, let's hope she only met some common Irish criminal."

I tell her about Penny and our bogus conversation. "I didn't have to pretend to do the scared part. I'm not as fearless as Penny."

"With me around, you don't need to worry," she says in her quiet, confident way.

"I like you being around." I feel a bit flustered but keep going. "Not just in your capacity as ninja warrior. I ... well ... I like you being around ..."

Before I can regret what I've just said, Tash leans over, takes hold of one of my hands and with the other, gently holds the back of my neck, pulling me towards her. *Oh shit this is really happening.*

My first kiss with a woman is unforgettable. Tash knows how a girl wants to be kissed and I'm immediately swept away on a wave of wild passion mixed with exquisite tenderness. It's as if we've been independently practising the perfect kiss for years in preparation for this moment. There's no awkwardness, just mutual understanding.

This goes on for what seems like an age and a matter of seconds at the same time.

Tash pulls away first, searching my face for my reaction. I probably look dumbfounded, but at the same time I'm smiling from ear to ear.

This is good enough for Tash. She picks me up like a child and carries me straight up to the mezzanine. I can feel the strength of her as she carries me. There's not an ounce of flab in her entire body. I've literally been swept off my feet. But panic starts to set in. *What in God's name am I going to do? Where do I start? Is this it? The moment I cross to the dark side? Does that one spectacular kiss mean I've already gone there? Do I care?*

Tash senses my tension: "No need to be scared. We're just going to share a bed. No funny stuff. I promise." I'm both relieved and disappointed.

She lays me down gently on the bed and proceeds to take all her clothes off, her vivid eyes locked on mine. I can't help but stare. Part shock, part awe. Her physique is airbrushed, Hollywood good.

She laughs. "Stop being so Irish, Floss."

She covers me with the duvet and climbs underneath with me. I hear Leon softly whimpering. I think he wants to join us.

"What do we do now?" I ask.

"Nothing you don't want to do, Floss. How do you feel about spoons?"

"Ecstatic. Can I be the little spoon?"

"But of course," says Tash gallantly.

We settle into a cosy clinch, with Tash snuggled in behind me. I'm still fully dressed and intensely aware of her naked frame against my back. I try to relax but the hands that move around and settle across my stomach are not helping. She starts to move her right hand in slow, concentric circles around my belly button. Each languid circle is slightly larger than the last. My mind starts to race ahead. I know where these circles are heading. My breath quickens with a mixture of nerves and anticipation. I can feel Tash's calm exhalations on my neck, no noticeable change in her. This continues in the same delicious dance, with me holding my breath for what seems like hours. By the time the circular trajectory of her hand glides lightly over my right breast, I nearly pass out with the rush of blood and electricity that zings through every part of my body. I feel as if I will come if she keeps this up for much longer.

With a rush of sudden embarrassment, I cover my face with my hands.

"Hey you," Tash whispers.

I hide behind my hands, trying to gain control of my breathing.

"Are you ok? I promise no more funny stuff."

"I ... well ..." I stammer. "I really like what you're doing, I just don't know what it ... what I ... what we ..."

She takes hold of my hips, flipping me around so I'm facing her, and gently draws my hands down from my face.

"Hey, hello in there," she says, giggling softly. "I do know. It's not problem. Slowly. Slowly." She lifts my chin up and places a light kiss on my lips.

"Time for sleep now, Floss," she adds, rolling me back into our original spoons position.

My heart is still galloping but Tash's strong embrace calms me down. And just like that, I spend my first night with a woman. No messing. I feel protected and pampered. *I could get used to this.*

In the morning, I wake to an empty bed and the smell of strong coffee brewing. Soft music is emanating from the iPod speakers in the form of Breaks Co-Op.

"Morning!" I shout down from the mezzanine.

"Oh hello, sleepyhead!"

It's seven o'clock. Tash looks like she just stepped off the catwalk. She's wearing nothing but an oversized man's shirt. Leon is following her every move in the kitchen.

I check myself out in the mirror along the back wall of the mezzanine. *Oh shit.* When she said sleepyhead, she was not kidding. My hair is completely ridiculous. I look like an Irish version of Cher, suffering from an acid trip and severe humidity.

"Do you have a bobbin, by any chance? I need to get this animal under control," I say, pointing at my hair.

"It looks good. Kind of wild. But I'll get you bobbin before we leave."

"Thanks. The general public is not quite ready for this."

"Can you get Penny to meet us at the post office?" Tash asks. "We will need her and her car."

Did I dream last night? I hope not.

Whatever, we're back on the case.

Aoife Sheridan

26

We get to the post office on James's Street just before 8am. A uniformed postal official is opening up shop as we arrive. He's in his mid-fifties, stocky, with a ruddy complexion that hints strongly at a liking for strong liquor. Unlike most postal workers, he seems to be happy in his job. He's whistling the tune to 'Maybe it's because I'm a Londoner' as he unlocks the dark-green security shutters.

Penny is parked about three spaces away. I see she's wearing her full hooligan outfit today. As she's looking over, I nod subtly in her direction so she knows we've seen her.

Tash and I follow the cheerful chappy into the post office. The space is divided into two main sections, separated by a short entranceway. The section to the left contains the counters and back office; on the right is our area of interest: wall-to-wall PO boxes.

As we agreed in advance, I approach the guy directly.

"Good morning, Marcus," I say reading the name from his name badge. "My name is Margaret Beechwood and this is my colleague Nadia Blinsky. We're here for the annual Guide Dog Collection. Are we ok to set up here in the hallway, so we can catch people coming into both areas of the shop?"

Although I used a tone that implied it was just a formality, he looks mightily confused, but I can sense he's a dog lover by the hand that has involuntarily reached out to stroke Leon. Leon plays him like a pro, nuzzling his snout gently under his hand.

"Erm ... I don't have any note of a collection here on the daily logbook. Beaut of a dog. What type?"

"He's a Leonberger. Don't be scared of his size. He's an absolute softie and I can tell he likes you."

"Jaysus, but he must eat you out of house and home," he says with a big smile.

"No kidding!" I say laughing and trying to butter him up. "He eats more than the average bear and he's fussy with it!"

"I can imagine…" he says, smitten.

Tash hands over her letter of supposed authorisation. I can tell he's now also a Tash lover. His face softens under the weight of her direct eye contact. Been there, buddy.

"This letter gives you all you need for your logbook. If there's problem, you dial number at bottom of letter," says Tash. It's our office line, but we're not expecting him to ring; if he does, he'll be auto-forwarded to Penny's mobile so she can cover us.

"Eh … grand so. I'll just make a note in the book and take a copy of that letter. if that's alright."

"No problem, Marcus," says Tash with one of her trademark, dazzling smiles.

"Can I get yiz a cup o' tea?" he asks now the formalities are over.

"That'd be lovely. We brought biscuits."

"Sound," he says and heads out the back.

We set up our desk, chairs and collection bucket, and position Leon out front. Tash ducks into the room with the post boxes and quickly finds and points out the Freedom Holdings box to me so we know which one to keep a close eye on.

Marcus comes back with the tea.

"Ah, you're a honey, Marcus. Thanks for this. Here, take a

couple of fig rolls for yourself. We've loads," I say handing over the packet of biscuits.

"Thanks Margaret. They're me favs," he says, taking two.

"Don't let us get in your way. We're all set here," I say in my most cheerful voice possible.

He nods at this and heads back in about his business.

The morning is slow; few visitors go through to the post boxes. But we make a packet of money. The combination of Leon and Tash works wonders. I act as 'the bank' in the background.

Around quarter to ten, a young African woman approaches box 4877, right next to the Freedom Holdings. I get a text from Tash two seconds later:

> Your eyes nearly pop out of head when she opens box. Be cool.

I nod in her direction with a slight smile. She really is a lot better at this stuff.

At 12 noon on the dot, the door opens. We somehow know immediately that this is our guy. Perhaps it's the flashy suit that is blatantly failing to camouflage his tough-guy looks. Tattoos peep out from under his sharply cuff-linked wrists.

He breezes past us and makes a beeline for PO box 4876. *Bingo bongo.*

I text Penny under the table:

> We are in motion. Sharp, shiny grey suit, Raybans and receding hairline. Think Jack Nicholson but nastier.

As he passes us with the day's collection of post and parcels, he nods and says a polite "Howareya ladies" in a sharp Dublin brogue. The plan is for Penny to follow him and for us to follow her in case she gets spotted.

I run next door and knock on the glass at Marcus's window. "Emergency back at the office! We'll hopefully be back later. Thanks for the tea!"

We're out the door just in time to see a black, four-wheel-drive Mercedes with tinted windows ease away from the curb. Penny pulls out into the traffic, keeping two cars between them. Not even a glance our way as she passes us. Well done Penny.

Tash, Leon and I jump into the Volvo. We move out quickly into the traffic, with Penny in our sights. We head along James's Street, down past Christchurch Cathedral and over the bridge to the northside of the River Liffey, heading down the quays towards O'Connell Bridge.

"God, I wish we could see through those bloody windows," I say.

Penny calls. "He's stopping at the Bridge Pub. I'm going to sail on by. Over to you guys now. I'll pull in at the taxi rank on the far side of O'Connell Street and wait for you there. I'll keep you on speakerphone."

We pull in about twenty metres short of the Bridge Pub. The Merc's parked just beside it. The driver door opens and Vlad Mursky himself steps out. He's larger and far more scary in real life. The mug shots must have snapped his good side.

"Holy fucking moly. If it isn't Vlad the Bad Ass."

He moves around to the rear passenger door on the pavement side and opens it. Our slick-suited guy from the post office steps out and heads into the bar with Vlad in tow. They look like a greyhound and a bull mastiff in convoy.

"I'm willing to bet a large sum of money that Flash Harry there is none other than Cecil Reid. What do you think?" I ask.

"I think you're right."

About five minutes pass, they re-emerge, squinting in the sunlight. Tash is shooting away with her bazooka-like camera.

"Smile you bastard," she says under her breath.

Vlad is carrying a brown paper bag in his right hand. "Is that a packed lunch or cold, hard cash, do you think?" I say.

"Protection money," replies Tash.

I speak to Penny on the mobile. "They're on the move. Be on your toes."

We give them a bit of space, keeping about four car lengths behind. We move at a steady pace along the quays, around by the Custom House and Busáras bus station. On Amiens Street, they stop at a laundromat. We cruise on past as Penny moves in behind us and parks a safe distance from the Merc.

"Tag. You're it, Pen," I say into the phone.

We repeat this alternating procedure at two more city-centre pubs and a newsagent's. Then we move north out of the city, with Tash and me on the trail of the Merc. I start to get excited that we might be heading for Little Munchkins crèche, but the car pulls in suddenly into St Ignatius Convent off Mount Prospect Avenue in Clontarf. We can't follow without calling attention to ourselves. We park along the road nearby. A few minutes later Penny tucks in behind us. She gets out and comes up to my window.

"Getting some form of holy blessing?" she suggests.

"Wholly unlikely. Why don't you have a look through the railings over there by the bus stop," I say. "We'll stay back here in case they recognise us from the post office."

A minute later, she calls on her mobile: "The skinny guy's heading to the front door … someone's answered … looks like Sister Agatha from here. Right, he's gone in. Vlad is doing sentry duty at the door."

"Cool. Now, look in the direction the buses come from and check the timetable every now and then." Tash nods approval of my suggestion. I smile to myself. Yes! I'm getting better at this.

"On it," says Penny at the other end.

At least fifteen minutes later Penny calls again: "Ok, he's out and back in the car. Do you pair want to follow first?"

"Sounds good. Did he have anything in his hand when he came out?"

"No, empty-handed."

"So, no protection money there. Interesting," I say.

She rings off. I turn to Tash and say, "They're on their way and we're up next."

She just nods calmly and starts the car.

"I wonder what the hell they were doing in there. They could both do with a good confession," I say. "We can drop in at a later date to visit Sister Agatha. She's the head nun there."

After Penny and I left primary school we graduated to St Ignatius all-girl convent school. It was a bit of a shock to the system to go from a 100 pupil mixed environment to a 1000 plus affair. We both have mixed but generally positive memories of the place.

"Ok, here they come," says Tash.

The Merc pulls out slowly and heads towards the Howth Road.

We follow at a safe distance. As we pull onto Collins Avenue, I know exactly where they're going. "Boom!" I can't help shouting. "First definite connection to Larisa and the crèche. In the bag. Yes!"

"Let's pull in before they do," suggests Tash. "I want to get photo."

She puts her camera in burst mode to take shots in quick succession, capturing the car, registration plate and the two men on their way to the crèche – but Vlad alone gets out this time. He rings the doorbell and one of the uniformed crèche workers answers. She goes back inside while Vlad remains on the doorstep.

A few minutes later the pale face of Larisa appears at the front door. I can hear the rapid-fire clicks of Tash's camera throughout.

The conversation is short with Larisa mainly shaking her head, and saying little. Another warning perhaps? It's all over in a minute and Vlad heads back to the driver side of the Merc. "Ok Penny, your turn," I say into my mouthpiece.

After another stop to pick up coffee and snacks, they head back towards the city, eventually pulling up outside a terraced four-storey house, on the North Circular Road, which looks the worse for wear.

We pull in at a safe distance behind Penny. Both Vlad and Cecil get out this time. Penny suddenly jumps into the back seat of our car. "Well, that's the most excitement I've had in a long time. A proper trail and stakeout. A-mazing!"

"This could be where the girls are kept," Tash says, pulling out her iPad. She has all the cool gadgets.

Tash enters the address. "It's coming up in the White Pages

only. Listing is for a Mary Donergan. It must only be residence."

"Or a brothel filled with trafficked girls?" asks Penny.

"God, do you think so? You could be right," I say feeling slightly intimidated by the prospect of sitting outside a real live brothel.

"And there's only one way to find out."

Oh no. She's got her determined look on her face. "Which is?" I ask nervously.

"We break in."

I find myself shaking my head and turn to Tash for moral support in resisting Penny's madness, but she's is nodding in agreement. "Tonight," she says without batting an eyelid.

O to the M to the Oh my God. We are about to be highly illegal.

27

It's 10pm. We're all back in Tash's car in front of 99 North Circular Road. Is this the hub of our Russian trafficking network? The house looks decidedly threatening in the half moonlight that sneaks out every now and then from behind the clouds.

Tash and Penny are chowing down on Mickey Ds and I'm busy chewing through what's left of my nails. The thought of committing a major felony pretty much kills my appetite. They're scoffing away like they're out for a summer's day picnic. At this moment I hate them both – Penny for her adrenaline-junkie-fuelled excitement and Tash for her absolute and unnerving calm. I'm busy berating myself for the fear that is running riot throughout my body. The nails are just the start of it. My bowels are in flitters.

We split up earlier in the evening to get kitted out for our break-in and to allow Penny time to nip home to put the kids to bed. Conor thinks she's out at her book club. He still hasn't noticed that the club have been reading the same book for roughly six months.

Now, in the car, we all look ready to paint the town red: plastered with make-up, mashed into slinky cocktail dresses and death-defying heels. I was disappointed not to be dressing in commando gear, and blackening my face with burnt cork, but when Tash explained the game plan, I couldn't argue with it. Three allegedly pissed gals, on their way back from a boozy office night out, would cause a lot less suspicion than black-clad-burglar-lookalikes. Better plan.

Penny looks like a housewife moonlighting as a hooker, Tash like this year's Miss Lithuania, and me like a fish out of water – I haven't been this dressed up since the Belvedere debs in my last year of secondary school. I've let my hair run riot for the occasion and have thus been relegated to the back seat. My hair just takes up too much space.

One of Tash's team watched the place while we were getting ready and reported that Cecil and Vlad, or Neander Man as we now call him, left the building at 9.28pm and went to Chapter One restaurant. They may be trafficking thugs, but they've got good taste.

Penny and I are both looking to Tash, the alpha female in our pack, to lead us. "Ok," says Tash. "I hope everyone ok. My team watch them, so we know if leave early. There are three floors in house. Floss takes top floor." I nod, trying to look confident. I'm petrified.

"Penny, for you, is first floor." Penny is almost half way out the door with the excitement.

"Wait!" says Tash, stopping Penny in her tracks. "I take ground floor. This way, I meet bad guys first. Ok?"

Now I'm nodding enthusiastically. And, in the back of my mind, I register that I'm on the top floor to both keep me out of harm's way and because I'm completely useless.

"Remember. Girls on night out. Having good time. Very drunk, very happy."

"Drunk, I can do," I say, feeling confident for the first time.

Penny takes out a naggin of Paddy whiskey, dabs some of it on her neck and wrists like perfume and passes it to Tash.

"Delicious, eau de whiskey," I say.

"Don't mind her," says Penny, "it's just the nerves. She prattles on when under pressure."

I give Penny the filthiest look I can muster via the rear-view mirror, but she just passes the whisky bottle back without looking. Tash hands Penny a half-full bottle of quite expensive wine and me a bottle of Bulmers, while holding an empty wine glass herself.

"Great, I get the cider. It's like being a teenager at the back of the Grove disco all over again," I moan from the back.

"Swapsy?" Penny offers.

"Nah, you're alright," I reply.

Tash is looking on with a look of vague amusement.

"Finished?" she asks.

"Yes," chime Penny and I in unison, feeling suitably reprimanded.

"Ok, let's go," says Tash.

And in seconds, we are out on the pavement in full character. Anyone looking at us would think we are at the end of what had started out around lunchtime. I become the natural leader as 'world's most blotto bird' as Tash and Pen wobble along on either side of me, providing highly unstable support. I'm intensely aware of Tash's firm grip on my arm.

"Could ya believe the state of your man at the door?" says Penny starting us off.

"He take my last cigarette," Tash adds.

"Sure, like, ach …blurrrrrshhhh," I contribute.

"He tried to pinch me arse," says Penny. "I said … that's a married arse you're grabbing there, mister, mister. I'll get me husband after you."

"He was too drunk to be scared," replies Tash.

"Aargh ..." Another one of my insights.

And we continue on in this vein until we reach the front door of Cecil's place. At this point, Tash starts mumbling about her keys. She's teetering about on her high heels, looking vulnerable for the first time ever. But there is nothing vulnerable about what she is doing. She's mooching about in her handbag with one hand, but her other hand is furiously working with a set of skeleton keys on the front-door lock. I'm looking on in awe, completely forgetting to be loud and intoxicated, when we hear the lock click and the heavy wooden door opens slightly. It took her just five seconds.

"Hooray! Drrrrrrink! Feck! Girrrrls!" I shout, getting back into character while also doing my best Father Jack impression.

We sneak inside and shut the door. Tash takes off her heels and nods to us to do the same. "Hurry!" she whispers, already moving off to investigate the ground floor. Penny and I sprint up the first flight of stairs. I continue to the second floor, my heart pounding like a base drum in my chest. It's so loud, I'm sure Penny can hear it below.

There are four doors off the landing, one straight in front of the stairs, two to the right and one behind the stairway, which must be the room facing onto the street. I try the first door. It's a bathroom which has not seen a cleaner's hand in some time. The stench would make a public urinal seem like a perfume shop. The bath is filled with dirty clothes and rusted gardening equipment. No female attire, just old-man gear all the way. Dodgy M&S cardigans, woollen tank tops and greying y-fronts. *Delightful.*

I move on to the next room. A dump room – purgatory for home furnishings. Lots of retired old furniture that hasn't made it yet to the scrapyard. I root around, looking for any stored papers or files in drawers. Nothing, not even a scrap of paper.

The next room looks like a replica of my Granny Eithne's old guest-room in her house in Finglas: two twin beds, Ernie and Bert style, with proper woollen blankets rather than duners. A dark, wooden dresser and matching wardrobe. Dust everywhere. I suspect the room hasn't welcomed a guest in many years. The drawers are all empty, except for some lavender sachets. The wardrobe contains the dresses of an obviously elderly lady and shoes: square-toed, brown leather, with sensible square heels.

No sign that says 'captive young foreign girls here!'

I move to the last room, behind the staircase. The door's locked. I knock and say quietly, "Is there anyone there?" Silence. I move to the bannisters and lean over, whisper-shouting: "Hey Tash. I need your door-opening skills up here." I hear a faint "ok" from two floors down.

I'm just about to turn back to the door when my mobile phone rings shrilly (the great detective forgot to put it in vibrate mode!). I nearly jump out of my skin. It's my mother. Perfect timing.

"Jesus, Mum. You scared the living shit out of me."

"Florence Maria McFarland. Do NOT use that language with me." In an instant, I've been transformed from glamorous cat burglar to small child. My mother can undo me with a single sentence.

"Sorry, Mum. I'm just on a bit of a stealth mission here and wasn't ready for my phone to ring."

"If it's so stealth, why is your phone on?"

"Good point. You have me there."

"I'm worried about your father ..." she starts, off on one of her rants.

"Mum, I can't really talk now ... I'll drop into you tomorrow, ok? Talk in the morning." I hang up the phone before she can get in another word. I can feel the Irish guilts rampaging through my subconscious.

I'm about to call her back, when I hear "Hey!"

I swivel around. "Fuckidity duckitidy fuck!" I bleat, my hand on my heart. "Why is everyone trying to scare the absolute shite out of me today? My nerves are in rag order as it stands."

It's Tash, who has done one of her bi-location tricks. Those stairs creaked like an old ship for me and yet I didn't hear a thing as she came upstairs.

"Did Scottie beam you up here or something?" I ask, still recovering from the shock. She looks confusedly at me. The Star Trek reference was obviously lost in translation. She reaches out her hand and places it over my hand on my chest. Deliciously sensuous. And my nerves are instantly soothed.

"This door?" she asks, removing her hand.

"Yep, it's the only one that's locked. There's nothing in the other rooms but remnants of old people. Zero hint of brothel or young girls anywhere."

"Downstairs I found some mail with Cecil and Europa Holdings, so we are in right place. Just maybe not absolute right place."

She starts working the door. It succumbs to her will in seconds. With her combination of beauty and ferocious strength, nothing resists her: man, woman, animal, or metal object ...

I hold my breath as she opens the door. It's a small box room with a single, military-style bunk in the corner, a washbasin under the window and, along the back wall, sits a cheap IKEA wardrobe that's meant to look vintage. The room is tidy and definitely lived in.

I'm convinced we've found a holding cell for a single girl on her arrival from abroad, but Tash opens the wardrobe – the clothes are all black and in off-the-scale, giant size. They can only belong to one person.

"Neander Man?" I say.

"I'd say so," says Penny from behind, causing me to jump yet again.

"Ok, everyone needs to announce their arrival in advance. My nerves can't handle all this sneaking around."

"I think enough excitement for one night. We have what we need here," says Tash.

"What's in the pink box?" asks Penny, pointing at a medium-sized, puce-pink cardboard packing box in the base of the wardrobe, partly covered by the hanging trousers.

I bend down and pull the box out. It's light. The label reads 'Frills and Thrills – for your Loving Pleasure'.

"Who's a naughty Vlad then?" I say, opening the lid. The box is crammed with dildos and sets of fur-lined handcuffs.

"The bloody pervert," says Penny. She hates this sort of thing.

"Ok," says Tash. "Not prove it's brothel here. Only prove that

Vlad like sex toys. Let's go."

We descend the stairs and head out the front door in the same style we came in. Loud, drunk and disorderly. We zigzag our way back to Tash's car and jump in. If anyone was watching us they would be forgiven for calling the cops to report a drunk driver. We don't hang around.

We drop Penny home first, still buzzing from the break-in. "Thanks Tash," she says as she gets out. "I don't think I'll be able to sleep tonight after all that excitement. Bloody brilliant! Thanks again."

She runs up to the front door and waves as she heads inside.

"Your place?" Tash asks me.

"Yes, please. I need to have some Leon cuddle time to calm me down."

"Nothing I can help you with?" she asks cheekily.

"To be honest, Tash, between breaking into a house and spending the night with a woman, both first time events in my life, I might add, I think I could do with a bit of head space to figure what the hell is going on with me at the moment."

"No problem", she says brightly, but I can tell she's disappointed.

"I'm sorry, Tash. My head works like an actuary's, you know? Logical and boxed off. Everything has to be balanced and accounted for. This?" I say pointing at us both, "this is the opposite of balance. But all this is rollercoaster followed by free-fall with no bungee cord. My mind feels as if it's been cut loose."

"Sometimes this is not bad thing, no? This cutting loose?" she says, smiling.

"For some, maybe. Penny for example. But me? I don't know if I'm cut out for this stuff."

"I think you have potential. With some training, you could be very good!"

"Which? At being a detective or a lesbian?" I say, genuinely curious.

"Maybe both," she says with a giggle.

We are silent on the drive to my place, both of us lost in our private thoughts. My head is about to split in two. I'm torn between wanting to jump into her lap and diving out the door of the moving car. The furore in my head must be audible.

We pull up in front of my house and I can feel Tash immediately tense up. There's the outline of a dark shadow sitting on my doorstep. She puts her hand protectively across me, indicating I should stay put. She's about to get out of the car when the shape moves out into the light of the streetlamp.

It's Milo McCarthy, bottle of wine in hand.

Aoife Sheridan

28

Seeing Milo McCarthy fails to settle the tornado of thoughts that is whirling between my ears. The combination of flattery and raw attraction makes my heart skip a beat, but Tash is right beside me. I desperately do not want her to think there is something between Milo and me.

I turn to Tash to begin trying to explain why Milo is sitting outside my doorstep just before midnight. But it's pointless. What guy loiters in front of a girl's house late at night, with a bottle of wine, thinking merely friendly thoughts?

"I see you tomorrow, Floss. You were very good tonight," she says. Her tone is icy, like a coach giving a kid obligatory feedback after a game they're both gutted they lost.

"Look, Tash, I don't know …" I begin.

"You have company. I need to get back to working." She revs her engine slightly to reinforce her message.

"Ok, but just so you know, it's unsolicited company, ok?"

She just nods. I get slowly out of the car, a bit wobbly on my high heels, feeling frustrated and sad at something that is beyond my control. The car door isn't even closed before she starts reversing quickly down my short driveway. I stare after her for a while, wondering if I should call her mobile immediately.

"Hope I'm not interrupting anything?" asks Milo from the steps, a mixture of sarcasm and curiosity in his voice. As I turn around, my Milo-meter has gone to the 'knee him in the nads' end of the scale. *Infuriating.*

"What? Tash? No, she's just helping us with a case," I say, trying to sound casual.

"I can go if you like? I know it's a bit late, but I just thought we should celebrate the Trilby case ... you look like you're already dressed for the occasion."

"What's in the bottle?"

"The finest Chardonnay Dunnes Stores has to offer."

"You'd better come in then." He's done his research. The least I can do is be polite. Plus, I need some alcohol to still the commotion in my mind. If I can't clear the confusion, I might as well just pickle it.

I unlock the front door and turn off the alarm. Leon barks like crazy from the kitchen. I open the door and he's all over me. Bless him, he's been alone all day and he still just wants to love me. Why can't all relationships be this simple? Unconditional love.

But Leon then catches a whiff of Milo. He drops down on all fours and lets out a low growl.

"Hey buddy," says Milo, reaching out a hand, which agitates Leon even more.

"I wouldn't put your hand out like that if I was you. Leon hasn't been fed ... Easy, fella, Milo is ok. He's one of the good guys." Leon stops growling but sits down defensively in front of me, keeping a watchful eye on Milo.

"Is he like this with everyone?" Milo asks.

"No, funnily enough, just with you."

"What about with Tash?" he asks, ever the detective.

"He absolutely adores Tash."

"Doesn't everyone?" he says, leaving me wondering again how they really know each other.

"How about that glass of wine?" I ask, keen to change the subject. We move into the kitchen. I fish out two clean-ish glasses and a wine opener, and then a tin of dog meat and a fresh water bowl.

As Leon forgets his protection duties and starts wolfing down his grub noisily, we assume our positions at the breakfast bar. Milo hands me a generous glass of wine and raises his own.

"To ... us?" he asks tentatively.

"To a solid team effort," I reply. We clink glasses and I take a very large gulp to steady myself.

"Mmmmm...that's exactly what I needed. You did well," I say.

"High praise. I really have to work hard for the compliments from you, Floss," he says, smirking.

"I can imagine you're more used to women draping themselves all over you."

"Actually, yes I am. But lately, the shine seems to have worn off the whole flirtation game. I find myself permanently distracted ..."

Holy fucking moly. Is Milo McCarthy, stud muffin extraordinaire, going to proclaim his undying love for me?

Two more large chugs of wine for me. He tops it up attentively. Another large gulp.

"I'm kind of scared to ask the obvious question as to what has you so distracted? Which is what you want me to ask, right?" I say, surprised by my own directness.

"You see? That's exactly what I mean." He's pretty animated

and borderline shouting. Leon looks at Milo as if to say 'I don't like your tone' mixed with 'where are you going with this, dude?'

"I'm not following you," I say.

"If I went out on a limb like that with any other girl, they'd be jumping at the chance." I laugh out loud and add an eye-roll. "But you ... you just seem to be immune. And there's this constant feeling of you seeing right through me and laughing. Always the laughing ... not with me, but at me."

God help me, I can't help but feel sorry for him at this point. Here is a man who has spent most of his life getting whatever he wants. He's not used to women armed with Milo McCarthy antibodies. But, at the same time, he's not scared to show his frustration and vulnerability. It makes him instantly more appealing. The Milo-ometer is wavering back from 'warm' to 'hot'.

"Milo McCarthy. First of all, I'm a woman, not a girl. Secondly, you're the guy that every mother warns their daughters about. I've been trained to repel overtures from your type since I realised there was such a thing as hot boys. And thirdly, you're probably only attracted to be because I don't do what the other girls do."

"I'm sorry, all I heard is that you think I'm a hot boy?" he asks, both eyebrows raised.

I can't help laughing, feeling giddy all of a sudden. That's what you get for trying to be honest with a guy who really is just on the make.

He starts laughing too and we both start giggling uncontrollably. Then he suddenly reaches out, grabs my hand and gives me a look that simply says, "Well? How about it, sweetheart?"

A thousand thoughts and possibilities rush through my head in the space of a second. What would be the harm? Wouldn't it help me get over this weird Tash thing? Why not throw myself at the manliest man in the stratosphere? Fight an alpha female with an alpha male? Problem solved? But what if Tash found out? I'd hate that. But what do I want to happen? That is the question ...

Milo can sense the indecision run through me. Like the proper hunter he is, he knows his prey has momentarily let its guard down. It's all the encouragement he needs. The hand that holds mine pulls me forcefully to him and I'm instantly lost in the most delectable kiss. All man: subtle aftershave, day-old stubble, an urgency that makes his intentions abundantly clear. My body is responding to him before I know what's happening. He starts edging me toward the couch, using his hips for steering. I grapple with the buttons of his shirt and help him pull it down and off over those sculpted biceps. Leon lets out a resigned whimper and lies down in a corner.

As Milo lowers me gently onto the couch, I can feel the sheer strength in his arms. *God, I really want this.* He kneels in front of me, easing himself gently between my legs, lips never leaving mine the entire time. His hands are gently supporting my neck before one of them breaks away and begins to move determinedly southwards. I let out a moan as his hand firmly cups my breast. I've dreamt about this moment for a long time without ever admitting it to myself. He groans in response and I can feel his breathing shorten. I want to urge him on, feeling the need to be properly nailed (yes nailed!) by a real man. This is the medicine I've been seeking to put me right again. I fumble with his t-shirt, trying to pull it up and off him. He helps me get it off and then focuses all his attention back on my breasts, his mouth brushing them through the fabric of my dress. His hands now move slowly down over my stomach and hips, his fingers fluttering over Zelda. After suffering from months and months of neglect, Zelda is already on fire. His touch nearly sends me over the edge. He has the end of my dress in his hands and begins to raise it slowly upwards. Just as I'm about to start helping him, my front doorbell rings shrilly.

I hear myself saying "don't stop". *God, did I really say that out loud?* I have turned into a sex-starved maniac.

But Milo has indeed stopped.

"More gentlemen or gentle-lady callers at this late hour?"

I shake my head. "Mormons, maybe? Just ignore it."

Milo pulls away from me. He heads out towards the door with an equally curious Leon in tow.

Fuck it. The spell is broken.

"Use the peephole," I shout and struggle up off the couch, straightening myself and following him out into the hall. When I get there he's looking through the small, glass window to the outside world.

"There's a boy outside sporting very large glasses." I can hear the relief in his voice.

"What!?" I decide to look for myself. It's Jeremy, Boy Wonder, on my doorstep.

"Jeremy?" I ask out loud opening the door.

"Jeremy?" asks Milo, as if to say "Who the fuck is Jeremy?"

As I open the door, Jeremy says, "Hey Floss. Sorry to call around so late at night." He glances briefly at Milo, who is standing brazenly in his bare chest and jeans.

"Does your mother know you're out? And how do you know where I live?" I ask, going into maternal and paranoid mode simultaneously.

"My folks are away and my granny is looking after us. She's deaf as a post, so I can come and go as I please after she's gone to bed," he says shrugging his shoulders.

"Ok, sounds plausible, and my address?"

"What can I say? It's what I do for a living," he says smugly.

"Right. Of course. Well, come in quickly before the neighbours start talking." My neighbour Betty would not have seen this much action at my house since ... well, since never!

"No, I've got another job to do. I just wanted to give you this," he says, handing me a flimsy piece of paper covered with dense, tiny print. It looks like it's been downloaded directly from the Matrix. I try to make sense of it, but the residual fire in my groin seems to have temporarily numbed my brain.

"What am I looking at here, Jeremy?"

"Your Russian buddy with the girls ... Piedr Korsak? He's on the move again. He's booked to arrive in Dublin tomorrow afternoon at 2.15 and he's got two female travel companions. Terminal 2. Flight number's there for you. Thought you'd like to know."

He jumps on his BMX, which is stashed just to the right of the door, and is gone before I can say thank you.

I turn to Milo who has been watching with mild amusement. "I can't help feeling that I've been upstaged by young Einstein there." He's chuckling but I can hear the regret in his voice.

"I'm really sorry, Milo. But this is just the break we've been waiting for. Piedr Korsak is the guy who is bringing in the girls from St Petersburg. It looks as if we just hit the jackpot."

"Be careful what you wish for, Floss. These guys will be dangerous. I know I've said it before, but this is the real deal. Any chance you're in over your head?"

"Any chance? Every chance! We're in way over our heads but we can't stop now. We're almost there. I really, really want to get these guys."

"At least let me help you."

I swallow my pride and utter a meek 'yes'. Back in the living room he puts on his t-shirt. I realise, with regret, that our little moment of escapism has come to an end.

"Coffee?" I ask as I flick on the kettle.

"Cup of tea for me".

"We're going to need everyone on this," I say more to myself.

"Tash included," Milo says. I look at him. No hidden meaning. His face shows total concentration. He's in the zone now, miles away.

I send two texts, one each to Penny and Tash, explaining Jeremy's discovery and that we'll need everyone on deck tomorrow. Despite the late hour, I get responses almost immediately:

> No way?! St Francis and all his poor scholars. We are detective genii! ;-) I won't be able to sleep a wink at the mere thought of tomorrow. Well done! Pen xx

Penny, fearless as ever. And then Tash:

> Good. Talk tomorrow. T

Tash, warm and gushing as ever. Looks like I've a bit of repair work to do there. Is she jealous or is there something more going on here that I don't understand? Some history between Milo and her is complicating this weird triangle even further.

Milo is back at the breakfast bar, sipping on his tea, slightly slumped and looking deflated.

"You and Tash," I say. He straightens up. "Remind me how you two know each other?"

"We worked together a long time ago," he says guardedly.

"If I know you and your 'working relationships' with the ladies, I can only imagine the rest."

"It was strictly business, I assure you. I don't hit on every attractive bit of skirt, you know."

"Bit of skirt? Really?" I say horrified to think of any woman, never mind Tash, being referred to as a bit of skirt.

"Sorry, every attractive woman," he says slowly, with a touch of petulance.

"Ok, so what type of business?"

"She was consulting to the force back then ... look, let's make a plan. It's been an eventful day and I'm pretty stuffed."

"You're right. Sorry," I say, re-focusing.

We stay up for another hour, me filling him in on the details of the case and what we've been up to. He's blown away by us breaking into Cecil Reid's place, but I can tell he's quietly impressed.

We make a simple plan. Penny and I will stick with trailing Cecil Reid, while Milo and Tash follow Piedr Korsak from the airport. I'd rather split them up – would be better to have a trained professional each with Penny and me – but we agree that Comrade Korsak is likely to be on high alert as he departs the airport. Better to leave him in the care of people who know what they are doing.

Milo gets up. "We should both get some rest before tomorrow. I'd better get going."

"Of course. Right, right," I say, trying to hide my disappointment.

He gets his jacket and I walk him to the front door. As he leaves, he puts one hand on my hip, using the other to tilt my chin up towards him. He kisses me lightly on the lips and then he's gone.

I close the door and turn to Leon who has come out to make sure Milo has actually left.

"Alone again."

29

I hardly sleep a wink. When I do, I'm plagued with disturbing dreams – which elude my memory upon waking. By 7am, I'm showered and dressed, having already taken Leon for his daily constitutional.

I munch on some Sugar Puffs and a strong coffee while I go over the plan again in my head. Tash and Milo will take the airport run and follow Piedr Korsak and the girls wherever they go. Hopefully, this leads us to the house where the girls are kept. In the meantime, Penny and I will stick with Cecil Reid and his offsider, Neander Man. We're to stay in mobile contact at all times and regroup at the end of the day wherever the girls end up. At that stage, the plan is to make a new plan.

I've put on my Esprit combat pants, along with some grey runners and a black, tight-knit jumper. I'm ready to kick ass. I'm a big believer in dressing for confidence. Today, I need to feel like a Marine. This is the closest outfit I've got.

At 7.30, I can't wait any longer. I drive straight over to Penny's, having texted her my estimated time of arrival. A few minutes after I park nearby, she emerges in a grey woollen trouser suit. She looks like she could be off to the races – if it was 1967! She has a sizeable backpack slung over one shoulder, which I assume has her change of outfit.

"Morning, sport!" She jumps in.

"Hey Pen. How are you doing?"

"Brilliant. I can't believe how close we are to catching these guys. I'm about to burst!"

"Alright, alright, keep your knickers on. We've actually got the duller side of the deal today," and I run her through our plan of attack.

"But Christ Almighty, Floss. Watching Cecil is like watching paint dry. You'd see more action in an old folks' home."

"I know, but talking to Milo last night, I realised we might not be cut out for the high stakes stuff."

"Hold on a second. Roll back there a minute. What happened with Milo last night?"

"Nothing. An impromptu drive by ... and maybe some light petting," I say sheepishly, the colour rising in my face.

"Florence McFarland, you dirty stop-out. You're playing with fire there, you know."

"I know. He's exactly the guy you're supposed to run a mile from ... but he did all the running in my direction. I just got a little carried away in the heat of the moment. He is very ... persuasive."

"Sweet Divine Jesus. I'm getting hot flushes just listening to you. Don't say you haven't been warned. It'll be little old Penny picking up the pieces of Floss after what is guaranteed to be a train crash."

"Nothing happened, Pen."

"Yeah but ... oh shag it. Let's get out of here."

As we pull away from the curb I can see Conor and the kids waving from the front room. I nudge Penny and she just manages to wave in the nick of time.

We head straight for Cecil's place on the North Circular Road. Penny crawls into the back seat and gets into her now standard hoodlum outfit. By the time we arrive, she has transformed from middle-aged gallery receptionist to hooded vagabond, with the only constant being the giant glasses.

We park around forty yards short of Cecil's front door and, coincidentally, across from a half-decent-looking coffee shop. Penny nips inside to get two lattes.

"Fuel for the engine room," she says as she climbs back in.

"Not that we're going to need it, following that old codger and his guard dog around all day. We'll both be able to take turns having nana naps."

I laugh at this, while staying focused on the front of the house. An hour and a half later, my eyes are beginning to droop when we see the now-familiar black Mercedes pull up outside Cecil's place. The car horn beeps three times in rapid succession. The giant form of Neander Man steps out and leans against the car door, waiting.

"You seeing this Pen?"

"You bet ya. He'll probably dent the car door just by leaning on it."

"He's one ugly mofo alright. I wonder where he stayed last night if he wasn't in the box room in Cecil's. You ready to rock?" Penny's on driving duty today as we may need her speedster skills.

"Floss ... I was born ready."

We see the curtains move briefly in the bay window on the right-hand side of the door. Two minutes later, Cecil Reid walks out in a dapper navy-blue suit, with a grey, woollen coat slung over his arm. Vlad opens the door for him as usual and we're off.

"Apart from his trips around the city picking up suspicious

brown paper bags," I say, "his only real crime so far is his association with Neander Man, coupled with his ownership of Freedom Holding. Nothing concrete yet. But I know in my heart of hearts that under that natty little outfit is one of Dublin's very, very bad guys."

"I'm with you, hon," Penny agrees. "Oh please, Cecil, please do something highly illegal today. It would make our day!"

I giggle. Detective work is a strange business, when you end up willing a civilian to perpetrate a crime.

We spend the next two hours following the Merc around town, its occupants making their daily rounds of visits and pick-ups. No major departure from their previous outings, with some overlap on the locations visited. When they stop off for an early lunch, we pick up some soup and paninis from an Insomnia café nearby.

On our break, I call Tash on her mobile, eager to make sure they are all set for the airport, but mostly to see if we are still ok after her brusque departure last night. I don't know what I want to say to her but I just have to call.

"Hi Tash?"

"Floss." *Mmmm ... not the warmest hello.*

"Just ringing to see that you are all set for the airport with Milo today?"

"Yes." *Oh shit, I am in trouble.*

"Right, well ... that's good ..."

"Anything else?"

"Well, yes. I just wanted to check that you are alright ... that we're alright." As I stutter this into the phone, I can feel Penny's laser-beams zero in on me. This is news for her. "You know, you left in a hurry last night, before I had a chance to explain."

"There is no problem. Nothing to explain. I know where I stand."

"Do you? How can you know, if I don't know? Surely I have some say in this." Penny's eyes are almost popping out of her head.

"Well, Milo then. Milo has a say. Is this fair?" she asks. It's a fair question.

"Look, he just turned up out of the blue. He'd helped me with a case and wanted to celebrate over a glass of wine."

"You forget I know Milo. Enough to know why he was on your doorstep."

"Ok, he might have tried some stuff on and I'll be honest and say I was tempted. Very tempted. But nothing serious happened."

"It's ok, Floss. You don't need explain."

"Yeah, well why don't you explain who that 'good friend' of yours was? The one who was giggling away in your bedroom when I called you that morning. And what exactly did go on with you and Milo back in the day? What do you actually do for a living and what is your second name for fuck's sake? A few mysteries there I'd like to solve," I say petulantly, almost out of breath at the intensity of my own outburst.

"Floss. You must be calm. You need to focus. For Nika and Anna. We forget everything today."

I hear a blip blip in my ear that tells me another call is coming through. I check the screen. It's my mother. Excellent timing as usual.

"Tash. Hold on. I've got another call. Let me just deal with it. Stay there." I put her on hold and answer the incoming call.

"Hiya Mum?"

"Hello love. How are you? I haven't heard from you in a while."

"Yeah. Sorry about that. Listen, I'm right in the middle of something at the moment. Can I call you back later? I promise I won't forget."

"But I'm worried about your father and his new religious fervour."

"Ok, Mum, I'll call you later. Bye, bye."

"Floss, are you still ..." I hang up and try to switch back to Tash but she's gone. She must have hung up.

"Fuckidy fuck fuck!" I shout in frustration.

"Floss, what in Jesus' name is going on here? First you're fending off Milo's advances and now you're having what sounds like a lover's tiff with Tash. Care to share?"

"Does it sound to you as if I know what's going on?"

"Fair point. Do you want to talk about it? I'll dispense some conservative advice, but I promise I won't judge," Penny says with a genuinely sympathetic look.

"I know, Pen. Maybe later, ok? It's like ... well, at the moment, the thoughts aren't sufficiently straight in my head to be able to articulate them to anyone else. Even to you, who speaks fluent Floss."

She chuckles and pats me on the leg.

"Alright, hon. Let's park it for the minute and focus on catching some bad guys."

When the Merc pulls in again at the convent, I turn to Penny: "I totally meant to talk to Sister Agatha about Cecil. She taught me French, which was not easy on either of us. She'll definitely remember me."

"Good idea."

"Look, as soon as they leave, I'll jump out and drop in and you can keep following the guys. Stay well back out of harm's way, though. If you think they've clocked you, just get the hell out of dodge. I couldn't face Conor if something happened to you."

"I'll be careful, I promise."

We have to wait around for thirty minutes before Cecil and Vlad emerge from the convent. It is Sister Agatha again who has let them in and out, so she will definitely know why they are there. I slink down low in my seat as they pass by. When they are out of sight I jump out, and walk up the winding driveway to the convent door. It's an impressive old granite structure, built in that typical 19th century oversized austere style. The front door is a huge studded archway, but only half of one side actually opens. I ring the bell and can hear the sound reverberating through the long corridors within.

The door opens about a foot and I see the familiar face of Sister Agatha. She's all of five foot two, bunty of frame, with a large round face and a kind and gentle demeanour. Her eyes always had a sparkle of mischief, enough to make you wonder what she missed out on by following 'God's calling'. Time has not been good to her. She must have been in her early fifties when teaching me, so is now in her mid-sixties, but she looks not a day under 80. The twinkle in her eyes has been all but extinguished. Teaching French to forty girls at a time must have taken its toll.

"Sister Agatha? Hi, it's me, Florence McFarland. You taught me French many moons ago."

"Is that yourself, Florence? I wouldn't recognise you except for the hair. What brings you here?"

She is still behind the door and I'm on the doorstep. "Oh, I was just wandering around the old neighbourhood. My Dad has taken to coming here for mass, so I thought I'd wander up to see what's changed, but to be honest, it looks the same as when I left it back in the day."

"Yes, yes, very good, dear," she says, nodding away.

"I was on my way up the drive when I saw a chap on his way out. Can't remember where I know him from, might be a friend of Dad's? But I think his name was Cyril ... no ... that's not it ... Cecil, yes, that's it. Cecil Reid." Sister Agatha glances behind her and looks decidedly uncomfortable.

"Oh really? You know Cecil? Yes he's one of our ... regular patrons. Well, I must say, it was lovely talking to you, Florence. I must be getting going now. Preparations to make for meals-on-wheels and then evening mass. God's workers can never rest, you know." Her voice has taken on a slightly squeaky tone.

"Oh right. Of course. Well, sorry to interrupt you when you're so busy. I'll leave you to it."

"Thank you, dear. Goodbye now."

The door is closed in my face. I pause for a second to reflect on what just happened. I'm not the best judge of anything, but I know one thing for absolute sure. Sister Agatha looked scared, and it wasn't of me.

30

I get straight on the blower to Penny as I walk back down the convent driveway.

"Thank God, Floss. Please save me from following these guys! Saying they're as boring as watching paint dry is an affront to the paint drying process."

"Are you quite finished?" I ask, patient as ever.

"Yeah, sorry. I thought we were going to see action today."

"Well, I've just come from getting the 'bum's rush' at the convent. I was hoping for a cup of tea at least, but I didn't even get across the threshold. Sister Agatha was not in the mood for small talk."

"Strange. It's normally such an open house up there," says Penny.

"But get this, when I mentioned Cecil Reid, she got all fidgety and clammed up like a clammy thing."

"Don't tell me he's putting the squeeze on the nuns for protection money? Even for a low life like him, that's a bit off."

"I know. Look, change of plan. Why don't you pop back here so we can both keep an eye on this place for a while? I've a feeling in my boobs that something's not quite right here and I'd like to get to the bottom of it."

"Yes!" I can almost hear her fist pumping the air. "On my way. There in five."

When I reach the bottom of the drive, I sit at the bus stop

where Penny loitered the last time we were here. I check in with Tash. "Hi Tash. How's it going?"

"Flight delayed. We are having coffee."

"Oh great, you can catch up on old times." My efforts at keeping a business-like tone have not lasted long.

"Yes. It's fun for me. Not so much for Milo. We even talked about you."

"All good I hope?"

Silence.

"Well, just to let you know that Penny and I have changed our plan of attack slightly. We're staking out the convent coz we think there's something weird going on there, and Cecil & Co don't seem to be deviating from their normal routine."

"Which convent?"

"St Ignatius School and Convent on Mount Prospect Avenue in Clontarf. It's just down the way from Sybil Hill old folks home."

"Ok, I know roughly where this is. Be careful. Stay well back from danger."

"So you do care?"

"Yes. I will keep in touch." Dial tone.

Well, at least that was better than the previous phone call.

The convent is behind me now so I have to use my mobile phone as a sort of mirror to check it out through the railings. It's not ideal, but I can at least spot if there is any movement and alter my position as required. All is quiet there at the moment.

Around five minutes later, Penny swings by and picks me up. We head on past the convent, do a U-turn at breakneck speed and come back to park on the far side of the road. From this spot, we have a good view of the convent front entrance and driveway.

"Any word from Milo and Tash?" asks Penny, as if she hasn't just nearly killed us with her rally driving manoeuvres.

"I'm going to try not to comment on that stunt you pulled back there."

"Good, then I'll try not to comment on your crazy love triangle."

"Yes, I did hear from them. The flight's delayed. They'll keep us in the loop."

"I wish I was tailing Piedr and the girls," says Penny. "That's where this case is going to break. Wherever he takes them after the airport will either be an interim safe house or their new prison."

"Easy there, tiger. We all have our part to play. And if I need a getaway car any time soon, you'll be the first person I call."

As it approaches lunchtime, we begin to see a bit of activity at the convent. Cars begin to arrive, maybe 15 in total. This must be the rush for either meals-on-wheels or mass. We take a note of all the registrations and drivers. All male. Then a delivery van from Pallas Foods swings by and drops off supplies for the convent.

"Fancy a coffee? I could do with stretching my legs," I say, grabbing my purse.

"Ooooh, yes and cake! Definitely cake!"

As I'm about to get out of the car, I glimpse the back of a pink van entering the convent driveway. There's signage on the side, but I'm not quick enough to make it out. It pulls up in front of the convent and a delivery guy jumps out and starts unloading boxes.

"Pass me the binoculars there, Pen."

I focus in on the van but still can't see the signage because the doors are pulled back and obscuring it from my view.

"I can't see where the van's from…." But as I say it, the driver shuts the van doors and I can see a sign on the side of the vehicle:

Discreet Deliveries.

"Interesting. That font looks familiar," I say, almost to myself. I zoom in on the guy lifting the boxes out of the van. They are puce pink and even without being able to read the writing on the side, I know where I've seen these boxes before.

"Bingo fucking bongo. Any idea what Sister Agatha and the girls would be wanting with a rather sizeable delivery of sex toys from Frills & Thrills?"

I turn to see Penny's jaw dropping.

"Give me those." Penny snatches the binoculars. "Holy Christ, Floss. I think we may just have found where the girls are stashed."

I start chewing my nails and wondering what our next steps should be. I'm making a list in my head of who we need to call and in what order. It goes something like:

- Mick Clancy – garda
- Milo & Tash – General update
- Sheila Brennan – Turn Off the Red Light

As I'm preparing the list I'm also dreaming of the headlines in the newspapers:

CTB cracks deadly Russian trafficking ring wide open

8-page pullout inside

We'll be on 'Morning Ireland', the Pat Kenny show and maybe even on a 'Prime Time' follow-up investigation. Jesus, if we made it to the dizzy heights of the Joe Duffy show, Mum would be so proud and maybe finally throw a bit of moral support in the direction of CTB.

Penny drags me back from my reveries: "You know we could take a closer look at the convent. A little recce. An innocent nosey-around. We could go in the school's back entrance via the old sports hall."

"Are you fucking joking me? No way, José! Penny Firth, I know you're getting all excited, I can practically feel the adrenaline oozing out of you over there, but I'm going to have to overrule you on this. We need to bring in the professionals."

"What's the harm? It could save us a bit of egg on our faces. Imagine that Cecil Reid just happens to have a soft spot for nuns and say Sister Agatha has recently taking to organising sex-toy parties to keep the younger nuns entertained. Just a couple of coincidences that lead us to make an incorrect and very unfortunate conclusion. Then we call in the SWAT team and next minute, Sister Agatha with a giant dildo is plastered all over the Irish Times. Courtesy of CTB Investigations. Is that the type of press you want?"

She has a point here and Penny, being herself with icing on top, knows that I've already been imagining the potential headlines. She can sense my weaknesses like a schoolyard bully and she never shies away from exploiting them.

"Mmmmm ... well, we should at least call Mick Clancy and tell him. That way if we disappear off the face of the earth, he'll know where to start looking."

"No, I would definitely advise against that. He could misinterpret us mooching around the convent as breaking and entering."

"And he wouldn't be far wrong," I say.

"Floss, we always talk about making the hard decisions. This is CTB's 'cut the blue wire' moment. We have to grasp it with both hands."

"I suppose you have a pair of pliers in your giant bag there?"

"No, but I do have a set of skeleton keys."

"Where in God's name did you get those?" I ask, both horrified and impressed.

"Whacker gave me them as a sign of his gratitude for bringing him home after his beating. He gave me a few short demos and I've been practising like a lunatic at home ever since."

"You never cease to amaze me, Pen."

We gather our things and then the most dreadful thought pops into my head. If our suspicions are correct and we've discovered a brothel....my Mum's worries over Dad's recent upsurge in mass attendance ... mass at the convent ... is Dad's mass a cover story for ...? *Eeeeeweuch!* It's disgusting to even contemplate it. Is my Dad actually a "John"? That bloody Des O'Connor. I've always known he was trouble. .

Penny is looking at me with a concerned expression. "What's the matter? Are you getting cold feet? The colour has completely drained from your face."

"It's not that. I may have uncovered a nasty family secret. I have to make a call."

I dial home.

"Floss darling, thanks for ringing me back. I was saying earlier …"

"Mum. Put Dad on the phone." I say struggling to keep the anger and disgust out of my voice.

"No need to get all het up, love." she says hearing my stressed tone.

"Please, Mum, just put Dad on the phone." I'm using the firm voice that works on small children (and now mothers, because I hear her cupping the phone and shouting at Dad).

Some mumbling followed by shuffling and then Dad is on the other end of the line.

"Hello Floss?"

"Hi Dad."

"How are you getting on?"

"I'm under a bit of pressure, Dad. I've a very important question to ask you."

"Go on …"

"Why the sudden interest in attending daily mass at the convent?" Penny's head practically does a full three-sixty when she hears this.

The expression of horror on her face is matched only by the feeling of disgust in my stomach.

"Just trying to be a better person."

"Oh cut the crap, Dad. You and I both know that is a

complete pile of horse shite. Mum mentioned Des O'Connor. What has that rascal got you messed up in?"

"To be fair, it was his idea," says Dad, crumpling instantly under the pressure.

"Oh God, Dad. How could you? It's disgusting … it's illegal and … it's completely immoral."

"Hold your horses there Floss. I think that's a bit harsh. We're only looking. Appreciating a beautiful thing from a distance, if you will."

"Oh pants. It gets worse! What is it? Some type of voyeuristic thing? Is it dogging? Are you telling me you're a dogger? I feel like I'm in a scene from Eyes Wide Shut."

"Hold it right there, Floss. First, I don't know what dogging is, but I'm pretty sure I don't do it. Secondly, I've never seen that movie. Thirdly, what is the great crime in a couple of old codgers like Des and myself sneaking a look at a pretty young nun in the front row at mass? We're not doing anyone any harm."

I'm about to continue my rant when his last sentence registers with me.

"Hold on. What did you just say?"

"We're not doing any harm."

"No not that … did you mention pretty nuns?"

"Yep, there's been an influx of young pretty nuns at the convent. Des heard about it and suggested we spend a bit more quality time at mass."

I release a long, slow sigh of relief. Dad, in fact, is not paying trafficked girls for sex. This is good news.

"Well it's not exactly exemplary father material, but it's a lot better than what I thought you were up to," I say feeling a lot calmer now.

"What exactly did you think I was up to? And what's dogging?" he asks.

"Got to go, Dad. Bye to Mum. Love you. Bye, bye."

Penny's in flitters laughing.

"I take it you got the gist of that piece of family farce?"

"Sorry, Floss! I'm only laughing because I'm so relieved for you!"

"Like hell you are! Right, back to work. Where were we?"

"We were going to break into the convent."

"Right," I say with renewed gusto. "Let's cut that bloody blue wire."

Aoife Sheridan

31

We drive the car around towards the school's rear entrance on Mount Prospect Drive. The convent and school cover about 10 acres of land, including the sport pitches and tennis courts. We pull into the car park on the edge of St Anne's Park, next to a bank of recycling bins. This will be our second break-in of the week. And this one is will be in broad daylight. It ups the ante slightly. My stomach has gone into free fall. Penny has gone into hyperdrive.

She's changing back into her woollen suit. Her thinking is that if we get caught, it might be easier for her to talk her way out of it in a respectable elderly lady outfit. Dressed as a hoodlum, she wouldn't stand a chance. I'll just have to hope her respectable attire makes me credible by association.

"Ok, let's do this," I say with more confidence than I'm feeling.

We get out of the car and stride purposefully through the open, wrought-iron gates of the school, attempting to give the impression that we've a divine right to be here. As it's Sunday, the place is deserted. We walk around the back of the gymnasium, location of many physical humiliations for me in the form of ballet classes. Mum always hoped I'd transform into a butterfly. But I never got out of my chrysalis.

The small emergency door at the back of the gym is the spot we're aiming for. As kids, Penny and I used this door frequently as our escape route when bunking off classes. It used to be open during school hours so PE classes could warm up outside on the hockey pitches.

The handle, however, is firmly locked.

"Guess it's time to put that new found skill of yours to the test, eh Penny?"

She's not quite as adept with skeleton keys as Tash, but after six minutes of wiggling and rattling, we hear the lock yield.

"How did you do that?" I ask, genuinely impressed.

"I've no idea to be honest. I just wiggle them around, throw out a few prayers to the Big Man and it just generally works."

"Right. Wiggle and prayers. Got it."

"If an alarm sounds, run for the hills," Penny suggests. She gently eases the door open, both of us cringing in anticipation of a piercing alarm shattering the silence.

Nothing but a deathly quiet greets us and a smell takes us both back to our school days. A mixture of antiseptic, old wood and dust permeates the air. If you did a blind sniff test on any ex-pupil, they'd be able to name that smell in one.

We didn't agree a plan for what to do once we get inside, mainly because I did not really believe we'd make it this far. Time for a quick team talk.

"Ok, how do you want to do this?" I whisper.

"Let's whip through the classrooms first. They're unlikely to be hiding anyone. Then we can move into the convent itself."

"Sounds like a plan. Are we sticking together?"

"Yeah, I think so," says Penny and relief runs through me.

We make our way stealthily through the corridors. The school section of the building is a shaped like a capital H – hence the nickname Cell Block H for the school. It's spread over two floors, with halls and floors painted a hospital blue.

Most of the classroom doors are open. As we pass the main toilet block, we take a peek inside. Penny takes one entrance door and I take the other. We count to three together and open both doors suddenly in an attempt to catch anyone inside. Something hits me on the head and I nearly pass out with the fright of it. I look down on the floor and see a wad of dried up old toilet paper. I look up at the ceiling and notice the familiar sight of toilet paper missiles stuck to the ceiling. Wow, we really were easily entertained back then. I nod to Penny to let her know I'm OK and we head back out, my heart rate slowly returning to something approaching normal.

When we get to the science block, some of the lab doors are closed. Penny takes out her magic keys, but I shake my head: "Let's just check through the windows." Nothing of note. Nor on the second floor.

"Ok, now for the hard part," I say. "The convent."

We head back down the main stairs and go to the end of the hallway, where the school ends and the nuns' living quarters begin. It's blocked off by a large, arched wooden door.

"Work your magic, Firth."

This time Penny cracks the lock in less than three minutes.

"Practice makes perfect," I whisper. She beams with pride at this.

We open the door as quietly as we can and are greeted with complete darkness. The doors of all the rooms must be closed. I take out my phone and switch on the flashlight app. The corridor is instantly bathed in an eerie blue light, which bounces off the matching blue walls. It feels like we're in an empty swimming pool. The corridor is around fifty metres long with eight doors, four on each side. It ends in a T-junction, where – as I recall – it meets another corridor. As we approach the junction, we register the sound of male voices. We pull up immediately, backs flat against the wall, and strain our ears.

It sounds as if the conversation is coming from one of the rooms down the left hand corridor. They're not speaking English. My money is on Russian. We can smell cigarette smoke.

I tap Penny on the shoulder, and whisper that we should move away. She nods. We turn right instead of left and make our way to the end of this new corridor. Another four doors each side. At the end we come to the back stairs. My heart's pounding away inside my chest. I'm keen to put some distance between us and the room with the scary man voices so we go downstairs.

In the basement, the hallway is pitch black, and exactly the same layout as the one above, but we can see light under the gap at the bottom of a door. Before I can stop her, Penny is knocking gently on the door. I gasp out loud at the audacity of it.

We hear light footsteps and then nothing. Whoever is there must be listening on the other side of the door.

Might as well be hung for a sheep as a lamb.

"Hello? Hi there," I whisper into the door frame.

"Da. Door locked."

It's a girl's voice, and she has a Russian accent. Penny whips out her skeleton keys again. Three minutes later, she nudges the door open. A tall, slim, mousy-haired girl is standing before us. Actually, she's not slim. She's malnourished. Skin and bone.

"Hello," I whisper with the most non-threatening expression and tone I can muster. "My name is Floss and this is Penny. We're here to help you. Can we come in?"

Her English must be alright because she immediately opens the door to let us in. We step into what would have been a nun's quarters, but has now become a prison cell for this young girl. And girl she is, no more than 18 years old. Her room has just a metal-frame bed, a sink and a half-size wardrobe. No window. No natural light or air.

"What's your name?" Penny asks gently once the door is closed.

"My name Zlata."

"Ok good. Where are you from?" I ask.

"From Russia. But they take passport. Door locked. Bad men." She glances upstairs. I notice a shadow around her right eye.

"Do you know how many girls are here?" Penny asks.

"No. I see only three same girls – we go to mass on Thursday. That's our only break from here or up there." Again, the glance upstairs.

"Are they forcing you to do things ….." I struggle to try to articulate the question I want to ask …"that you maybe don't want to do."

"Yes. For money." The tears start to flow. She starts sobbing. Penny, mother fantastic, is in with her arms around the girl to comfort her.

"It's ok, Zlata. We're going to get you out of here," Penny says looking over her shoulder at me, a look of grim determination on her face.

"But passport. And … if they catch us, big trouble," she says, punching her right fist into her left hand.

"We're not going to get caught," I insist. Suddenly, my fear has disappeared, replaced with a steely resolve to liberate these poor girls. "Ok?"

She nods.

"Ok, sit tight. We're going to get the other girls out as well. We'll come back and knock twice on your door and you'll know it's safe to come out. Right?"

"Yes. But quick. Dinner is bring soon, I think."

"We'll be quick, I promise," I say as we sneak back out the door.

The coast is still clear. We start working on the next door, and then the next, all the way down the corridor. Behind each door is a similar, sad story. Some of the girls are in bad shape. The face of one of them is swollen and bruised, and she struggles to walk. She will need some help to get out of here.

Eight girls in total – but no sign of Anna or Nika.

The second last room is empty.

Behind the tenth and final door, when we ask the girl her name, she replies "Nyet". She is shaking and frail, the picture of suffering.

"Don't be scared," Penny says. "We're here to help you."

A shake of the head.

I risk a different tactic and say in my sternest voice, "Stay here or come with us? Your choice."

She looks straight at me now and there's the beginnings of some defiance there, but she's still hesitating.

I turn to Penny and quietly say, "We don't have time for this. Nine girls now and still no sign of Anna or Nika."

The emaciated girl in front of us visibly startles at the mention of the two girls' names. I take another closer look at her and suddenly catch a glimpse of the girl we've been searching for now for two weeks. Anna Durchenko. But she's lost the gloss and shine of youth that jumped out from the photos that Nika showed us. She seems to have aged around ten years in the few short months she has been held captive in Dublin.

"Anna?"

She nods slowly and her shoulders slump.

"Hello Anna. My name is Floss. Your friend Nika asked us to find you. We're going to get you out of here. This is Penny."

She does not say a word but simply lowers her head and weeps silently. My heart is breaking just looking at her.

"Please don't cry, Anna. I promise we'll get you out of here, ok? But tell us, first, before we go, do you know where Nika is?"

She looks up and shakes her head.

"No see Nika. Nika great friend."

"Alright. Alright," I say softly, giving her a reassuring squeeze on the arm.

I turn to Penny. "I need you to get the girls out of here, I'm going to look upstairs for Nika and any other girls. There must be more rooms up there."

"Upstairs is sex rooms," Anna says quietly.

Penny shakes her head. "I don't like the idea of splitting up. Too risky."

"The most important thing is to get these girls out of here. As soon as you get out, call Mick Clancy and tell him to get a gang of gardaí over here as soon as possible. I'll be right behind you. Just give me those key thingies."

She hands them over reluctantly. "Let's get these girls out of their rooms first, Penny. You take the first four doors and I'll take the rest. Anna, stay close behind Penny, ok?"

She kind of nods and shakes her head at the same time. I take it to mean she's alright but can't believe we're about to do this. I'm with her on that. I'm having an out of body experience. Or rather my body has been taken over by some crazy, braver version of myself.

We ease open the door to Anna's cell and make a dash down the corridor, Penny and I knocking twice rapidly on our assigned doors. The girls all emerge hesitantly, but are immediately encouraged by the sight of one another. Two of them help the girl who can barely walk, supporting her on either side.

We move to the back stairs. They move in quietly behind me. At the top of the stairs, I stand aside and let them pass, pointing towards the T-junction so they can go through to the school. We can hear the quiet murmur of voices from the room down the corridor at the far end as before.

They all look petrified, but there is hope beginning to appear in their faces too as they sense the slight possibility of freedom.

Penny squeezes my hand and mouths 'be careful', and off she goes with the girls. The tune of 'All By Myself' by Eric Carmen starts belting through my head. I climb up the stairs to the first floor. The doors are all partly open and I'm horrified at what I see. If downstairs was the prison, upstairs is the brothel.

Double beds with cheap red velour covers and enough sex paraphernalia to make a Dutch prostitute blush. Blackout blinds on all windows.

None of the rooms are in use. No sign of Nika. Have we missed something? Is there some other section to the building that I don't know about? I'm just turning back the way I came when my mobile phone starts to ring in the deafening silence. I'm such a fucking numpty for not remembering to turn it off. The volume's not that high so I'm hoping like hell the guards downstairs won't have heard it through the closed door.

It's Milo.

"Hello," I whisper.

"Floss, our buddy Piedr has two new girls in tow. Stop whatever you're doing. We've been trailing them since the airport and we've just pulled in to the convent."

"Shhhh … I'm here already."

"What? You're where? The convent? And why are you whispering?"

"I'm in the convent. We found the girls. Penny's sneaking them out the back as we speak. Go round to the back entrance on Mount Prospect Drive and meet her there."

"Shit! Tash, turn around and go around the block. Floss is already inside the convent. This is a fucking train crash!" I can hear tyres screeching.

"Shhhh …" I say trying to calm him down, worried the guys can hear from downstairs.

"Floss McFarland. You listen to me. You get yourself the hell out that building right this second. Do you hear me?"

"Yes. Loud and clear."

I end the call and quickly make my way back to the top of the stairs. I stall briefly to listen out for any movement downstairs, but hear nothing. I'm down the stairs in two seconds flat. I head for the corridor that leads back to the school, but can't help turning to take a quick glance at the door where the Russian voices were coming from. The door is wide open. My heart, which has been uncharacteristically calm for the past few minutes, now starts the familiar rumba of fear. I'm about to turn back towards the corridor when I hear a faint swooshing sound from behind me, followed by the loud crack of a very heavy object connecting with my skull.

I can only imagine that I must have crumpled to the floor, because for me now, there is only darkness.

32

I've got a brain-splitting headache. I reach upwards to feel the source of the pain, but I can't move an inch. My hands are bound tightly behind my back. My feet are tied together and secured to the legs of the chair in which I'm sitting. I open my eyes slowly, taking in my surroundings. The artwork on the wall comes into focus and looks vaguely familiar. I know I've been here before. I shake my head to try to clear the fuzziness that envelopes me and take another look around. Then I notice the familiar sight of my desk and things click into place. I'm back in CTB's prefabricated office, strapped to my own leather chair.

This is not good.

But it could be worse. I could be somewhere else.

I wriggle around in the chair, trying to see if there is any movement, but whoever has tied me in here has done a bloody good job. I look around for something to untie myself with. In a movie, there'd be a knife or scissors just out of reach for me to focus on and strain for. But the industrial cleaners, who tidied up after the break-in, did a stellar job. Everything is shipshape.

I move my wrists a bit to see if there is any give, but cry out in pain as the binds tighten and cut into my skin. When the pain has subsided somewhat, I try to move my ankles. Same thing there. No movement.

Think, Floss, think.

My mobile phone? Where was it before I got clocked from behind? In my jacket pocket. But, even if they didn't remove it, my arms are pinned behind my back and I have the suppleness of a plank of wood.

I'm starting to panic when the door to the office opens and in walks none other than Cecil Reid, followed by Vlad Mursky, aka Neander Man. He stands over by the main window, blocking out all daylight.

Cecil Reid may project a dapper, gentlemanly appearance from afar. Close up, he exudes menace. His skin is pock-marked and oily and his eyes, bright green in colour, are those of a lizard, partly thanks to a total lack of eyelashes. And his heavy breathing spreads a sinister, Darth Vader vibe.

Without a word, he crosses over to Penny's desk, sits himself down and leans forward on his hands as if he owns the place. He stares across at me with his reptilian eyes. I suspect he wants me to fill the silence out of blind fear and panic. I clamp my mouth shut. It's torture. But it works.

First blood to Floss.

"Florenth McFarland, I wish I could say it was a pleasure." He speaks in a strong Dublin accent with a distinctive lisp, which only adds to his whole bad guy routine. He pronounces my name as Florenth...I'd really like to hear him try to say 'Floss'.

"Mister Reid. Illegal importer of underage girls for the purpose of prostitution, I presume." I manage to conceal the fact that I'm petrified.

"I prefer to think of it as liberating girls from their domestic tragedies," he replies, while checking out his nails.

"Out of the frying pan and into the fire more like. Don't try and dress up your thuggery as anything other than that."

"It's a matter of perspective."

"I saw the state of the girls in that convent. Or should I say cells? Most of them either half-starved, half pummelled or both. Don't kid yourself with your Mother Teresa routine, Cecil," I say, getting angry now and warming to my theme.

He laughs. It's a deep gurgling sound like the laughter is being strangled in his throat. I revise the likeness from Darth Vader to Jabba the Hutt.

"My, my, you are a spirited young thing aren't you, Florenth? I'd really like a bit more time to get to know you more … intimately, shall we say?" He looks me up and down, very slowly.

Euech! My skin is crawling. The thought of Cecil 'Slime Bucket' Reid coming anywhere near me is nauseating. I need all of my poker skills, honed over years of Friday night games, to maintain a calm exterior.

"Charmed, I'm sure." I say, still not wanting him to know he's getting to me.

He laughs quietly, but there's a twitch in his left eye. His 'tell'. It's bothering him that I'm not cowering in fear.

"Well, Florenth, it has been lovely chatting, but I have a busineth to run …" He gets up from behind Penny's desk.

"Wait!" I almost shout. If Cecil leaves, I'll be left with Neander Man. Up to this point, he has just been staring impassively at me, but there's a glint in his eye that suggests he's keen for the chat to finish so he can get on with the task at a hand.

"Yeth?" Cecil asks.

"Where's Nika?" I demand.

"Sorry, who?" asks Cecil, showing what appears to be genuine curiosity.

"Nika was not in the convent."

"I don't distract myself with names, Florenth. These girls are just numbers to me. Currency if you will. Each one like its own mint, printing money morning, noon and night."

"You bastard."

Vlad starts laughing his giant-man laugh behind me.

"That's more like it, Florenth. That's the little terrier I'd come to expect."

"What have you done with the nuns?"

"They've been used as collateral, let's say, to keep Sister Agatha in line.

"But where are they now?" I'm pleading openly now.

"What does it matter to you? You're about to die in an unfortunate demolition accident and you're worried about a bunch of dried-up old biddies who hide behind high walls thanking the Lord for their solitude. Your energies would be better spent making peace with yourself before you go to meet your maker."

"I'd rather use my time to plot how I'm going to make you pay, you freak of nature."

"Feisty to the last. Bravo, Florenth, bravo. It's a shame to have to snuff out that fighting spirit of yours."

He gets up and moves around to the door. He gives Neander Man the nod, a flamboyant wave of the hand to me.

"Adieu. Oh, and pleasant trip!" and he's gone.

Neander Man has started his booming evil laugh again. He enjoys his job. "This will be fun for both of us," he says in a pronounced Russian accent, his voice surprisingly high for the size of his frame. "Would you like me to tell you what's going to happen now?" He moves slowly towards me.

"Fuck you!"

"No? Not interested? Not even bit curious? I think I would like to tell you anyway. Your lovely office is attached to crane. I'm going to lift entire trailer up to height of 100 metres. Then I will hang you over Liffey for while, to let fear build inside. Maybe jiggle office about . Then I will hit release button on crane and you will come crashing to death. And nobody will be able to put Humpty Dumpty Floss together again."

And he laughs out loud at his own cleverness.

"What's the matter? Cat got your tongue?" he asks.

He has me there. I begin to realise that I'm completely and utterly poked. There's no point in rising to his bait. It will just make him enjoy it all the more. So I've clamped my jaw shut once more.

"Well, I'm going to go now. Have fun! I've always wanted to be crane driver."

He pats my head gently on his way past me. I jerk back my head to let him know I'm not happy about it. He shrugs his oversized shoulders and heads out the door without a backwards look.

As I sit there in the chair, waiting for the end to begin, I can't help but think back on where I went wrong. A call to the police before going into the convent would have been, on reflection, the smarter way to go. Separating from Penny was just plain stupid. My new-found courage and steeliness seemed to get the better of me. All logical sense went out the window. Oh well. If there is a next time, I'll know better.

I wonder where Penny is. Did she get the girls out ok? Are they all safe? Did Milo and Tash free the two newly trafficked girls? Would Tash ever have spoken to me again? Would I have won her back? Do I want her? Do I want Milo? Was that clinch with Milo just a random incident? Shit, my Mum and Dad are going to be really pissed off about all this.

I hear heavy steps above me. Vlad must be attaching the crane hooks to the four eye rings on the roof. I feel the cabin shake as he jumps off. A few minutes later, the whole cabin shakes slightly, several times, as if he's testing. A moment's pause ... then a sudden jolt, and the whole cabin starts rising slowly upwards, swaying a little from side to side. I'm airborne!

My chair suddenly topples over. Thank God for that! Otherwise the chair wheels would have me ricocheting around in here as if I were inside a pinball machine. It hurts, though. Maybe I cracked a rib against the arm of the chair as I landed. I'm finding it hard to breathe.

The cabin is now swinging more vigorously from side to side, like a fairground Viking ship. I end up facedown, cheeks plastered against the front window, praying that the glass is sealed good and tight. Eeeks! The car park is way down below me. I can see Cecil standing there looking up at me, with an expression of faint amusement on his face. Above, I can see the crane cab, with Neander Man inside, laughing away as he swings the cabin like a wrecking ball.

It finally dawns on me that this really could be it. My time to check out. But I'm not ready to go! I've loads more living and loving to do. I'm not so much scared as furious. The anger surges inside me like a volcanic eruption. I start roaring: "Fuck this! It's not fair! Let me down, you primeval monster!"

I'm shouting at the top of my lungs and crying at the same

time. It can't be a pretty sight, not that anyone's watching me.

Just as I'm about to run out of breath, I see a blurry black movement at the foot of the crane. I can't quite make it out but it's moving swiftly up the frame of the crane. I strain my eyes, and eventually realise that it's the figure of someone dressed in black who's climbing rapidly.

It's Tash! Aikido legend and now crane climber. She makes it look easy. I get a rush of both dread and joy. I want desperately for her to come and save me, but at the same time want to warn her away from Neander Man. Karate Kid she may be, but how will she cope when face to face with the Man Beast?

Neander Man is fully focused on perfecting his cabin-swinging skills. Although my ribs are killing me and I have to distort my neck to see what's going on below, I can see flashes coming from the side of the car park. Cecil is running as if to seek shelter, but he drops suddenly to the ground and lies sprawled with his arms outstretched. Has he been shot? Please God, let it be so. If I have to die to take him out of circulation, I can cope with that.

It's like I'm watching a silent movie, the only score being my racing heartbeat and raging curses.

I look back up. Tash is almost at the door of the crane cab.

"Careful, Tash!" I scream.

In one fluid movement, she raises herself up level with the door, opens it with one arm, catching Vlad momentarily off-guard. I can see him letting go of the crane controls. The prefab plunges, then jerks to a halt, but my stomach is back up somewhere above me in the sky. As the cabin dropped, I rose a little into the air and, when it suddenly halted, crashed heavily back down against the window while my tender rib slammed against the chair handle once more. The window will surely break! I close my eyes tight in anticipation of the end.

But when I open my eyes, I see I'm almost level with the crane cab, just in time to see Tash, who's dangling from the crane with one hand, whip out what looks like a Taser and fire it at Vlad. He staggers for a moment, then seems to waver as the 50,000 volts course through him. It only slows him down for a split second. He takes a swing at her, but he's too slow and clumsy.

Now she's back up at the door of the crane cab, holding on with her left hand as she delivers a few rapid right-handers to Vlad's face. His arms are flailing about trying to connect with her. Her punches, which would floor a normal person, don't even make a dent in Vlad. She's clearly hurt her fist, as I can see her holding it for a second. Vlad takes the opportunity to grab hold of her ponytail and jerks her violently backwards. She's still holding onto the crane with one hand but only just. If he let go of her, she could fall.

He raises his right arm as if about to swing at a baseball.

"Noooooooooo!" I scream.

Tash has spotted what's coming. She reaches behind her back, pulls out a Dirty Harry handgun and, before Neander Man has a chance to launch his attack, fires two rounds into his face. Three flashes, then a spray of blood on the back wall of the crane cab.

Neander Man slumps forward onto the controls. My office again plunges downwards. I'm in free fall! I see a look of horror on Tash's face as I plummet past her. And then darkness. Again.

33

I dream that I'm at the controls of some kind of flying machine, soaring high above a burning New York City, saving people who are stranded at the tops of their buildings. I fly to each building, picking up two people at a time, and whip them across to the safety of Staten Island. The Statue of Liberty is cheering me on and waving her flame about like a pom-pom. I'm quite the hero. On my way back for the last trip, I suddenly forget how to fly. My engine stalls in mid-flight. I'm tumbling towards the ground far below. As I fall, the Statue of Liberty chants "Floss, Floss, Floss ..."

I wake with a start just before I hit the ground. Milo McCarthy is saying my name repeatedly and gently tapping my face.

"Floss, Floss, Floss, can you hear me, Floss? Are you ok, Floss? Floss? Talk to me ..." He actually sounds desperate.

"Please stop hitting my face," I say.

"Oh my God, you're ok! Sorry!" He starts laughing. "Christ, you gave us quite a fright, Floss. But it looks like you haven't lost your bolshie spirit."

Fright? What's he talking about? Sign? Ordeal? I'm still half in and half out of my dream, so what he's saying fails to compute. But as he starts untying my hands, the memories flood back. I see Tash dangling from the crane by a single hand.

"Tash! Is Tash ok? Where is she?" I fear the worst.

"She took a couple of knocks but she's going to be ok. They build them pretty tough in Vilnius. She's outside being seen to by the ambulance crew."

"What happened to Cecil? Was he shot?"

"Yeah, we got here in the nick of time. He was watching the aerial show and really enjoying himself. We gave him a couple of chances to turn himself in, but he wanted to go out in style. He whipped a gun out on us and started firing and running. About seven officers let rip and basically turned him into a human colander."

He gently unties my feet and helps me up. I try to stand but my knees buckle like a new-born giraffe. Milo catches me and pulls my arm around him for support, then begins to ease me out of what's left of my office.

"How far did I fall?"

"All up, about seventy metres. Tash managed to hit the brakes before you hit the ground. She saved your life, kid."

These last words stir me deeply. I begin to cry uncontrollably, full body heaves and sobs. Milo holds me close until I'm cried out.

I pull away.

"Shit, I've destroyed your jacket." I say, surveying the snotty mess I've left behind.

"It's an honour and ... I'll send you the dry cleaning bill with my invoice!" he says with a double-wink.

The car park is full of squad cars, gardaí and ambulance teams. A medic quickly wraps a blanket around me and sits me down in the back of an ambulance. I can't see Tash anywhere.

Milo heads off to talk to some of his police buddies. Somewhere in the background, cameras flash repeatedly.

Suddenly Penny - my oldest and dearest friend - is in my face and hugging me.

"Ouch ... my ribs!" I whine.

"Oh sorry, Floss! But my God, it's so good to see you! You don't know how relieved I am. We were so worried when you didn't come out of the convent. They must have taken you out the front way while we were all at the back entrance. I'm so sorry I left you. I should never have let you stay to look for Nika. It was so stupid. I've been kicking myself ever since."

"Pen ... don't be silly. I'm the stupid one. I got a bit carried away. The rush of finding the girls ... of being right for once ... it just went to my head."

"Anyway, you're safe now and we did it! We flippin' well got the bad guys!"

"What about the nuns?"

"They found two of them huddled in a heap in the attic at the top of the convent – some pretty makeshift accommodation had been set up for them. Cecil & Co needed to keep them up there to give some semblance of a working convent. As far as I know they're the only teaching nuns left. The rest of them were transferred to their sister convent in Cork. The poor things are in serious shock, half-starved and praying to anyone who'd listen. It will take them awhile to get over it, but they'll be ok."

"God, those poor women. It's a bit more than they signed up for." I say still grimacing from the pain of my ribs.

A mobile phone rings. It's mine. I reach around, letting out a squeal as the pain rips through my rib cage.

"Is that yourself, Floss?" It's a gravelly Dublin brogue.

"It is, I think."

"It's Mick Clancy here. Rumour has it you caused quite a mess along the Quays there!" he chortles.

"You could say that. How are you, Mick?"

"In better shape than you, to be sure. I'm having a celebratory pint here in Mulligans."

"Great. What are we celebrating?"

"I found your little Russian friend."

"What? Nika?!"

"That's right. Little Miss Nika. She's been banged up in the Mater Hospital for the last week or so. Seems she never got as far as the trafficking guys. She was asking questions in the wrong places and one of the pimps must have taken offence. Gave her a right going over. Unconscious for a week or so. Came through asking for Floss McFarland. One of the nurses remembered me asking around and gave me a shout."

"Is she ok?"

"She's bruised and battered but I told her you'd found her friend. She seemed to rally a bit at that."

"The poor little minx. Brilliant work, Mick. You're a good man, you know that? Thanks for calling."

"And listen, McFarland, don't go pulling any stunts like that again. You were lucky this time. Might not work out so well for ya next time. Know what I mean?" he says in a fatherly manner.

"I think I might be retired," I say with a sigh.

He laughs at this and hangs up with a "Bye, bye. I have to go. The tide is in!' His fresh pint has obviously arrived.

"Did I get that right?" asks Penny. "They found Nika?"

"Yes, good old Mick Clancy. A dark horse in shining white armour. Think how productive he would be if he could stay sober."

"Well done, Floss," says Penny as she gently squeezes my hand.

"Hey, we're a team, you and I. Cagney and Lacey, remember?"

In the distance I see Tash and Milo slowly coming towards us. Tash's right arm is in a sling and I can make out the black eye from here. But she's smiling radiantly. Smiling at me.

Milo has a hand resting under her elbow, helping her along, while stealing sly glances at me. Something about his demeanour tells me there's nothing going on between them. Purely platonic. How stupid I've been!

Suddenly, the sheer enormousness of what has happened to me overwhelms me. My entire body begins to shake and the tears pour down my cheeks. I'm struggling to maintain control.

"Jesus, Floss. Are you ok?" asks Penny. "You're shaking like a leaf, hon."

I shake my head through the tears.

"Look! Here come your other knights in shining armour!"

Through my tears, I look up at my guardian angels, who between them saved my life, walking towards me. They both look at me with a mixture of anxiety and expectation. And then the two great loves of my current life suddenly blur into one.

Seriously ... how *is* a girl to choose?

THE END

Aoife Sheridan

ACKNOWLEDGMENTS

Crikey! Writing this is harder than the entire book itself. But here goes …

Firstly, it's important to acknowledge that this book is a complete work of fiction. Any errors, inaccuracies and misrepresentations are entirely my responsibility. If any character in the book actually exists in Dublin, it's an incredible coincidence and I'd really like to meet them. There are references to real Dublin locations in the book but I'm not going to tell you which ones. With one exception: The car park, where the portable office of Cut the Blue Investigations resides, does exist as a barren wasteland as I write this today. In the future, I hope it will become something stunning and characterful to further enhance Dublin's quays. Maybe, as you read this, it already has.

It's important to note that the organisation Turn Off the Red Light does exist in Ireland. They do immense work to combat human trafficking, but their office location and staff exist only in my imagination. Don't let that stop you from making a donation though! Go on … it's easy: www.turnofftheredilight.ie/donate

Thanks to my editor David Quin of SwiftWrite. How glad am I that you alone responded to my polite inquiry? You were quite the find.

To Summer Q. Damn girl! Try not to be quite so accomplished. When I sent you the manuscript, I thought it was finished.

To my merry band of test readers: Liz Wilson, Melissa Furze,

Derv Mullan, Colette Sheridan and Karen Winkworth. Your feedback was really appreciated and more importantly, felt like a group of cheerleaders egging me on.

To Cora Murphy of Mesh Design for the stunning book design. I really hope people judge this book by its cover.

To Rhona Byrne for Floss' map of Dublin. There are elements of you in Penny, but you're way hotter (at least 23 times).

There are a couple of choice expressions in here, borrowed from friends and family – it's important they get their day in the sun:

- Speed bumps between my brain and mouth – Bob and Lesley Meline
- Smacked bulldog's arse – Paddy Donnelly
- Bingo bongo – Graham Abel
- The title 'Cut The Blue' itself – Kris Rogers

To the Sheridan family, both the originals and the "blow-ins". I grew up surrounded by the art of the possible, a shedload of love, laughter and Liverpool Football Club. I try to thank my lucky stars every day for you all.

To Mum and Dad. For absolutely everything.

To the Pocket Rocket, my co-conspirator and partner in crime. Although this book is dedicated to Eithna, it is written entirely for you.

Aoife (Eefa) Sheridan
Dublin 2013

Printed in Great Britain
by Amazon.co.uk, Ltd.,
Marston Gate.